CARING FOR YOUR CLOWN

BOOK THREE

LETTING GO OF THINGS

OLEANDER BLUME

WARNING THESE BOOKS ARE ABOUT ABUSE AND
CONTAIN TRIGGERING CONTENT

The Caring for Your Clown Series is about childhood trauma and
abuse and the process of healing from childhood trauma and abuse
and thus will depict instances and aftermath of traumatic events
and child abuse.
The types of trauma and abuses depicted, discussed or alluded to
include and are not limited to the following topics.
Physical abuse
Psychological abuse
Emotional abuse
Traumatic neglect
Child sexual abuse
Sexual assault
Miscarriage
Bullying
Transphobic rhetoric
Medical abuse
Negative self talk
Suicidal ideation
Panic attacks
Flashbacks
Anxiety
Death of loved ones
Please be advised that if any of these topics are triggering and/or
deeply discomforting, it is recommended to not engage in this
material.

Just the Way You Left it

"**D**ouglass!" Oliver charged past the other students as they congregated in front of the middle school. His friend stood somewhere near the door, entirely unprepared for him to come vaulting over the picnic table and crashing into him.

"O-Olivia, don't run, you'll get in trouble again!" Douglass braced himself, only for Oliver to grab his hand and shove a prescription pill bottle into his palm with excitement.

"What's this?" Douglass inspected the little orange bottle, turning it over to read words he could barely pronounce. "Are you sure it's okay to bring these to school?"

"Blockers!" Oliver bounced, an enormous grin spreading across his face as he beamed down at the drugs. "My mom took me to the doctor over the weekend— I know it's sorta too late, but I don't have to pretend to be a girl anymore!"

Douglass blinked, cocking his head in mild concern. "You're really sure about this?"

Oliver responded with a face, some mix between slight hurt and frustration before he huffed and took his pills back. "Of course I am, I've never been more excited in my life! My dad even took me clothes shopping so I have a whole new wardrobe for next year!"

The boy tangled his fingers up in his long hair, pulling half of it back so he could tie it up in a sloppy bun on the top of his head. "No more dresses, or skirts, I won't have to shave anymore— I'm gonna get SO HAIRY!!"

Oliver leaned in, pressing his palms into Douglass's chest as he lowered his voice and whispered into his ear.

"You got a what?!" He squawked back, "I didn't even know they made those!"

"They do! But I don't really know how to use it so I'm probably not gonna wear it or anything. It looks sooo real though, you wouldn't believe!" Oliver adjusted his skirt, pulling it down from where it gradually hiked up around his waist and garnering a somewhat intrigued look from his friend.

"You're not wearing it right now, are you?"

"Oh my god, no!" Oliver punched him lightly in the shoulder. "I'm not looking to get suspended or anything just yet. The high school is already making it a whole thing— they don't want me to use any of the 'gendered' bathrooms. And I'm not allowed to go in any of the locker rooms either. If they found out I was packing or god forbid— if it fell out?! They'd totally kill me."

"That doesn't seem fair," Douglass remarked, casually scooting his friend toward the bench nearby so they didn't have to stand in the doorway.

"Ehh," Oliver shrugged, "it is what it—"

He was cut off by an eruption, an explosion bigger than either of them had ever seen. The boys turned, along with every other student that stood in the middle school courtyard.

Off in the distance, on the north eastern side of town across the bridge, was a fire. Smoke billowed up into the air, turning the sky a murky brown when it met with the low hanging clouds.

"Woah." Oliver's gaze turned downward, and he half-mindedly patted Douglass on the shoulder in order to get his attention. "The lab's on fire."

Douglass didn't need him to say it, he was looking at the same thing. The entire back half of the building was ablaze, shooting flames up into the sky as sirens from a fire truck screamed and honked down the road.

"You think our parents are alright?"

"Probably, stuff happens all the time there." Oliver reassured him. "I mean, I was there last week and my dad accidentally set something on fire. It happens—"

"Olivia Tarsul to the front office, Olivia Tarsul to the front office please, you have a phone call." The loudspeaker cut him off, prompting Douglass to give a much more concerned look toward the boy as he cautiously opened the door to the school. Douglass followed close behind, his heart sinking with every step as a feeling of overwhelming dread rested over him.

"It's probably my mom." Oliver offered a slightly less reassured smile. "I bet Dr. Abadi accidentally mixed up his samples again."

He opened the glass door, holding it for Douglass before picking up the phone on the counter.

"Yeah?" Oliver turned, elbowing his friend in the chest as if to make sure he knew everything would be okay. "Yeah, the whole school is outside, we can see it from here."

Douglass craned his neck in effort to hear the muffled, garbled words from the other end of the phone.

"Yeah, I can't really hear you, the firetruck is too loud. Dad—" Oliver grew stiff, drawing Douglass's attention the moment he heard the boy's breath hitch and drag into his lungs with a slow, shaky gasp.

In an instant, his heart dropped to the floor as he watched his friend's face drain of all color. Oliver moved slowly, turning one dreadful step at a time as his eyes drifted from the window and the fire across the mountains to Douglass, who stared at him with immediate grief.

"Olivia—" he choked, "Olivia what happened?"

For a small, almost miniscule moment, their gazes met, just before the phone in Oliver's hand slipped out and clacked against the office desk. The boy's eyes grew wide, and Douglass could see him struggle to focus as his pupils dilated back and forth. Then they constricted, so tightly, as the horrific realization drifted over him.

"She's gone."

***

Oliver stared out the airplane window, watching the vast expanse of blue underneath him pass by with little indication of the direction he was going. He was going home. That's all that mattered.

Two or so weeks in Surat over the winter as dictated by his father. 'A change of scenery might help things.'

India was very far away from the States. It wasn't the first time he'd been; he'd been when he was eleven. It was for a wedding. This time he'd gone because Jon had it in his mind that if he were away from Pineton, he wouldn't be affected by the aftermath of what happened there.

The thing he hated most about the whole ordeal was that it worked.

But now he was coming back and every mile he zoomed closer to Pineton's mountains, he felt all his set aside atrocities weigh further down on him.

"How was it?" Jon asked after an hour-long car ride in utter silence. He sounded like he was trying to be happy. *It isn't working.*

Oliver toted his suitcases up the stairs straight to his room without a word. He didn't want to talk, and honestly didn't want to be here at all— but he didn't want to go back to India.

His father followed him regardless of his efforts not to interact.

He took one of the suitcases from Oliver and opened the door to his room for ease of access, knowing full well the boy had no inclination for conversation.

"How is Baba?" Jon ventured, lingering in the doorway, well and away from his son's horrific quiet.

"Her dementia is getting worse," he answered after an uncomfortably long silence. Oliver unzipped his bags and began sorting out his clothes, some of which weren't what he'd taken with him. "She thinks I'm Mom, or Dāda most of the time."

"Yeah...Manpreet was telling me about that," Jon said, apparently opting for a light tone. Oliver imagined this was him trying to work his way up to the real questions. "How's everyone else? The shop doing well?"

Oliver gave a short nod, neatly folding fancy new garments Manpreet had hand sewn for him so he looked somewhat presentable at Temple.

"I helped with some new designs for her summer collection," he answered almost coldly. It was little more effort than drawing intricate mandalas for silk prints, but Manpreet always adored using his artistic skills for her tailor business. "The new shop opened up in time for Pancha Ganapati too, it's doing okay."

"That's good." *This is an empty conversation.* Both of them knew that, but Oliver was pressed to make his father undeniably uncomfortable for as long as he could.

"Rajan calls me Hijra now," he muttered after a moment. He overheard a disappointed groan from his father, who knew just as much as he that it was intended as entirely derogatory.

"I'll talk to my sister about that," Jon answered, opting to close in on his kid and actually help him put away his clothes.

Oliver pulled away from him though, and sidestepped to increase his distance. "Why'd you make me go?"

He glared at him, watching the man sigh and rub his face in what looked like relief that he'd said it at all.

"I needed time—"

"For what?"

"To take care of— of things," Jon answered, hoisting Oliver's other suitcase onto his bed to dig through.

"Like covering up what happened?" The boy bit softly. "I know that's what you were doing and what you didn't want me to see."

"That wasn't—" Jon hesitated, lowering his voice to keep himself from arguing. "That wasn't the only reason, you— I figured you needed time. To process things, I know how hard things have been and with—"

"Dindet dying too?" Oliver cut in, jerking his suitcase to the other side of his bed so he gained a solid three feet between him and his father. "You can say it. They're both gone. You just think I can't handle it cause of what's wrong with me."

"That's not true—"

"Is it?" Oliver threw down the shirt in his hands and shot his father another glare. "You shipped me off to India because I ran away right? Cause I'm broken. Cause I let her die. And you were worried that I'd get worse, right?"

"Oliver, you're not..broken." Jon raised his hand but kept his voice gentle, prompting the boy to drop his gaze with a disdainful little huff.

"I didn't have any," he answered before the question could be asked. "No panic attacks and no flashbacks— I'm doing *fine*."

He wasn't lying this time, for once. The entire duration of his stay with his extended family was occupied by the shop or the temple, and if neither of those it was forced sight-seeing or taking care of his grandmother. He didn't have time to be reminded of anything— let alone what happened a few weeks prior.

Oliver slowly returned to his suitcase and began pulling out more clothes Manpreet had either bought or made for him.

"She told me to say thank you," he said after a while, "for sending some of the settlement to her. It's what made her able to open a second store."

Jon nodded curtly, he'd almost forgotten that he'd done so. Shortly after the custody case he'd sent a large sum of the lab settlement to his sister.

"So, Hijra, huh?" He changed the subject softly, hoping his son was comfortable enough to talk about his stay instead of the reason he left.

"Yeah," Oliver mumbled, picking up on his ploy. He obliged. "I didn't know what it meant at first, so I didn't really care— but now he won't call me anything *but* that."

"And Manpreet didn't have anything to say about that? What about Tanvi?"

"Well...Tanvi kept trying to spin it as a compliment, I can add it to my roster of things I've been called now, ha." Oliver forced a small laugh at the thought. It was far easier to make a game out of slurs than feel the way they were meant to make him feel. "Can't let anyone at school hear that one."

Jon nodded along, his lips twitching into a frown at the thought of his child's poor coping. "Speaking of that, I talked with some of the administrators at the school..."

Crap.

Oliver heaved an uncomfortable sigh and kept his gaze on the floor. *He's gonna wanna know about the rumors. About Markus...*

"Mrs. Bradshaw— your counselor, mentioned some of the students had seen you using the 'wrong' restroom." *False alarm.*

"It's not the *wrong* restroom if I'm literally only allowed to use their stupid, crappy, unisex one," Oliver countered, a flicker of frustration in his voice at the absurd idea. *I should be allowed to use the boy's restroom. They are the ones that decided I shouldn't.* "Besides, it's not even like it matters."

"It is a pretty stupid rule," his dad agreed, gaining a small smile out of the kid. "But it's still a rule, and you've already been suspended once."

And the smile was gone.

"They just hate me," Oliver grumbled, finishing emptying his suitcase and moving to return all his unpacked clothes to his closet.

"They don't *all* hate you," his father gave very unconvincing reassurance, "they're just...slow on the uptick. Patricia's been on our side from the start— even if she doesn't act it."

Oliver shot him a look from his closet that reeked of sarcastic disbelief, prompting his father to change the subject once more.

"Douglass misses you by the way." That made Oliver pause and poke his head out the closet with mild intrigue.

It was shortly replaced with forced nonchalance.

"Yeah, I'm sure he misses being my knight in shining armor," he responded sardonically, deliberately staying in the closet to hide how hot his face got.

"He came by *every day* once he got back from Maine." Jon chimed, leaning back to see his son attempting to bury himself in his clothes to hide his embarrassment. "Was asking about you, how you're doing. He's absolutely head over heels."

Jon snickered at the sound of his son fumbling with his suitcase, thoroughly enjoying the way Oliver wheezed with unconscious frazzlement.

"He— I— he probably just wants to see me in a dress again!" Oliver retorted, glancing back to see his father's cheeky grin in the crack of his door. "I already turned him down once anyways— and then he got a dumb crush on a freaking *alien*, so it's not like he doesn't have other options!"

"*You like him!*" Jon grinned, pulling the closet door open with his foot so he could put away more of his son's clothes.

Oliver sputtered nonsensically for a moment before he stole the clothes from his dad in poor defiance. "No, I don't! You're just saying that 'cause it gets on my nerves!"

Jon eyed him incredulously, poking the boy gently in the stomach, "then how come you're all anxious?"

Oliver slapped his hand away and stuck his tongue out. "I am *not* anxious."

Absolute lie.

His dad's grin widened with Oliver's increasingly flush face and he tickled him lightly. "I'm not the one with butterflies in my stomach."

Oliver wriggled and an unceremonious little giggle erupted from him at his father's second successful attempt at easing the previous tension.

"Dad! I'm not twelve!" He laughed, letting his father wrap his arms around him in a tight hug as he dragged him out of the closet.

"I oughtta carry you all the way across the street so you can *officially* announce your return," Jon remarked, prompting the boy to writhe a bit in his arms.

"*Don't* do that! It'll be so weird! He's gonna think I'm dumb!" Oliver replied through his half choked giggling.

Jon swayed him back and forth for a moment, holding him high enough that his feet couldn't touch the ground before he fell back on Oliver's bed with a soft thud and content hum.

"I missed you too, you know," he said after Oliver's laughter finally quelled. "And I don't mind if you wanna help him and Chris out. It's really kind of you...I'm proud of you."

Oliver blinked, and his little joyous distraction faded as he thought about his words.

"I don't...know what you mean," he said after a minute. He

wrapped his dad's hands around himself, drinking in the warmth and safety of it.

"The money? I saw a good chunk of it missing from my wallet before you flew out. And I know Douglass brought you home before then too." Jon gave a gentle laugh and patted his son's stomach, lost on the soft seriousness of his answer. Oliver twisted around on top of him, resting his head on his chest in a moment of thought. *Should I?*

"No, I just—"

No...don't tell him. He doesn't need to know.

"I know we got a lot from the lab..." He felt his father shift under him, and his hand moved from his back to pet his head.

"And you figured it would be irresponsible not to help them out?"

*I can't tell him...*Oliver hummed softly in response, letting himself sink into the comfort his father provided. It was safe. Genuine. He didn't deserve it.

Death in the Family

liver stared at the gravestone from the cemetery gate, still trying to recollect something other than the last memory he had with what was supposed to be, and should have been, *her.*

His hand stayed shoved in his pocket, turning over a very warm little orange thing that was also supposed to be alive.

It was an easy cover up. A volatile experimental substance that amplified Chris's electrical current ten fold, no one got dangerously hurt. The electromagnetic fluctuations cut out the lab cameras. It was all cleaned up within the evening. It was easy.

It's supposed to be easy by now. You've done it before. You've been here before.

It wasn't.

After everything, he figured at some point he would be able to deal with at least his mother.

He couldn't do two at the same time.

So for the last week off from school, he went back and forth from his house to the cemetery, thinking that something would change and he could find some kind of catharsis in talking to a rock on top of an empty box in the ground.

He didn't.

What else can I do? Dad's been back to work since— there were too many accidents at the lab..and being at home was complicated.

By the time he got back, it was dusk almost, and the attic light was on for a change.

"Jon, I don't know what to do— and with AKAN breathing down our necks—" Oliver overheard Mr. Furkin from upstairs and did all he could not to bite down on his lip in effort to keep his tongue. Instead of going to his room and risking interaction, he dwelled for a bit in the living room before moving to the back porch to sit with his ghosts.

***

Jon leaned out of the attic doorway once he heard the sound of the front door close and hushed his colleague with a small wave, just in case his son heard them. "Take the blueprints, and any parts to my machine. I'll wire something over for you."

"What about—"

"It's fine, Chris." Jon shot down his objection with a slightly pained smile. "It's fine."

Chris lowered his gaze, letting it drift off toward the modified blueprint Dindet had made, and let out a shamed sigh. "I thought what I saw wasn't real...to think you were working with one this whole time."

Jon's smile faded and he rolled up the blueprint, handing it briskly to his friend. "Her name was Dindet."

Chris nodded, keeping his eyes to the floor in his incomparable guilt. He took the blueprints from Jon's almost too tight grip. *If I had known...it doesn't make any difference now.*

"By the way," Jon added, preventing him from leaving just yet. "Thank you for accepting the money."

Chris paused, sifting through his immediate memory in search of what his friend could be talking about. "What money?"

"The cash Oliver gave Douglass? He took it from my wallet at some point— figured he wanted to help you guys out." Jon offered a smile, one that slowly fell as he scanned the man's look of confusion. "It was a little under 800?"

Douglass would have told me about it if it was that much. "Jon, I don't know what you're talking about."

***

Oliver fished Dindet's bean from his pocket and rolled her gently in his palm in the brisk winter air.

He figured, if she was alive at all, he could at least keep her safe.

Every harsh word he had last said to her rocked around in his head and more than anything, he just wanted to say he was sorry. He just wanted to talk to her.

He held her up in the fading sunlight, squinting to see some tiny, hope inducing heartbeat silhouetted against the light before giving up and dropping his hand back into his lap.

He had forgotten that she was so small and soft and frail. That all of her was just this tiny round thing that held all her thoughts and feelings and that it could so, *so* easily be crushed if he squeezed just a little too hard.

He hated this, all of it. Far worse than he hated everything after his mother got taken from him. Moreover, Oliver hated himself.

He stood up, tired of being in a place where two people he cared about used to be, and slid the door open to go back inside.

"Oliver," Chris fumbled back to avoid the kid as he nearly ran into him. His eyes flickered down from Oliver's glare to the thing in his hands and he pressed his lips together in an uncomfortable frown. "Is that—"

"Don't touch her!" The boy cut him off, pulling his friend out of the scientist's reach and taking a few steps up the stairs to even further their distance.

Chris nodded meekly, submitting to his guilt and the grave repercussions of his ignorance, and let the boy go up to his room to sulk.

Oliver fell back against his door and let out a cold sigh before heading to his bed. He stopped, for a moment, his eyes catching the picture on his desk and he quietly placed it face down and set Dindet next to it. Then, promptly dropped face first into his mattress with a tired groan.

Sleep would be a miracle, but every time he closed his eyes, his brain filled up with the echoes of Dindet's agonized screams— at least with his mother he didn't see it happen.

He used to be able to imagine it, now all he could imagine was her screaming just like Dindet before being ripped apart into nothing.

Scattered. That's what she said. He figured it was something akin to Dindet's electrocution. It was the only sound comparison he could make.

A soft knock on his door lifted him from his thoughts and Oliver rolled over and turned his head, just as his dad crept it open with gentle hesitation.

"I'm sorry I haven't been able to talk to you." Jon began, taking half a step into his room. "Work has had me running around all week."

"It's fine," Oliver replied, resting his head back on his pillow and staring up at the glowy stars on his ceiling. Jon hung in the doorway, then finally built up the gall to come into his room.

"I know you're upset because we couldn't get...her back." At that, Oliver sat up, almost baffled by his father's blatant omission of who else was gone now.

"I'm sorry about Dindet too." Jon added, much softer, still awkwardly hanging back by the door rather than moving to console his child. It was the same bitter coldness he received the day Marie had gone.

Oliver seemed to fall into a pit, and everytime he got footing enough to climb back out, something else would topple over him and knock him back down to the bottom.

Jon did his best to understand it.

"It's my fault she's gone." Oliver interrupted the silence, keeping his attention trained on the stars on his ceiling, rather than the look of pity his dad gave him.

Jon shook his head and came closer, resting his hand on the down-turned picture and placing it upright again.

"It's not your fault, you couldn't have known," he tried, staring at the photo for a moment. Oliver turned over to face away from him.

"I'm going to bed," he said, signaling for his father to just give up on it already. The scientist reluctantly obliged, taking a small moment to look at the bean in solemn silence before letting his son alone.

Oliver lied. Odds were, he wasn't going to sleep at all. And his dad saying it wasn't his fault, that he couldn't have known? *I told her to go. I told her to leave, and when she didn't, I left her there in the cemetery. That's how she got found, because of what I did.*

It doesn't matter that I didn't know she got taken, it doesn't matter that I didn't know she was just across the street.

The principal of it was that you didn't care. Not at the time. Not until after she was gone.

She's gone now because you didn't care enough to look for her, all because you were so caught up in some stupid idea that you could bring back mom and everything would be perfect again. It didn't work like that.

Life doesn't work like that. The dead don't come back and mom and Dindet are as good as dead, and all you can do is be stupidly mad about it.

***

Oliver sat up as the sun started to peek through his window and rubbed his tired eyes, turning over to drop off his bed only to stub his toe hard on something cold, metal, and painful. He sucked in a breath with a grimace and bent down to see what he was about to chuck against the wall in a drowsy rage.

It's that music box toy. The one Dindet got from old lady Deauxtree the night she first came here.

He turned the rusty toy over in his hands for a bit, finding the key and twisting it up to hear the little circus tune it played before the lid popped open and a ratty jester doll flopped out with a dirty smile. *Of course that would be something she'd like.* He set the open music box down next to his lamp in exchange for Dindet and headed downstairs for an early breakfast.

Bad People with Good Friends

liver wanted to fall back asleep, but apparently the universe had other intentions for him, because not even thirty minutes into his couch nap did he get woken up by a knock on the door.

The boy sat up and begrudgingly went to the doorway, peeking it open to see Douglass half-mindedly messing with the mostly dead plants on the front porch.

"Oliver— hey, uh, how's your last day of break?" he asked, accidentally ripping off a leaf from the plant in his startle. *Has it been a week already?*

"It's fine. What do you want?" Oliver replied gruffly, waiting while Douglass twisted around to pick up something.

"I got a bunch of stuff during Hanukkah at my mom's this year. She's still trying to get me to stay with her and Gary. I— I figured since Dindet went back to her country for a while, we could play some video games?"

Right...that was the alibi I gave.

Douglass offered a small smile and held up a brand new gaming console, complete with several discs and downloadables in a bag around his wrist. "Uh, I also brought some movies, I know horror is your favorite."

"No." Oliver tried to shut the door but Douglass stuck his foot out to keep him from doing so, and glanced back toward his house with a look of mild unease.

"Can I *please* hang out with you? My dad's in a bad mood and I don't wanna really mess with him," he pleaded, giving the boy some high quality puppy dog eyes.

Reluctantly, Oliver let out a sigh, pushing the door open all the way and stepping aside so the kid could come in.

Douglass grinned and carted in his games, setting the stuff down on the coffee table and getting a good look around the living room as Oliver shut the door, already starting into the kitchen for obligatory guest snacks.

"Thanks for letting me hang out. Did you hear?" Douglass asked as he began setting up the console for the television. "My dad's project got all screwed up and it broke down before he could even show it off."

"Yeah." Oliver grit his teeth at the mention of it. "I heard."

He stuck a pot on the stove and poured in some macaroni to boil, not keen to remain on the subject.

"I wish I could have seen it."

"No, you don't," Oliver muttered under his breath, now adding powdered cheese and a bit of the good stuff to make it more than just crappy, watery mac and cheese.

Douglass was messing with the plugs behind the TV now, and briefly popped his head up in search of a remote.

"It worked just fine before," he stated, spotting the remote on the end table. As he moved to grab it though, he noticed Dindet's bean sitting next to it. "Hey, isn't this—"

"Don't touch that!" Oliver swiveled around, nearly tossing his wooden spoon over the edge of the pot as he sprinted over, stealing the precious thing out of Douglass's hands before he could even react.

The kid's eyes narrowed and a sly little smile crept across his face, garnering a meaningful glower from his friend.

"Did she give it to you?" he asked, raising an inquisitive eyebrow.

Oliver rolled the bean in his palm and flicked him in the forehead in response to his absurd implications.

"Oh my god, you *do* have a heart!" He laughed, rubbing the spot Oliver flicked and flicking him right back. "You liked her too, I knew it!"

"Douglass, you sweet, bisexual idiot. I'm gay." Oliver casually pushed him back toward his game. "I never liked her like that."

Douglass turned flush and averted his eyes, quickly changing the subject. "Have you been in your pajamas all day?"

Oliver blinked, glancing down at himself and his rather dirty, stained, pj's. "So?"

Regardless of Douglass's opinion, he felt some small obligation to change his clothes and quickly trotted upstairs as his friend followed.

Douglass milled around outside Oliver's door. "Are you allowed—"

"Yeah, it's fine," Oliver interrupted, waving him into his room.

"I mean— is it alright for me to uh...since you're..." Douglass trailed off, shrinking back when Oliver cocked his eyebrow at him, as if waiting for the stupid question.

"It's *my* room, I can have whoever I want in here. What sort of movies did you bring?" Oliver wandered into his bathroom and came back out with actually brushed hair. He then moved to his closet to change into a different pair of what were most definitely still pajamas, leaving Douglass to stand idly and awkwardly between the closet and bathroom doors, waiting to give him some of the DVDs he'd brought.

Oliver returned, picking one out and handing him back two of the three movies, then headed back downstairs to set up the television to watch whatever, probably bad, ghost horror flick Douglass had brought.

If he had to oblige having someone over, he didn't mind at all that it was Douglass.

He was a good kid. Despite how...complicated he made Oliver feel.

Douglass returned with a bowl of popcorn just as Oliver set up the movie and made himself as comfortable as possible on the couch next to him.

"So, what's this one about?" Oliver asked. He desperately craved the distraction, regardless of whether asking would serve any purpose in the long run.

"Some girl finding out about a secret cult worshiping town that kidnapped her family and want to...I dunno, sacrifice her to the old gods? Something dumb. Probably." Douglass chuckled a bit, offering his friend the bowl of popcorn as the movie started up with a scream.

"Ooh, replacing the studio theme with a scream. Definitely not cliché." Oliver gave him a small smirk, forcing back his bad thoughts as he stuffed his face with a handful of popcorn. "Okay— challenge. Every time something really stupid happens, stuff as much popcorn in your mouth and try not to swallow it or spit it out."

Slowly but surely, the distraction worked, and Oliver grew more comfortable as the movie played out its egregious clichés and Douglass's presence melted away the dark parts of his brain.

"Okay— okay!" He batted Douglass's cheek to try and get him to fail the dumb challenge they'd set up. "The next crappy jumpscare I'll put *two* handfuls in my mouth."

Douglass furrowed his brow, and sputtered something along the lines of, 'no, *more* than that.' But all that really happened was a few slobbery kernels came tumbling out of his mouth, followed by a trail of drool down his shirt.

As if on cue, the loud rise in music made the two kids jump out of their seats, Douglass spewing his mouthful of popcorn all over Oliver as he struggled not to cry from the hilarious and also ridiculously stupid snorts of laughter.

"Sorry!" Douglass gathered his nasty popcorn off his friend and tossed it into the trashcan he'd moved next to them partway through the movie. Oliver didn't reply, save for laughs through little grimaces as he held his side to keep from getting stitches.

"Ohoo..it hurts but it's so funny!" He moaned, wincing a bit through his smile. He threw his hand into the nearly half empty bowl and shoved as much popcorn in his face as he could, with absolutely no intention of ever swallowing it. "Nhwhshyooshheefamwonsher—"

"I have no idea what you're saying." Douglass snickered, poking him in the nose till his head tipped back and the kid struggled to keep his mouth shut from his stupid giggles.

"Mrphh!"

"*Use your words*," he said, trying to coax him into spewing. Oliver crossed his arms and shook his head, catching onto the dumb trick and focusing his attention back on the bad horror movie. Douglass laughed and gave up on his ploy, opting to wait for another scare to act as the force that'd make him lose the game.

They sat there for a bit, their silence being filled by the badly edited jumpcuts and screams of the protagonist until a surreal, dreamlike torture scene started playing out.

"Electroshock? That's kind of stupid, don't you..." Douglass's snide comment trailed off as he shot a quick glance at Oliver. The kid had turned terribly stiff, and his fingers dug into the couch.

His mouth dropped open and the challenge stopped mattering.

"Turn it off." Oliver barely even breathed the words and Douglass immediately bolted from the couch to turn the television off. He relaxed almost immediately, and looked ten times more exhausted than before as he curled up his legs and leaned against the arm of the couch.

"I'm sorry– I didn't think something like that would have been a tri–"

"It's fine. It's alright," Oliver cut in softly, "I'm alright. I'm okay– I just wasn't ready, is all."

Douglass murmured something softly to himself, and awkwardly picked up the popcorn that had been spat on the floor. "You haven't done that in a while...not since..."

Matthew came back? Or at least...not in front of...you.

Oliver kept to himself, opting not to remark on Douglass's obvious concern. So, his friend changed the subject entirely.

"Hey– remember my bar mitzvah?" he asked, throwing the last of the popcorn in the trash before he got up to snag some of the mac and cheese Oliver had made.

"Yeah," he answered, turning his head to follow him as he returned with an extra bowl and a couple glasses of water.

"Yeah, you stuck out like a sore thumb the whole day cause you had on that red saree." Douglass recalled, offering the little meal to him.

"Baba and Manpreet were over that summer and they didn't know how formal it was supposed to be," Oliver explained, growing only slightly less skittish as he spoke, "I still have it— and the big punch stain is still there too."

"That was an accident and you know it!" Douglass plopped down next to him.

"Was not! And even the dry cleaner couldn't get it out— it was silk!" Oliver rolled his eyes, and shoved a spoonful of macaroni in his mouth with a little mutter of his grievance.

There was a silence that drifted between them, long enough that Douglass was wont to fill it, but Oliver cut out any remark with a few innocuous words. "You wanna braid my hair?"

Douglass pulled his spoon away from his lips to stare at him.

"Like you used to, when Jojo lost all her hair..remember?" Oliver clarified, making a point to look away from him as he spoke.

"But it's so short now," Douglass answered in the tone that indicated Oliver's trite proposal flew right over his head. And probably out the door with the rest of his common sense.

"You can do a bunch of tiny ones?" Oliver picked up a tuft of his bangs and braided it in a couple of seconds to demonstrate. "It's just...I know you miss her, and you weren't in town for the anniversary this year...and we— we haven't done it in a while..."

"I thought you didn't—" Douglass caught himself. Finally catching up to what the poor kid was actually asking of him. "Yeah, uh, yeah it's been sorta rough. I'd like that."

Oliver gave a quick nod, followed by the tiniest of relieved sighs as he slid off the couch and situated himself on the floor in front of his friend.

"Let me know if I pull too hard, okay?" Douglass asked, politely reaching over the boy to grab the ashtray full of tiny rubber bands on the coffee table.

Oliver awkwardly fiddled with his fingers, offering a small nod and grabbing the remote so he could distract his thoughts with whatever badly written television series he could find on the satellite.

"I forgot how much hair you have." Douglass mused, methodically pulling tiny strands of choppy blond hair into braids at the nape of Oliver's neck. All of it was cut haphazardly in a way that clearly indicated he did it himself. Probably early in the morning before the first day of school, judging by how grown out it was.

"I guess? When I cut it, it got more wavy. Makes me kind of look like—" Oliver stopped, not keen on reminding himself how similar he looked to his biological father. *At least it isn't the same color.*

The two of them fell into a much more pleasant silence, allowing the background noise of the television to drown out the discontent of the previous quiet while Douglass idly plaited Oliver's hair.

It was nice. *Really nice.* He had forgotten these stupid little moments with Douglass and how he was so good and making things better. *It isn't the same way Dindet had done things.*

She had made things easier by way of distraction yeah, but no matter what, there was always a lingering...feeling, like she was bigger than anything else in the room.

The surface tension with her was thin and easily broken.

Douglass is like a little puddle in comparison. Small and unassuming and simple. Unapologetic.

"You still have my book by the way." Oliver broke the quiet. "The copy of Pride and Prejudice? You never gave it back."

"Huh?" Douglass nodded, retrieving himself from his daze of braids in order to answer. "You threw it at me, I didn't think you *wanted* it back?"

"I don't, I just...I remembered that. I'm sorry I threw it at you." Oliver handed him another little hair band. "In my defense, you *did* call me a vampire...dick."

"I only said that cause I'd never seen anyone hooked to a blood bag thing before!" Douglass defended himself, bending forward to press his chin into the top of Oliver's head. "Plus you're like..super pale— I mean not as much as Dindet, and I was twelve and dumb."

Oliver turned underneath him to try and shoot a pointless glare at the kid, only to scrape the tender part of his forehead on Douglass's chin and jerk out from underneath him with a gentle hiss of pain.

"S-sorry! Did I pull too hard?" Douglass loosened his grip on the strands in his hand and Oliver promptly leaned back between his legs with a disgruntled huff.

"No, I just forgot is all," he mumbled, rubbing the mostly healed scar Matthew had left from their last altercation. It had opened up again after he made the *very* extra smart decision of bashing his head into a glass case.

"Matthew hit me pretty hard with one of his beer bottles when I was at the motel." He answered, though the fresh memory that played in his head was the splintering of glass and Dindet's agonized shrieking.

Oliver felt his friend's fingers tense around his head before Douglass let out a shaky breath and relaxed. "Are you alright?"

"Yeah." He shrugged, ignoring the stress in the boy's voice. "I had to get a few stitches, and it's kind of ugly, so I'll probably never brush my hair back ever again. But it doesn't hurt as much as it used to. I was stupid and hit my head again is all."

"You're not stupid," Douglass corrected softly,"Can...can I see it?"

Oliver obliged the request and pulled his fingers through the front of his hair and tilted his head back into Douglass's lap to show off the newly uncovered wound. It was massive, wide where a piece of broken glass had sliced open the skin from his hairline and down, where it tapered off just above the kid's eyelid, cleaving his left eyebrow in two.

Oliver stared up, watching Douglass's lips twitch as his eyes traced over the half healed scar. The boy's expression moved from intrigue to concern and straight into rage before he blinked and refocused his attention on how long Oliver had been staring at him.

"It looks worse than it is," he said as nonchalantly as possible, opting to avert his gaze from Douglass altogether. "But you know— not like you can kiss to make it better or anything."

Oliver forced a small laugh at the insinuation to hide how hot his face got at the idea.

"I can if you want?"

What??

"Hhh," Oliver sputtered, "you're just saying that cause you've had a crush on me since I moved here."

"Yeah, and?" Douglass gave him a look of abject innocence, as if he had no idea what ugly little thing he caused to flutter up inside Oliver at the notion. "It doesn't have to mean anything."

"Well, it *wouldn't*." Oliver huffed, folding his arms to cover up how ridiculously fast his heart beat.

"So do you want me to or not?" Douglass offered a gentle little smile, the genuine kind that caught Oliver completely off guard. *It isn't like that. It wouldn't mean anything cause it's just a dumb kiss on the forehead, right?*

You don't even like him back.

Obviously.

You can't.

It's the same as when mom did it or something.

Exactly the same.

"Go for it, I don't really care." Oliver brushed away his silly anxieties and hunched forward, only to feel Douglass's fingers glide up the back of his head and gently tug him back into his lap.

He dropped back, staring up at the boy as he leaned closer and planted his lips on the quietly stinging scar.

Douglass had his eyes closed, which was probably a good thing because he wouldn't have been able to confuse the heat of a healing wound for the rush of blood that flooded Oliver's face and turned him bright red, if they were open.

He definitely couldn't see the way his pupils dilated back and forth in effort to remain focused on the present. The only thing

Douglass was privy to was the boy's hands reaching up and tangling in his curls.

Oliver on the other hand, had his eyes wide open. For every excruciating second. It was nice, of course. He liked it a lot. Way more than he thought he would.

But time moved increasingly slower as the seconds ticked by and he stared at Douglass's forehead. At first it was nothing, normal, usual. But then, as if a crack had formed in the back of his thoughts, the thing he was looking at began to morph and shift. It turned black and blue, manipulating the shadows to fit the image that forced its way to the front of his mind. Twisting something Oliver liked...into something he didn't.

The heat of his face grew stronger, louder, like an awful static in his head likened only to the one Dindet had. It flooded his ears and hitched his breath and in one fell swoop it dropped down into the deepest part of his stomach and crushed him.

Oliver reached up, brushing his fingers through Douglass's curls as he struggled to shove down the sudden and inextricable fear that latched itself to every thought that raced in his head.

"Get out." Deadpanned, the words drifted up from him into Douglass's ears, prompting the boy to attempt to pull away. But Oliver's fingers had already dug themselves into his hair, proving the attempt to be fruitless.

"Wh—"

"Get out of my house, Douglass," Oliver said, finally unlatching himself from the boy. Douglass sat up, a look of utter confusion on his face at the distance in Oliver's voice.

"Oli—"

"Get OUT!" Oliver bolted up, bringing the poor kid with him as Douglass's fingers caught the unfinished braids in his hair. He let out a hideous yowl and clambered over the coffee table in search of safety he didn't need.

"I— I'm sorry!" Douglass let go of him and stumbled back, balancing himself on the couch as Oliver swiveled around to glare at him with tears in his eyes.

"Just go! I don't want you here anymore!" He held the back of his head, taking a defensive step backward as Douglass tried to draw near.

"You said it was—"

"I know what I said! Leave!" Oliver spat, shuffling from the fireplace to the corner. *I need him gone. I need to be alone!*

Douglass rounded the coffee table slowly, keeping his hands up in some attempt to get his friend out of whatever spiral he'd so suddenly been shoved into. "You're not making any sense, was it bad pictures—"

"Why do you care?!" Oliver cut in, trudging up to him and forcing the boy to take a step toward the front door.

"It's your fault!"

"What—"

"You thought you could— could *trick* me, right?!"

"Oliver, I don't wanna trick you! I— I don't even know why you're upset?!" Douglass ducked away from the pillow Oliver chucked at him and took another few steps back as the boy left whatever defensive mode he was in and dove straight into offense.

"GET OUT!" He shrieked, throwing another pillow at Douglass in a frivolous attempt to make him stop caring. *Stop being worried and just leave. Please!*

"What's *wrong*?!" Douglass barked back, prompting the boy to fling another decorative pillow his way. "You're being crazy! I just wanna help!"

"You think I don't *know that*?! I don't want your help, you idiot!" Oliver shoved into him, knocking Douglass off his balance as he pushed him toward the front door. "I WANT YOU TO LEAVE!"

"I just—"

"DON'T YOU GET IT? YOU'RE THE PROBLEM!!" Douglass was not the problem.

Oliver threw the door open and forced the boy out of his home.

Douglass whipped around in effort to get back inside, until the door slammed in his face and he was locked out and left staring in utter bafflement at whatever just happened.

Oliver slammed his fists hard into the wood and immediately crumpled down to the floor in a heap of gut wrenching sobs. Each one hurt far more than the last and god, all he wanted was for it to stop.

"You *idiot!*" He bit, referring only to himself as he smacked his palms hard against his head. "Why are you like this?!"

He was just trying to help! You stupid, worthless piece of shit. You always do this. Every time. He was just trying to help.

Oliver stupidly punched the door, letting out another wail in effort to quell that awful and ugly irrational fear that bubbled up in his innards and threatened to spill out of him like the bile in his throat.

"Douglass is *good.* He wouldn't hurt you like that. Why are you afraid?!" Oliver curled up against the door, banging the back of his head against it in order to make his brain start working again. "You *like* him...stop being so stupid. He won't hurt you. you stupid, stupid, *stupid*—"

But he could.

That's all it was. A tiny, horrific thought that rose up amongst his efforts to push down pictures of blood and sweat, and Matthew. Markus.

It was something Oliver had forgotten. That everyone had the same capabilities. *That it was so easy. That if they wanted*—

Oliver's attention was pulled away from the ugly thoughts with the soft buzz of his phone on the coffee table. It made him crawl to his feet.

It was Douglass. No doubt still standing outside his door. He stared at it as it rang, half of him dearly wanting to let the call end and the other half desperately desiring the opposite. He picked it up.

"Douglass—"

"I'm not mad," his voice cut in softly. *He should be. He should be so mad at you.* "Oliver, will you please let me back in?"

***

Douglass changed out the movie that was playing, switching it for a romcom that he knew for a fact wouldn't trigger his friend– aside from maybe his gag reflex.

"Is it at least one that's actually funny?" Oliver returned from upstairs, plopping down on the couch and making himself comfortable. He kicked his legs up on the boy's lap once he sat down and eyed Douglass incredulously.

"I think it's a funny one," he replied.

"I like that one with Shakespeare– or was it the knight one?" Oliver got up again, heading back to the kitchen to make some of his personally patented hot cocoa and kicked the quilt over the both of them once he handed one of the mugs to Douglass.

"You only like that one because it's got a girl that pretends she's a guy."

"I get my rep where I can, alright? I don't ask for much."

Douglass settled in next to him, stretching out on the couch until he took up roughly half of it and Oliver promptly shoved his foot in his face.

"Sorry for freaking out," he said, as casually as he possibly could.

"It's alright, I'm not mad about it." Douglass poked his toes, causing him to pull his feet back with a slightly forced scowl as he sat up. "I'm just glad you let me back in... I figured you hated me after I kissed you."

For a second or two Oliver turned away from him, if only to hide how red his face turned at the kid's utter nonchalance with the topic.

"Do...you still like me?" He asked after a moment. "I mean, cause you know— I know you had a crush on Dindet for a while. I mean— it's not like I care or anything. I just don't want it to...cause— cause I've done...*do* things...that hurt you..."

Oliver's rambling ceased the moment Douglass's fingers filed between his and held his hand.

"Of course I still like you," Douglass's smile was sweet. Genuine even. It made Oliver's stomach flop over and twist itself into knots as he stared at him, so he dropped his gaze in tender shame.

"You don't want to like me," he muttered. Oliver curled his legs up to create some small distance between them and pressed his chin into his knees. Then pulled his hand out from Douglass's grasp. "I'm not...*good*."

Under New Management

"**D**id something happen?" Jon whispered, keeping close to his colleague as the two of them made their way into the back of the lab. Chris looked terrified and there was a wild look in his eyes as he kept pace with Jon.

"The new head director wants to know how the project is going and—"

"Gentleman." The voice made the two of them stop in their tracks. Dr. Hausman stood at the end of the corridor, directly in front of the hall that led to the despicable machine they were creating, and something far worse. "Director Miles is waiting for you."

Chris gulped dryly, glancing back at Jon for some silent reassurance, but the man stayed stone faced in the wake of their unknown. The woman beckoned them forward, and they abided, quietly following her to the center room that held the atrocity.

Some giant glass case, reminiscent of the one Chris had created to hold Dindet, stood in the corner. Newly constructed and attached to a large generator that on occasion buzzed and threatened the creature inside with its jolts of electricity.

Jon halted, grabbing Chris by the wrist to keep him from moving any closer and the three of them stared at the alien that had been captured some short while ago.

It was tall, taller than all of them. Its three pronged hat just barely grazed the ceiling, despite the fact that the jester was hunched over with its long claws perched under its chin in an expectant pose. A smile etched across its face, crinkling up the corners of its pupiless black eyes as if it were holding back a laugh.

"I appreciate your work in searching for the entity, however it seems we were looking in the wrong place." This new voice came from the right of the cage, where an incredibly tall, lithe and androgynous person stepped out of the shadows.

"Director Miles," they introduced themselves, unfolding their hands for the men to shake, "I've been brought in to oversee the transporter project."

Jon clenched his jaw hard enough that Chris could hear the grind of his teeth.

The director smiled and took the scientist's hands, shaking them vigorously.

"My understanding is that you two have been enlisting the assistance of an extra-dimensional entity to recreate a functioning molecular transporter and an electromagnetic disruptor—respectively."

"Director," Chris began, gently placing a hand on Jon's shoulder to keep the man from doing something reckless. "If I may be so bold...I don't believe that—"

"Yes," Jon interrupted, forcing himself to smile despite the ungodly amount of rage that boiled just beneath the veneer. He glanced at Chris for a brief second before taking his hand off his shoulder.

"I was worried that we weren't going to be able to find it," he began, "as we've hit some roadblocks for our project, I can't seem to figure out how to accurately measure the rate of vibration needed to move into the fourth dimension. That was our test, you see—"

"I don't care about the metrics, Jon, I care about results. And keeping things under wraps," the Director cut in.

"As you know, AKAN is now partnered with a— shall we say, *secret* military branch of the FBI. *This* was found by our research team," they explained, their eyes cutting to the enormous alien, "about twelve miles from your property."

Jon held his breath, keeping his eyes trained on the alien jester that smiled back at him.

The storm...it put itself here.

On purpose.

"Do you have anything to say for yourself?"

Jon let out the breath he was holding in an attempt to calm his nerves.

"I...have been working with it," he lied, "in an attempt to bring back Ma— my wife. I tried to get rid of it after Chris had almost killed it."

Chris blinked, quickly grasping what cogs were clicking in his friend's head and nodded, prepared to back his claims if need be.

"So, you are the one responsible for this?" Miles asked.

"Yes."

"Well," the Director clapped their hands together, donning a wide smile. "Then you understand the gravity of the situation?"

"Yes," Jon answered.

"I'm glad you do," Director Miles glanced toward the door, as the room began to fill with government agents that carried tools and machines. "I want to introduce you to your new colleagues, agents of the BERC, the Bureau of Extraterrestrial Reconnaissance and Contact."

Jon glanced at Dr. Hausman, trying to read the look on her face, but she simply bowed her head as Miles continued. "The objective hasn't changed, you're going to continue work on the molecular transporter, and assist BERC in studying these entities, their technology and composition. During your *conditional* employment, you and your families will be protected under federal law— so long as we don't have any more...hiccups."

"And boys," The Director paused, "None, and I mean *none* of this is to leave this lab, understood? If the public were to find out that an alien species exists among us, it would incite panic with the people. The president would be forced to get involved, this facility would be shut down permanently and you..."

The Director circled around Jon, gliding their fingers along the glass case. "Let's just say it won't be good for you or anyone you love."

Director Miles eyed Jon, patiently waiting for the scientist to bow his head in a stiff nod.

"I understand."

***

Jon quietly came in through the front door of his home, juggling bags of groceries along with his keys and coat.

He couldn't quite bring himself to come home, or see the look on Oliver's face when he'd eventually have to tell him what was going on.

So he went instead to pick up some groceries at somewhere around six in the morning and planned to avoid him as much as possible. Part of him hoped Oliver wanted the space.

He set the groceries down on the counter, pausing briefly from putting them away to hear his son murmuring in his sleep from the couch. Jon snuck around the back of it, catching sight of two kids instead of one.

Douglass took up most of the space, his head kinked up against the arm of the couch, and Oliver managed to somehow wedge half of himself in between his friend and the back of the couch, the other half was thrown over Douglass like a stack of pillows. Popcorn and movies littered the floor in front of the coffee table, and both boys had video game controllers shoved between themselves and the cushions.

"Ahhrm." Jon cleared his throat as loudly as he could without letting out the laugh in his voice.

His son made a little noise, no doubt some half murmur after staying up for way too many hours, thoroughly crushing Douglass in the game they had been playing— judging by the score displayed on the television.

"Ols, next time you have a sleepover, send me a text, alright?" Jon said, poking his kid's foot lightly enough to tickle him. Oliver's face scrunched up a bit, and his eyes flickered open to see his dad's cheeky, dumb but distracted smile.

Immediately he sat up, or at least tried too. He shoved his hand into Douglass's stomach and woke him up too, causing the boy to *also* try to sit up— despite Oliver putting all his weight on him in his own attempt.

"There something I should know about?" Jon chuckled.

"N-no!?" Oliver turned flush and promptly shoved a still very tired Douglass off the couch entirely. The poor kid scrambled up from the floor with abject befuddlement striping his face with blush.

"I'm just joking, Oliver." his dad tousled his hair and headed back to the kitchen to put away groceries. "Next time just give warning before inviting friends over."

"Uh, I'm..I'm gonna go. Now." Douglass casually retreated to the door, leaving before anyone caught on in effort to spare himself from secondhand embarrassment.

"We were just watching movies," Oliver followed his dad around, helping him put up the things he'd bought as he attempted to give an explanation. "Plus it's not like I *like* him!"

Jon gave an incredibly incredulous look, prompting the kid to let out a more than embarrassed huff.

"Where have you been all day?" Oliver changed the subject, "work?"

"Yeah," his father's demeanor shifted, almost unnoticeably, but his son saw it nonetheless.

"I thought you weren't gonna go back until January?" He picked at the sack of bread, and began setting various other groceries in the places they needed to go.

"There were some changes, and I've had to start working earlier than..anticipated," Jon answered, already beginning to unravel at the seams.

"Why?" It was a stupid question, but Oliver asked it anyways. "It's because of what happened isn't it?"

Jon stopped and drew in a breath, half preparing himself to tell his child what was going on, and half resenting the fact that it was happening at all. *I made this mess though.*

"Ols..." he hesitated, "it's really not anything to worry about. The lab covered everything up, but they decided to move to new management, and the new Head Director called me in to start working on a new project."

"What kind of project?" Oliver eyed him, moving back toward the couch to pick up leftover popcorn and cups.

"Eels," his dad answered, taking a moment to come up with a believable lie. "The biology department discovered a new species of deep sea eels in the Marianas, and sent a couple live samples over to the lab to study."

"You're a physicist though," he countered.

"Yeah, but they are really short staffed, due to the expedition team being out in Thailand," Jon turned to face him now, "they think that the species has mutated due to the radiation on the Marshall Islands, and that happens to be one of my specialties— so, they asked me to come in and study them for the time being. It'll only take a month or so."

Oliver paused, dropping his gaze down to the ground, and letting it drift off toward the back porch.

I said I was going to be here..

"Oliver, hey," his father moved, kneeling down in front of him so he could look him in the eyes, "I know things are rough, and I said I'd be there for you, and I am— it's just...not in the way we expected. Things are gonna even out, I promise."

"Are we in trouble?" Oliver's voice was soft, almost like he knew the answer, and desperately wanted him to say the opposite. Or tell the truth.

I should tell the truth.

"No," Jon mumbled, rubbing his hands over his son's arms in effort to comfort him, "no, no...everything is gonna be fine. I'm taking care of things."

Happy Birthday

liver stared at his ceiling. There were forty-two stars on it. Two hundred and ten points for each one.

He counted and recounted them over again, all night to keep himself from falling asleep.

He didn't want to have a nightmare. *Not today.*

He could hear the soft creaks of the floorboards as Jon crept up the stairs in an exhausted haze. He knew what he was going to ask.

"You sure you're alright to go?" His father murmured through the door. Oliver blinked, but kept his gaze on the stars.

"Yeah, I'll be fine," he said, "it's just another day."

It wasn't. Today was his birthday, February seventeenth. He was fifteen now. And another year closer to starting testosterone.

Normally, on any other kid's birthday, this would be cause for celebration. But for him it was just an ugly reminder.

Today was the day his mother was…

Scattered.

Oliver heaved a sigh and rolled onto his side, staring at his alarm clock. *Nine hours. Nine hours and school will be over. Three more and the day will be too. You can get through that.*

***

Cassidy quietly meandered the hall before class started, searching as inconspicuously as she could for Douglass. She wanted to ask if he knew why Dindet hadn't been coming to school since winter break, though she wasn't entirely sure if he knew her secret.

She would have asked Oliver on the first day back. But he missed it. And the day after that. And the day after that one too. By the time he *did* come back to school, he looked perpetually exhausted and like he wanted to punch anything that so much as mildly annoyed him.

Today was a bit different though, and she expected him not to come to school. So instead of looking for Oliver, she looked for Douglass.

"Douglass!" Cassidy called, catching the boy's attention as he pushed through the front entrance. She hastily waved him forward, pulling out the tiny pink box she held behind her back.

"What's up?" Douglass offered a gentle smile, his eyes drifting down to the little box with intrigue. "Ooh, you brought cupcakes?"

"They're for Oliver, cause it's his birthday, right?" Cassidy tilted her box for him to see. "You said he really likes Indian food?"

"I mean, he loves it, but Cas—"

"Oh good, cause I wasn't super sure."

"I'm not sure today's a good day—"

"It's supposed to be Gulab Jamun, but I don't know if I fried the donuts right," she continued in earnest, poking the clear film over her homemade treat to keep the sugar soaked topping from falling off the frosting. "I figured you could give them to him for me since he's probably not—"

"What are you guys talking about?" Oliver interrupted, prompting Cassidy to swivel around with her gift, and Douglass to don a look of pure regret as he curled inward on himself.

"Nothing—"

"Happy birthday!" Cassidy cut off Douglass's effort to end the conversation, thrusting her box toward Oliver with a small, nervous nod.

She watched as the kid's tired gaze drifted from her face down to the box in her hands. He stared at the sweets for far longer than Douglass knew to be a comfortable amount of time.

"...thanks..." Oliver reached out, deftly pulling the box from Cassidy's grasp. He stood there, for a moment or two, still staring down at the cupcakes as he wobbled unconsciously. Then he simply turned and left for class.

"*Why* did you do that?" Douglass finally said once the boy was well out of earshot. "This is the worst day to do anything for him! Today is the day—"

"That's why I did it," Cassidy interjected matter of factly. She readjusted her bag over her shoulder and began walking to the classroom. "It's the anniversary of his mom's death *and* his birthday. I think it would be especially cruel to not try and cheer him up."

"But he wouldn't want that, you know how he is, right?" Douglass followed, lowering his voice to a whisper as they neared the classroom. "He's not gonna wanna talk about it, or even acknowledge it, so why would you go to all the trouble?"

Cassidy stopped just before the door, forcing Douglass to halt in effort to get an answer out of her.

"Cause Dindet's gone too now," she said, briefly twisting her kinky curls into a ringlet above her shoulder. "He doesn't have her to talk to about it, he probably misses her as much as he does his mom...so I wanted to do something nice."

She was right, even if she were guessing. In fact, throughout the day, Oliver's thoughts crossed from his mother to Dindet and back again as he milled about.

He drifted from one location to the next like a ghost trapped in purgatory, only ever remaining cognizant enough of his surroundings to comprehend the most minimal of what he needed. In class he was quiet, bordering on sleep as the English teacher droned on about dystopian allegories for World War II.

Today was the only other day that Theo made a point not to bother him. She had her head shoved into a book, only glancing back once or twice to get a look at the cupcakes he had set at the corner of his desk.

"Mister Jariwala." Oliver blinked and his head jerked up in effort to keep himself from nodding off again.

"U—huh?" His glazed over eyes hovered between the current and whatever was left of the dream he was starting to have. Mrs.

Hargreaves stood at the front of the class, staring back at him with a pleasant, yet frustrated smile.

"Can you please get eight hours of sleep *outside* of my class?"

"Y-yeah...sorry." Oliver rubbed his eyes, pressing his fingers into them in order to make them stop stinging so much, and stared down at his copy of Fahrenheit 451. Then promptly fell back asleep.

***

Theophania Deauxtree ambled somewhat aimlessly down the school halls, her eyes scanning the scattered and taped over posters of the most recent missing student. Some upperclassman boy, apparently.

She wasn't really here looking for missing seniors though, but Oliver. Or Olivia.

She wasn't entirely sure anymore and as much as that frustrated her, she understood that today was a very bad day to act on that frustration. So instead, she had quietly snuck out of class behind the boy when he'd asked to use the bathroom, and was following at a reasonable enough distance that he hadn't yet caught her.

Oliver drifted like a half full balloon for a vast majority of his very long and mostly meandering trek to his designated bathroom, stopping every now and then to stare at the school's terrible motivational posters or the art classes pottery display for a lot longer than the average person likely would. After a while, Theo had nearly turned her quiet stalking into a sort of game, where she was the spy and he was the one being spied on.

Mostly because she hadn't gotten the nerve to actually speak to him, let alone attempt to console him on the anniversary of his mother's death.

Oliver stopped again, prompting the girl to duck behind the trash bin against the wall. Theo waited, cursing herself so briefly under her breath for how much of an idiot she looked like, hiding from a dumb boy-girl-*whatever*.

She peeked over the lid, and just as she did, Oliver's head turned and he stared directly at her with that same empty expression he'd been wearing all day.

"What do you want, Theo?"

Shit, shit, shit.

She lowered a tad and mustered her nerve to stand up.

"Nothing, obviously. Definitely not anything from *you*." She shot, completely failing in every definition of the word, to be either nonchalant or kind.

"Okay." Oliver deadpanned, turning to continue his balloon drifting.

"Wait—" Theo called, kicking herself in soft regret. She picked up her speed enough to stop him, though it didn't take much effort as he seemed not to really care about outpacing her.

She pulled in front of him, forcing the boy to a halt and he stared directly through her.

"If you're going to say something mean, I'd appreciate it if you saved it for tomorrow," Oliver stated, prompting the smallest and most stomach curdling form of guilt to bubble inside of Theo as she stared down at him.

"I— I was actually—"

"You don't have to remind me," he cut in, pushing her aside with Mrs. Hargreaves' fat wooden block of a hall pass. "It's my fault she's dead, just like you said the first time. I didn't forget, so you can go back to class…pick up your regular schedule after today."

"God, you— you are so *annoying*." Theo reached out, grabbing the kid's shirt and tugging it ever so slightly, causing Oliver to draw in an anxious breath that pulled her eyes away from the tight fabric of his binder.

She was taller than him, by at least a foot, but she towered over all the other girls in her class. And some of the boys.

"Do you like being this way?" Theo cut through his silence, fully unaware of how it landed on Oliver's ears.

He stared back at her, slowly pressing his palm into her balled fist to loosen her grip.

"I don't know what you mean." He didn't look scared as he spoke, only tired, and it was confusing because he still trembled. *She was always scared.*

"Do you like being like this?" Theo repeated, "that's what I wanted to ask you when you came back to school. Is it what you wanted? Now that she's dead?"

Genuinely, she was trying very hard to not sound as full of hatred and jealousy and anger as she was. But Theo couldn't help but grit her teeth at the gall Olivia had to claim that she could *only* feel grief on today of all days.

She stared at him for a moment, until his shaking became apparent enough that she let go, dropping her gaze in effort to alleviate the tension.

"I'm…sorry," Theo added, much softer and with such an air of discomfort that the apology sounded far more hollow than it did genuine. "For what I said about her..your mom—"

"No, you're not." Oliver interrupted, the sting in his voice not made any less painful when he moved his gaze to the wall. "You don't care, and even if you did, you always hated her so don't *lie* and say you're sorry when you're not."

Theo's brow furrowed and she couldn't stop her face from screwing up in stupid and vile anger at his response.

"I said it because it's true," she argued, retracting her already poor attempt at an apology. "You're just— just an idiot because for *some* reason, you think that pretending or— or forgetting, or *whatever you're trying to do* is just gonna change things like they never even happened! Like I didn't have to—"

"SHUT UP!" Oliver twisted around, showing off the first actual emotion of the day with his visceral glare. "You promised. You *swore* to not talk about it, and *you* were the one who made me leave— don't act like you're this– this *angel* when all you ever do is make me miserable. You made *everyone* believe your stupid rumors, and then— the one day. *The one day* I should be allowed to be upset, you follow me around for half an hour, just to tell me I can't be?! She was my *mom. My mother.* And now she's gone, forever."

"As if she was ever there in the first place," the girl scoffed coldly, struggling with her own vindictive desire to force Oliver to see things from her perspective, for just once. Theo tangled her fingers up in

Oliver's shirt and listened intently to the fast little breaths the boy heaved in effort to hide his panic. All it made her think of was that day in school when he wore that ugly white dress. And every day before that...when he lived just a few feet down the apartment hall.

She didn't imagine something so stupid as that would remind her how thin the walls were.

"I'm glad you got adopted."

Oliver blinked, his angry face softening with small shock at Theo's surreal honesty before she shoved him back a couple of steps and turned on her heel the opposite direction.

She paused briefly, dropping her chin and tilting her head just enough that she knew he could still hear her.

"You're better off without them."

***

Oliver stared at the girl as she left, some tiny and indignant part of him wanting so badly to yell and scream at Theo for her cruelty. Instead he just dropped his gaze off and away, pretending that not a word she'd said affected him.

She's the annoying one. I didn't even do anything to her!

What right does she have to—

His thoughts cut short when his attention was wholly stolen by something he'd least expected.

Wait...

Oliver leaned forward, taking a few steps closer and squinting his eyes at the missing person's poster tacked into the corkboard across the hall.

He moved closer and tugged at the paper, tearing it down from where it was hung so he could further inspect the image of the unfortunate student.

"I..know you.." he breathed, his eyes flickering back down the hall to make sure he wasn't overheard. The only other person around was that new therapist, but she was way too far away to hear or probably even recognize him.

Oliver scanned the paper briefly.

Missing

Cody James Mulligan, age 17. Last seen November 21st of last year at Ehil Inn off HWY 70, exit 180, wearing black jeans, Metal-Allica T-shirt with gray jacket, brown and green beanie hat and housekeeper's apron. If you've seen this boy or know his whereabouts, please contact Pineton Police, ext. Department of Missing Persons at 555-0162.

Just below the description was a large photo, undoubtedly a school photo taken of the senior the prior year. His fluffy brown hair flipping out from underneath his hat, coupled with the exact same shirt the poster described him last wearing.

It may have been a very brief time Oliver had interacted with the boy, but the moment the memory returned, ugly realization made his fingers crinkle the paper with quiet tension.

I saw him.

I saw Markus punch Cody before he

went…missing..

Walking Backwards

hree hours and forty-five minutes. That's all I have left before I can go home and the day…today will be over.

The sound of a cafeteria tray landing next to him shook Oliver from his thoughts. He lifted his head from the cool, plastic lunch table to stare at Douglass, who sat down next to him.

"Where's Dindet? Did she go back home for real?" he asked, sliding into the seat and pushing his tray toward Oliver to share. He didn't go through the line again and hadn't so much as touched Cassidy's sweets, so Douglass figured it would be best if he got food for the both of them.

"Sure," Oliver answered, placing his head back down and blatantly ignoring the offer.

"Is everything okay?" he asked, poking the kid in the head until he sat up with a reluctant sigh.

"*Yes*. Everything is fine."

Douglass furrowed his brow, and poked him one more time with a frown. "You're lying. What's wrong? Do you miss her?"

This time, Oliver dropped his chin into his chest and folded in on himself, murmuring a soft 'no' that was likely the least believable thing anyone had ever heard.

"You could call her?" Douglass tried.

"No."

"You could—"

"Why do you care so much?" Oliver cut in, tossing a glare at the kid as he stood up. *There isn't any point to this.* "No one wants your opinion."

Oliver shoved the tray back toward him, enough to knock it completely to the ground, prompting Douglass to shoot up out of his chair.

He reached forward, clasping his hand tight around his friend's arm and yanking him back with just enough force that Oliver let out a stifled gasp.

He could feel the wound Dindet had made on his arm tear and start to bleed again as Douglass wrenched him back.

His eyes darted from the wince in Oliver's face to his arm, landing on the stain of blood through the boy's sleeve that painted his fingers red.

"*What did you do?*" His voice was low, rife with concern, in such a way that Oliver fumbled to come up with an excuse in the moment.

"It's not what you think! I'm not like that!" He spat, But before he could react, Douglass grabbed him by the wrist and pushed back his sleeve, revealing four perfectly spaced bloody holes.

"*Oliver…*" his voice was wrought with disbelief, prompting the boy to shake his head and claw his fingers off of him.

"I— I wasn't the one who— I don't need this right now!" Stealing his hand back, Oliver retreated off to tend to the painful mess.

He didn't need this. He didn't need any of this and yet everyone just had to get into his business, because they had some preconceived notion that he needed to talk to them. *I don't. I don't need to talk to anyone.*

***

"I think it would be best if you sought counseling." Mrs. Bradshaw folded her fingers together and looked over her glasses at the very annoyed kid sitting in the chair across from her.

"No," Oliver grumbled, keeping tight to himself as he stared at the floor.

She shifted in her chair, "what I mean is, you will be suspended from school, again, if this behavior keeps up, therefore it is *in your best interest* to seek counseling."

"That's not fair!" He retorted, smacking his palms down on her desk as if to make a point. Though it served the opposite purpose. "I haven't even done anything!"

The school counselor rolled her eyes and thumbed through the files on her desk. "The first day of school you came to me saying you were hallucinating a clown. You've missed nearly half of the first semester. Your grades are falling significantly. You've skipped class, hid in the janitors closet, bullied other students, stolen school property, locked yourself in the bathroom for six hours. *You ran away from home.* And let's not mention the very concerning rumors that have been in the halls— of which I'm sure you are aware."

"Oliver." Mrs. Bradshaw dropped her papers down to look directly at him. "I understand that losing your mother, having your abusive father come back into your life—"

"*What* rumors?"

"–and housing a foreigner in your home all while going through transition is *hard*. It is really hard. But running away from home? Hurting yourself?"

"Hurting myself?" Oliver drew pale, and almost instinctively folded his arms in effort to hide the bandages under his sleeve.

"Whatever is going on is having such a negative impact on you, and I am *trying* to help you." The counselor seemed to completely ignore him. "So I've talked with your teachers and we have come to the conclusion that a mandatory session with the school therapist is the best course of action."

"What if I skip out?" He threatened.

"You will be expelled from school for ongoing disorderly conduct."

Oh.

"...you can't make me do this." Oliver scooted further back in his seat, pressing into the cold leather in order to try and keep his head from floating off his shoulders. *This isn't happening. I'm fine! Everything is fine. Really.*

"You're right," Mrs. Bradshaw replied, "I can't make you do anything. But I have already called your father and he agrees that, at the moment, this is best for you. So your afternoon class will be followed by a session with Miss Popiviolli, and she will escort you from room 309 to her office starting tomorrow."

"There's no way!" Oliver argued. *He wouldn't do that without talking to me about it first!*

***

It was well past dark when Jon pulled into the dirt driveway of his home and kicked through the snow on his way to the door. The cabin was dark, and he hoped that Oliver was already asleep in his room.

The exhausted scientist hung his coat and keys on the side wall, taking care not to flip on any lights and potentially wake his son if he *weren't* in his room.

He needn't worry though, because the moment he turned to the stairs, the living room lamp clicked on and Oliver's head swiveled around to face him.

"Ols it's almost two—"

"You're sending me to therapy again?" Oliver cut in, the rage in his unnaturally calm voice not hidden in the slightest.

"Oliver, it's late. We can talk about this over the weekend—"

"Oh really?" Oliver bit back, scrambling from the couch in order to block his father from going up the stairs and avoiding the conversation altogether. "Like how we talked about you deciding to send me to therapy? *Oh that's right!* You didn't!"

Jon rubbed his face and let out a soft groan, prompting an ostentatious eye roll from his son. "I was going to tell you, things have just been— they've been really hectic. For both of us."

"But I'm doing *fine*! I don't need any more therapy!" Oliver argued, barring his dad's second attempt to get either up the stairs or into his bedroom.

"You say that—"

"I am!" The boy held up his arms, mimicking Jon's efforts to evade and pushing him back into the living room. "I can talk now, right? What more do you want?"

"Oliver, I've been awake for almost twenty-four hours. The *only* thing I want right now is to sleep." He let out an exhausted sigh and pressed his fingers to his temples to alleviate the headache that had built up over hours of staring through a microscope. *Now isn't a good time.*

"That's not fair though! First you send me to India, and now *therapy* without even telling me, and— and you don't even wanna talk about it?!" Oliver grabbed his father's sleeve, though the man simply dragged him along with him as he frumped into his bedroom. "I'm not even mad that you're making me go. I'm mad that you didn't tell me. That you *lied*!"

"LIKE YOU LIED ABOUT STEALING?!" Jon snapped, spinning on his heel to face him.

Immediately Oliver relinquished his grasp on his father and retreated with a startled little gasp.

"I didn't lie. I just... with Dindet, Matthew and Marie, the transporter— Douglass told me how you'd..." Jon trailed off, his thoughts ceasing among the increasingly noticeable sound of Oliver's sudden and overwhelming panic. He turned, squinting in the shadows in order to get a better look. "Oh...Oliver, I– I'm sorry."

The boy stood with his eyes planted somewhere in between his father and nothing, gulping down quick and pointless breaths in order to stop trembling as much as he was.

Jon softened himself, his posture and his voice, "Hey, it's okay...listen."

He moved closer, kneeling down as he met Oliver's height and pressed his hand over his chest. "Just breathe."

At first the kid flinched, breaking his line of sight with the morphing shadows to flicker his gaze down at what had touched him. Then he choked down an attempt at one heavy breath, sputtering out the exhale as Jon breathed in unison.

"I'm sorry, I didn't mean to scare you. I'm not going to hurt you. I'm not mad...I'm sorry I yelled." He reassured him, coaxing out another deep breath along with the most subtle of nods. *This is why. This was why he needs it.*

Sooner or later, Jon knew that everything would catch up to Oliver the way it caught up to him after Dindet destroyed his portal. Of course, he was able to handle it— for the most part. He was an adult. But Oliver was still only a child, and such reconciliation didn't come nearly as easy to him as it did his step-father.

"I'm just worried," Jon admitted, gently rubbing his child's back as he felt his heart begin to slow. "It's been so much for me, losing her, the custody case...Dindet. I can't even imagine what it must be like for you."

Oliver gulped dryly, sucking in one final and calming breath before he stepped away from Jon in a moment of thought. "I'm doing *fine*. I can handle it on my own."

"Oliver—"

"I can." He cut him off in earnest, offering a sympathetic glance back. "You have a lot of work to do...with eels. And...I guess a few sessions wouldn't hurt."

***

Oliver did a particularly good job at making his father feel better about things. That didn't mean he wasn't still mad. He was livid, in fact. And it showed on his face the entirety of the next day.

"Oliv—"

"Don't. Talk. To. Me." He ordered, glaring at Douglass as he pushed past him to the hallway.

Regardless of his wishes, the kid followed him, easily keeping up as Oliver tried to outpace him.

"I'm sorry, it's just—"

"*Be sorry.*" He cut in, "it's your fault. I have to go talk to some stupid therapist I barely even know because of you. I don't even get a choice!"

"I'm just worried—"

"I don't care!" He spun around, slamming his palms into Douglass's chest to get him to back off. "You think you know shit but you *don't*! You think you're my friend, but you're not! I don't need you, I don't need therapy, I don't need *anything*!"

Douglass lowered his head slightly, almost as a show of submission, before his eyes flickered back up to glare at Oliver.

"I *am* your friend. Whether you think so or not, and— and you think you're the only one who has it bad? Who lost someone? I lost my sister! My dad's probably going to lose his house! But I don't hurt myself because of it!" He shoved back, lighter than Oliver was prepared for.

"So? At least your only friend is *alive*! You didn't watch them get TORN APART!" He shouted, shoving even harder this time, with enough force to knock Douglass a step back.

"SHE IS DEAD!" Oliver pushed him back further, preventing Douglass from regaining his balance, "DINDET IS DEAD!"

Aloud, it hurt even more, and Oliver's continuous shoving turned into meek pressure as he fought against the bile that rose in his throat and the tears that threatened to fall.

"And it's my fault." He whispered, "it's my fault. My fault, *my fault*!"

Oliver butted his head into Douglass's chest, smearing his tears into his shirt as he shook and trembled, forcing the boy to comprehend on some level how abhorrent a person his so-called 'friend' was.

"Th-that's not true," he murmured, pressing his hands into Oliver's shoulders to push him away, just enough to see the terrible anguish in his eyes. "...she just went home, that's all. She's not—"

Before he could finish, Oliver pulled away, staggering back as he stared at him completely dumbfounded.

"I— I lied..." Oliver's eyes flickered toward the emergency door as his head made a terrible decision. Then he ran.

He didn't make it far. In actuality, he slammed right into the slightly plump, pale, red headed woman that rounded the corner at the most inconvenient of times. The two of them collided so hard that the psych books she was carrying flew along with her and Oliver.

He crashed hard into the ground, face first, warranting a nasty bloody nose to compliment his tear stricken, blotchy face.

"Oh, my goodness! Are you okay?!" Miss Popiviolli crawled on her hands and knees toward him, immediately tearing off a piece of paper to roll up and shove up his nose. "I didn't even—"

She paused, looking him up and down for a moment before reaching over to grab a folder that had strewn papers everywhere on the floor. "Do I know you?"

Oliver's head shot up and he rubbed the blood off his lips, still dazed from the torrent of thoughts and this lady's random appearance. He was certain she wasn't standing there before.

She reached out a hand to shake, offering a soft smile until he deftly obliged.

"I swear I've seen you before. Oh! You're the boy that stole from the principal's office. Oliver, right?" She chuckled lightheartedly. "You don't look so good."

She held his hand for a moment, squeezing slightly as he attempted to take it back. Eventually she let go and began gathering her things.

"I guess we'll find out why in our session, huh? You can call me Poppy."

"I don't want to." He croaked softly, refusing to get up at all.

Miss Poppy let out a small sigh and shrugged, "nobody wants to go to therapy, love. That doesn't mean it's not any help."

She got to her feet and waited patiently for him to do the same. Though, Oliver was hard pressed to act at all and simply folded into a criss cross, glaring up at her like she were the devil herself.

"Make me." It was an unbelievably childish remark, but he didn't expect her to actually bend down and force him to his feet. So when she did, he promptly let out a small groan of disobedience as she dragged him off toward her office.

"You know, I'm not going to make you say or talk about anything that makes you uncomfortable." *Every topic that I could possibly conceive is uncomfortable.*

"And the rules of confidentiality still apply, so none of it ever leaves my office unless you pose a danger to yourself or anyone else," she continued, leading him by the arm to the door of her office, "you're a tiny little thing though, so I don't imagine you could harm anything."

Miss Poppy unlocked her door and gestured for him to enter. Reluctantly, he did.

She circled around a couch and motioned for him to sit while she flipped on a white noise maker and sat down on the sofa seat across from him.

This is stupid. This whole endeavor was stupid, and a waste of time and Oliver didn't want anything to do with any kind of therapy. Least of all with some stranger.

"I'm not talking to you. You know that, right?" He shot a look at her and frumped down into the seat, moving his eyes toward the clock on the wall.

Poppy nodded, practically accepting his obstinance and crossed her legs with a sigh. "Okay. We can just sit here in silence for ninety minutes if you like."

Poppy Seeds

"I want to go home."

Oliver glanced away from the office window, watching Miss Poppy as she fiddled with her clipboard, boredly waiting for him to say something else.

"Let me go home," he said gruffly, leaning back into the couch as his attention turned toward the clock. It must have been broken or something, because regardless of the ticking, he was still sitting here in silence in front of this weird woman, while time apparently stopped.

"You've been to therapy before? You mentioned that the last time we chatted. You were a lot more talkative then— what changed?" she redirected, flipping through a small file that was probably compiled by Mrs. Bradshaw. The boy glared at her, hoping that if he stared long enough, she would just let him leave, or spontaneously catch on fire. "It says here you used to see Mrs. Aguirra."

"She was better than you," he muttered.

"You ought to know how this works then?" She remarked, ignoring him entirely and crossing one leg over the other as she tapped her fingers on the arm rest. "I can't do anything if you don't talk to me. It's not like I can read your mind."

Oliver huffed, and narrowed his eyes at her, turning his attention entirely to the woman as he looked her up and down. She was pale, almost as pale as Dindet, with droopy, cat-like eyes and bright red hair that looked way too perfect to be normal. For a second, he thought she wasn't breathing at all.

"I don't expect you to," he answered, gauging her response as she simply smiled.

"You're tough, aren't you?" she said instead, leaning forward. "I read your files, hospital records, the court transcripts and Dr. Aguirra's notes…that's a lot for one person to try and handle…especially with your history of sexual abuse."

What?

Oliver blinked and quickly dropped eye contact, pressing further back into the couch at her words.

"Oh my," Miss Poppy's still face shifted into a look of soft regret and she set her clipboard aside. "I'm so sorry, I shouldn't have brought that up so carelessly. I had surmised as much from our brief session last year, the only thing that really confirmed it was the record of your recent hospitalization."

"This isn't how therapy works," he retorted quietly, closing in on himself as she stripped away the curtain around his life. "I'm- you're not supposed to talk about that stuff."

"Why is that?" The therapist twisted around in her seat, reaching back to her desk to pull off a binder full of papers and transcripts. She thumbed through the notes. "It's nothing to be ashamed of."

As if just saying that changes anything.

"It explains quite a lot, really," Miss Poppy continued quaintly, "children who've experienced chronic sexual abuse develop a myriad of social and developmental issues— especially in cases as severe as yours."

"Stop."

"An incestuous relationship with a parent from such a young age, especially in combination with such a violent household can lead to struggles with emotional regulation, behavioral issues, like your history of violent outbursts? Deep feelings of guilt and shame around intimacy, personal relationships— romantic or otherwise. Hypersexuality and tendency to enter into unhealthy relationships is very common for kids like you, having such a skewed perception of what is normal and what isn't. There's often a great desire for emotional dependency, coupled with anxieties around abandonment... I wonder if your mother was aware—"

"I'm not talking about that," Oliver interjected, only fueling the woman's near spiteful interest in the topic.

"Why not? It seems to have had a lasting impact on your life. Complex Post Traumatic Stress, Depersonalization, selective mutism? These are all very common results of experiencing such horrific—"

"I don't need you to list off everything that's wrong with me." Oliver grew increasingly aggravated with the gall this uppity woman had. He turned his gaze back to the clock in order not to face her. *It wasn't that bad. She's just making it out that way in order to get something out of you. Don't fall for it.*

"Still, that's a lot for a fifteen year old kid to handle."

"It was over three years ago," he corrected. "Matthew is gone now, and so is my mom so it doesn't even matter anymore."

"So...it doesn't matter that only four months ago you were admitted to the hospital due to a septic miscarriage you weren't even aware was happening?"

Dammit.

"It wasn't that bad. You're making it out to be worse than it really was," he argued impatiently, keeping his eyes away from her as he scanned the room.

"Do you say the same thing about what Markus did?"

....h–how does she. I never—

Oliver tensed, every fiber of his being growing taught with adrenaline at the succinct and deceptively simple remark. *She shouldn't. She couldn't know about that! I never told anyone. Not Jon, not even Douglass. Only Markus—*

"Hhh..." he struggled to respond, still reeling from the mere fact that she said it. That she knew.

Oliver's eyes flickered back to her, grazing over the bored look on her unnaturally still face. She stared back at him. Unmoving, aside from the blue stress ball rolling in her palm that caught his eye.

"Y-you're lying," he managed to sputter out. "I never said anything like that happened— it doesn't— *didn't*. You made that up just to get to me."

"I...try to respect the confidentiality of my patients, Oliver." The therapist closed her binder and leaned forward. "But I can't deny my suspicions. A previous patient of mine had made several mentions of you in relation to mister Mulligan-Higgs. He was concerned about you— that you had engaged in—"

"I said it was fine. It's what he wanted and I don't really even care anymore anyways."

Oliver stood up shakily, shooting one more pointless glare at her as he moved toward the door. "It's only bad if you say no, or don't say anything, right? I didn't even know he recorded it until after—"

Miss Popiviolli leaned back in her seat again, twirling her pen in her hand with a barely hidden smirk at how far his tongue had left him.

"You can go, if you're not comfortable. But I would really like to continue our conversation," she replied.

It doesn't matter. What she says doesn't matter. Markus doesn't, Matthew doesn't. I shouldn't have to sit here and talk about this if I don't want to.

I did it because— because I wanted to! So that makes it fine. That's how it works. That's how it's supposed to work, right?

"That boy," Miss Poppy continued, standing up to confront him further. "The one who was concerned about you, he's gone missing, Oliver."

Instinctively, he grew stiff, clenching his hand around the doorknob in preparation to leave. She came closer though, her fingers fanning out over his arm and hovering just above his wrist. She tapped him lightly, causing Oliver to tighten himself further.

"I worry that you may be...a target." Her eyes drifted down to his hand that gripped the door handle and Oliver hesitated to turn it as she retreated back to her seat with a tired sigh.

"You've done this so many times before, and you're angry and bitter because by now, you should be okay, but you're *not*. I understand that, I understand that my prying brings up all sorts of awful memories and feelings that are hard to control and contain." Poppy rested her head on her fist. "I want to help you, but I have to make sure you're safe and *feel* safe enough to talk about things..I'm sorry that I haven't accomplished that for you."

Oliver dropped his head, tightening his grip on the door.

"I…saw him last. Cody." he answered, quietly unclenching his hand from the knob.

Oliver pulled away, though as he did it felt like the floor had dropped ten feet lower and he hadn't followed. His mind turned soft and fuzzy for some small second and he blinked to stop the sudden and profuse tears that rolled down his cheeks. He wasn't even sure why they were there.

***

Oliver trudged through the spring rain to his house.

Douglass walked behind him, far slower, keeping a decent ten feet out of his way while he silently rampaged. There was simultaneously very little and very much to question about his friend, but he didn't have the gumption to speak at all.

He was certain he was hiding something, or more than one thing, and regardless of how hard Oliver tried to hide it, Douglass recognised quite quickly the way he seemed to walk backwards into a pit.

He kept his eyes to the dirt though, stepping around puddles of mud and water and eventually tearing away from Oliver as he continued to head to his house.

Douglass shoved his front door open and dropped his backpack the second he entered the front hallway, glancing left to right in case his dad was home. There wasn't any noise from the garage, and the master bedroom light was off, along with every other one in the house.

He flipped the switch, once, twice, before he realized that the power had been cut off. Again. *We must have missed a bill last month.*

He wandered into the kitchen to pull out a secret little stash of cash he'd saved up from working at the antique shop and folded it up into an envelope to send off later.

Douglass made his way back outside, catching Oliver just as he shut the door to his house. *Maybe I should go say something.*

If Oliver wanted to talk to me, he wouldn't have said so. He's the type of person that just holds everything inside until it explodes— and then he'll pretend nothing ever happened at all.

If I want him to say anything, I'd have to force it out of him. Or I'd just have to learn how to read people's minds.

Douglass glanced back at his empty house, then at the cabin before heading straight down the road to his friend's home.

*****

Oliver flopped down on the couch, fishing out Dindet's weird little bean to see if it still beat teeny tiny heartbeats.

Suddenly, there was a loud knock and he nearly jumped out of his skin. He stared at the door, praying it was just in his head, until a familiar voice called from outside.

"Oliver? It's me, Douglass...can I come over?" *Great. Another thing I don't need.* Begrudgingly, after several more and increasingly persistent knocks, he rolled off the couch and opened it to see Douglass idling rather uncomfortably on the porch.

"Oliver, hey—" before the kid could finish, Oliver slammed the door in his face.

"Go home, Douglass," he grumbled through the wood, peeking out the peephole to see if he would. Even though he knew he wouldn't, and didn't really want him to.

"Ols, I'm sorry," he whined back, knocking once more on the door. "I freaked out, it was dumb and I shouldn't have told anyone without talking to you first."

Oliver leaned back against the door, slowly sliding down to the floor. *Of course he would say that. Of course he would make me feel even more awful than I already do. It's not your fault Douglass.* "Just go away."

"Oliver, *please.*" There was a light thud on the door as Douglass butted his head into it, "I just want to talk...we never just... *talk* anymore..."

Oliver dipped his head before tipping back with the slightest wince of agony. He sucked in a preparative breath and got to his feet to crack the door open. Just enough to see the genuine concern in Douglass's eyes, which made it ever the more difficult to deny.

"Fine," he said, pulling the door open. But before the kid could come in, he stepped out, pushing him slightly off balance as he cautiously stepped onto the porch. "But not here."

He made his way around the back porch, leading Douglass off toward the treeline and taking particular care to not tread near where Dindet used to sit at night.

"Where are we going?" Douglass stepped around soaked earth as he caught up with Oliver.

"Dunno," he replied, keeping his eyes on the ground as he trekked further up the incline toward a cliff overhang. "I don't want to be home right now."

Really I want to just not be anywhere.

"Are you gonna tell me what's going on?" Douglass asked, "about Dindet?"

"If I do, you won't believe me," Oliver answered briskly, breaking a thin low hanging branch off one of the trees he passed under. "You'll just think I'm crazy and have even more reason to tell on me."

Douglass picked up his pace, rounding the kid and stopping in front of him to make him slow down. "I won't tell on you, and I promise, I'll believe you."

Oliver halted, smacking his stick on the trunk of a tree in contemplation. *It would be really, really nice if someone other than me and Dad knew about everything. Cassidy apparently knows to keep secrets too..I guess.*

He paused a moment, heaving in a breath and quickly combing his fingers through his hair before actually coming out with it.

"Dindet is an alien clown and she was helping my dad finish a machine that was supposed to bring my mom back from interdimensional space and we got in a fight and I told her to leave but then your dad found her and used her in *his* machine and it killed her and I think the government is coming to investigate or something I don't know."

He's not going to believe you.

Oliver clenched his eyes shut, hesitantly peeking to see the unmistakable look of befuddlement on Douglass's face. Immediately his hopes died and he deflated, averting his eyes back toward the ground. *Told you so.*

"You don't believe me," he murmured, venturing further up the mountain side until he reached a small clearing that led to a cliff edge another few hundred feet up.

"I— I believe you." Douglass affirmed, in the least affirming way possible. He followed his friend to the edge of the cliff, taking care not to step on the patches of packed snow and ice that still clung to the ground around the steep drop just to their right.

Oliver stopped at the edge and dropped down in the dirt, laying back to stare up at the little white dots that swirled around in the sky. "It's fine. It doesn't even matter anymore."

"It does to you," Douglass remarked, plopping down next to him and immediately picking at the tufts of grass that grew through the stone. "If it matters then it matters, and I don't think you're crazy."

Except for maybe psychotic. Dindet was weird and dressed like a clown, but an alien? Something is still wrong but there's no way Douglass would believe it's alien clowns. Stress, right? That can do stupid stuff to your brain? Make you think absurd things like that? He probably thinks I totally lost it.

"Does it..sound worse because I'm back in therapy?" Oliver asked, prompting Douglass to stop his grass picking to stare at him.

"Well...logically, yeah."

He doesn't really believe me. And even if he did, Dindet is gone. There's no real way to prove it.

"Your honesty knows no bounds." Oliver sat up, and casually chucked a small rock over the cliff side, watching it plummet down into the forest below. "It's because of what happened to Dindet...and other stuff also."

"Oh..what other stuff? like your mo—"

"No," Oliver cut in.

"Just like, stuff…it's really not super important but—" He grew quiet and fiddled with pebbles on the ground. "You know that kid who went missing over break?"

Douglass sat up.

"He's Markus's brother," Oliver continued, glancing up to catch Douglass's look of intrigue sour with anger, "I guess..he went missing the night we..."

"Went to see your mom…" The way Douglass finished the sentence only made Oliver drop backward on the ground, rolling over with a heavy sigh of submission.

"..yeah."

Red Words

Cassidy quietly made her way around the school halls, delivering the new batch of missing person's posters to the teachers as per the office lady's request. It was early in the morning, before anyone she normally talked to got to school because, unfortunately, they all rode the bus and she lived little more than a couple miles down the road.

She turned the corner into her homeroom class and stopped, caught dead in her tracks by something she didn't even think was possible.

Theophania Deauxtree stood almost face first into the desk behind hers, scrubbing with absolute fury to get every last marker stain off of the laminate. She was so thoroughly occupied by her endeavor that she didn't even hear Cassidy enter, let alone know she was there until the girl's voice startled her from her efforts.

"What are you doing?"

Theo jumped and twisted around, immediately planting her hands over the words written on the desk. "N-nothing! What are *you* doing?!"

Cassidy cocked an eyebrow at her and promptly set her posters down on Mrs. Hargreaves desk. "Delivering the updated posters of that boy to the classrooms. I do it for all the missing students before class starts. What are *you* doing?"

Theo rolled her eyes. "God, you are such a teacher's pet. It's not even important so why don't you go lick someone else's shoes."

Cassidy's flat face twisted up with a scowl at the girl's words and she edged closer, causing Theo to shift in order to prevent her from seeing what was written on the desk.

"That's Oliver's desk." She eyed her, trying to circle around the girl's attempt at blocking. "Did you write on it? That's destruction of school property! What did you write—"

"I wasn't the one who wrote on it, I'm just cleaning it off, *god*!" Theo swatted at her.

"Well who wrote on it? What does it say?" Cassidy demanded, trying to catch her hand and throw it away before Theo could slap it back down over the laminate.

"No! You can't—" too late. Cassidy ripped Theo's arm out from under her, forcing her to take a step back and reveal the huge red letters that spelled ugly words all over Oliver's desk.

She stared at it, cataloging every insult in her mind and coming to a screeching halt as her eyes flickered back to Theo's bright red face.

"Cady and Alexa started hanging out with Hailey," she explained, trying to shrug off her discomfort. "She told them some stuff and they decided to start screwing with him...I've been cleaning it off, but they keep writing more after basketball practice. I can't get the sharpie off."

Cassidy offered a dumbfounded little nod, still in the process of trying to wrap her mind around why Theo, of all people, would go out of her way to get rid of such nasty things. "But you *hate* him, I thought?"

"Ugh, why does everyone think that?!" The girl huffed and moved toward the teacher's desk in search of chance nail polish remover. "I don't hate her— him. He just— pisses me off."

Cassidy furrowed her brow and turned to face her.

"You're mean to him literally *every day*. And *you* started the whole thing about his mom! If that's not—" Cassidy stopped herself, her insides turning upside down with unabashed, if not slightly snide joy. Her whole face scrunched up with a grin. *"You have a crush on him, don't you?"*

Theo sputtered nonsensically in response and shot an ugly little glare at her. "No I *don't!* That's *gross. I don't like girls."*

"Well, yeah, *duh. Oliver's not a girl."* Cassidy remarked, not hiding the bite in her tone. She took a step closer to Theo, prompting the girl to move the other direction around the rows of desks. "It's okay if you like him, but I'm pretty sure he leans the other way, if you know what I mean."

Theo nearly slammed the bottle of cleaner she'd found on the desk and shot another wild glare at the girl. "María, madre de cristo— don't let me hit this stupid girl. *No.* I just don't like seeing this ugly crap right behind me! Especially because I already know about his—"

Theo cut herself off, cursing nothing words as she forced herself to focus on removing all the slurs on Oliver's desk.

"His...what?" Cassidy leaned in, her interest thoroughly piqued now.

"It's not your business." Theo chided, "and you have no room to talk, getting on to literally everyone and their freaking dog for saying anything mean at all."

Cassidy's gaze dropped and her enjoyment in the girl's embarrassment dipped down into something else entirely. "You used to live with him, right? The same apartment complex?"

Theo paused, refusing to look up from her work despite the severe shift in Cassidy's tone. She didn't answer.

"I only ask because I know the sort of stuff Hailey has been spreading about him."

Theo continued to scrub as if her life depended on it, and every second longer she stood in front of Cassidy, the weight of her followed silence bore into her until she couldn't take it anymore.

"The apartment next to mine, what of it?" She finally answered, adding a spritz of cleaner to the desk to try and work it into the laminate before the bell rang.

"Were you guys friends?"

"Sort of."

Cassidy let out a soft sigh of contemplation, briefly pulling Theo from her concentration and causing her to look at her. There was so much pensivity in her face, she could almost hear the cogs turning in her brain. Then Cassidy spoke, softly, with intermittent glances toward the classroom door as she continued.

"A while back Hailey got mad at me for sitting with Dindet and them, it was after he showed up in a dress," she said, "she went off about those rumors and stuff and I didn't really think anything of it, you know? But Oliver started freaking out...like *really freaking out.* I asked him about it and he just said she was lying…"

Theo scrubbing slowed to a halt as she listened to the girl speak. Every word was like a pile driver in her bones and for some awful reason, she couldn't stop shaking. Couldn't stop thinking about it, how she knew exactly what she was talking about and how loud it was through the walls of her room. Even when she shoved all her stuffed animals up to the side to try and buffer it.

She shook her head to loose the thoughts from her mind. "You shouldn't pry into people's personal lives."

"I— I'm not trying to," Cassidy backtracked, "I just, I know how bad it can get and with Dind— with everything else I know...it doesn't feel like...I think something happened."

Theo dropped her cloth on the desk and turned to stare the girl dead in the eye. "You *don't* know how bad it can get, and you don't know what you think you do. What Matthew did doesn't have anything to do with you and if you were *really* Oliver's friend you would leave it alone."

"What did Matthew do?"

Theo scoffed at the question, finishing up her successful attempt at removing the slurs on Oliver's desk as the bell rang and the first few students began trickling into the classroom.

"Ask Oliver yourself."

***

Oliver wandered through the hall during the class switches, taking his dear sweet time on his way to the one bathroom he was technically allowed to use. He'd opted several times over to go out of his way to use it because the more convenient option was in the hall closest to Markus. And he'd been avoiding that boy like the plague. Especially after his session with Miss Poppy.

"Oliver!" Cassidy's voice called from much further down the hall behind him and he immediately picked up pace. "Oliver, wait, I wanna talk!"

"I don't!" He waved her off, turning down the nearest hall to avoid her. Unfortunately, she was more well versed in the layout of the school and knew that particular hall was a dead end. So she cut him off at the neck.

"Please? I promise, it won't be like last time. I'm not gonna smack anyone or anything!" She panted, catching up with him when he was eventually forced to turn around and go back the way he came.

"Dindet's not coming back, I already told you. And *honestly* you shouldn't be talking about her anymore in the first place." He said, hoping that was exactly what she wanted to hear.

"I know that, I wanted to talk to you because I want to know more about you." She replied, prompting the boy to stop dead in his tracks and stare at her.

"No."

"What? Why not?" Cassidy followed him as he tried to escape once again. "You seem like a— like.. well, uh.."

"Oh, please, don't hurt yourself," Oliver remarked, shooting her a sideways glance in her attempt to call him 'nice'. "The only reason you hung out with me and Douglass in the first place is because you liked my clown. She's gone and I'm not interested."

Cassidy huffed and dropped her attempt at being friendly, instead moving in front of him and spreading her arms to block his path. "Why do you always have to be such an *asshole?!*"

That definitely made him stop.

"I'm not—"

"Yeah, you *are!*" The girl cut in, taking a step toward him and forcing him back in the process. "You're mean to everyone, all the time. Even when they're trying to help you. I just wanted to ask you about Matthew and you—"

"SHUT UP ABOUT HIM!" Oliver cut her off, startling her with the absolute desolation in his voice. "Those girls were lying, Markus was *lying*. Just leave it alone, alright?"

Cassidy lowered her arms, taken aback by how easily the boy lost all his aloof and distant composure. Like he was nothing more than a pile of heavy rocks pulled together with sewing thread.

He attempted to push past her but she dug in her heels and wouldn't dare let it go.

"Were they?" She countered, catching up with his half jog of a walk. "Cause I've never seen someone freak out like that before—and you practically ignored me for the rest of the year after. That doesn't add up."

Oliver swiveled around to go a different direction. *I can't do this right now. There's another way to get to that stupid bathroom right? East wing?? Or was it west—*

"*Oliver.*" Cassidy interrupted his thoughts, prompting him to shoot a shaky glower in her direction. It wasn't nearly as palpable as he wanted it to be. "I'm just trying to help, okay? I was talking to Theo and she mentioned someone named Matthew— Douglass told me he's your dad right?"

"*Stop.*" A pitiful response. Oliver side-stepped between the girl and the lockers, trying to get to the other end of the wing so he could circle back and hopefully lock himself in the bathroom again just to escape her interrogation.

"Did he do something?" Cassidy followed.

"Stop!" Oliver turned on his heel to face her, making the ugliest face he could muster in his desperate struggle to keep his nerves under control. "Did that stupid therapist put you up to this?! Is she using you to get me to say something?!"

"What? N-no, you're in therapy?" At her answer, the boy twisted back around and picked up his pace until he was panting from the effort it took to get away from Cassidy's prying.

Eventually, he came to a stop at a corner, hunched over and trying to drag in breaths to steady his heartbeat. *It's fine. It's alright. He won't come back. No one knows. Markus hasn't done anything yet. Stop freaking out.*

Oliver gulped and brushed the hair out of his face to gather his composure. Only to come face to face with the exact person he was running from when he stood straight.

"If he hurt you, you should tell someone." Cassidy stated, completely blind to the panic in Oliver's eyes when he stared back at her. He quickly evaded her and circled around the girl to edge his way closer to the bathroom. *It's down this hall I just have to get there. I just have to—*

"My mom is a social worker, we can do an investigation and everything," Cassidy added, still tailing him only a couple paces behind. *It's close. I'm so close! Just get there and it'll be fine.* "You'll be protected if he ever came back, we even have these kits—"

"Cassidy *please*!" Oliver's legs fell out from underneath him and he slammed into the ground in a spectacular display of his utter failure to keep walking. The only good thing it did was cause Cassidy to stop talking and stare at him, trying to figure out how he managed to trip over nothing.

"A- are you okay?!" The girl scrambled to his side and dropped down, trying to help him up. He swatted at her and dragged himself to his feet again, still struggling to pull in breaths.

"I— I'm so sorry, that looked like it really hurt, you're sure you're….alright." Cassidy met eyes with the boy for little more than a fraction of a second. It was all she needed to understand just how far she'd pushed. Oliver's whole face was red and blotchy, tears streaming down his cheeks as he fruitlessly sucked in air and looked back at her as though she had gouged a knife into his side and twisted hard.

"Leave— leave me alone." It was much more of a plea than a demand, the way the words fell out of his mouth. Immediately Cassidy pulled away from him to give him space and he sat on his knees, still rubbing his eyes and trying so very hard not to look like some lost little kid.

For a moment, she just stood there, waiting in silence as the boy gathered his nerves again, not knowing what to do.

"Oliver, I'm...I'm so sorry," she said after a while. He'd managed to stop crying uncontrollably now, and was just sniffling stupidly on the ground. "I...went too far.."

"Yeah," he choked out, forcing an anxious laugh into the response. Cassidy crouched down beside him, adjusting her skirt so she didn't accidentally step on it in the process.

"I just...I *do* actually care about you. Not just Dindet. I wanna make sure you're okay too."

"I'm fine," Oliver retorted, though the bite he wanted in his voice wasn't there. He got to his feet and brushed the dirt off his legs. "It's nice...that you care and all. But I don't need your help."

Cassidy's mouth dropped open in objection, but she held her tongue and took a step back to allow him more space.

"Usually you just use the boy's room." She changed the subject, glancing around to get a picture of her surroundings. She'd chased him all the way to the other side of the school where the unisex restroom was.

"I can't anymore." Oliver obliged the silent shift in topic. "Bradshaw threatened to expel me if I don't start following the rules."

"That's not fair," Cassidy responded, hesitantly following him the last few hundred feet down the hall to his destination. "Is...that why you're in therapy?"

Oliver stopped, his gaze locked on the bright yellow caution tape covering the wide entrance to the restroom. The door had been viciously ripped off its hinges and blood red paint splattered over the wood and tile. In the dark of the tiny room inside, the sink was torn off the wall and several plungers shoved into the toilet.

On the door, the floor and the mirror, in ugly red words were awful names and a single demand. 'Where is it, Olivia?'

"Yeah," Oliver answered, "it is..."

Perpetuation of Violence

Theo smacked her hands down into the desk, causing Oliver to jerk his head up and stare at her with abject confusion.

"Did your freak girlfriend go back home?" She chided, her eyes flitting to the desk behind him that now sat empty.

"She wasn't my girlfriend." He grunted, casually pushing her hands back off of his desk. Instead of leaving like he wanted her to, she sat down on the desk instead, flicking him in the head to get his full attention.

"Oh right, that would make it gay." Her eyes narrowed and a small smile pulled at her lips, "don't wanna disappoint your *new* dad."

For a moment, a very small one, he flinched, forcing himself to relax in order to look up at her.

"*You're* one to talk, Theo." Oliver shoved her back off his desk and promptly laid his head back down in effort to better ignore her. Frankly, he didn't even want to waste the energy.

Theo, on the other hand was apparently in the mood to only focus on him, and just as quickly bopped the back of his head, hard enough that his face slammed into the desk.

"Wh-what the hell?!" He reared back, rubbing the new bump on his head, before getting out of his desk to confront her.

"What?" She questioned, donning a look of mock innocence, "I didn't do anything."

"You hit me!" He retorted, instinctively gripping the bar of his chair to force down the shudder that threatened him.

Hit her back.

"It wasn't even that hard!"

"You out of— *forget it.*" Oliver shot another glare back at Theo. "I'm leaving, get out of my way."

He quickly ducked past her and out the door, immediately veering off toward the furthest place he could think of. *It's fine. Everything is fine. I wasn't going to do anything, I wasn't mad. I'm not gonna freak out.*

That stupid therapist didn't get in my head. Emotional outbursts?? Pffft. It's stupid. She's stupid. I'm fine.

Oliver threw open the door to the boy's restroom and quickly scanned the place to make sure no one was inside. Then moved to the sink.

It's dumb. Stop freaking out. You're fine! That would never happen and besides—

Oliver splashed his face with water, stringing his hair back with his fingers as every part of him fought the urge to crouch down and descend into that awful terror in the back of his mind. *She's making you do this. There's no reason to be upset. Stop being upset! It wasn't that bad. It's not that—*

"Just the kid I've been looking for."

Oliver jumped at the voice, twisting around to see Markus staring at him from next to the bathroom door.

"You like the little message I sent?" he said, looking him up and down.

"I was just—"

"Leaving? Without even saying goodbye? Rude." The senior cut Oliver off, taking a step closer.

"I can get you more money, if— if you want, I just have to ask my dad." Oliver side-stepped around him, opting to move to the next sink over so he didn't have to maintain eye contact.

Markus stepped up toward him, blocking his view of the exit and forcing him to stare blankly into his chest. He was trying to intimidate him, make him feel small, unsafe. It was working.

"See, I *would* trust you on your word. But we both know that's not what I'm here for." Markus's eyes locked on Oliver, making every part of his skin crawl with unease. "Where is it, Olivia?"

"I don't know what you're talking about," Oliver answered, moving around the senior. "I'm just trying to leave—"

"No, I think you're trying to avoid me." Markus cut him off, taking a step closer, simultaneously cornering him against the wall. "It's all a little too convenient."

"I told you, if you want more money I can get it for you—" Oliver tried to make his way around him but that option quickly dissipated when the senior grabbed him by the shirt and his back hit the bathroom door.

"The flash drive is gone," Markus' voice turned into a vicious hiss, "and it seems a bit too much of a *coincidence* that my stupid brother is missing along with it and you don't show your face for weeks. You and him were the only people at the motel, so I know it was you and him who stole it."

Oliver froze.

What?

He struggled to move, to force down air and actually grab the handle of the door.

By the time he did though, the older boy was already uncomfortably close, causing Oliver to instead press himself into the door as if it would do anything to help him. The doors opened inward. And right now he dreaded the idea of bringing himself any closer to him.

"He ran off, didn't he? He's always messing with my shit, ruining my stuff and bitching about who I fuck." The boy pushed into him and Oliver clenched his eyes shut to keep himself from crying.

"I don't know anything, I swear," Oliver answered, hoping his honesty would be heard.

The pressure against him moved away and Oliver's mind spun in effort to find a better exit route. But instead, before he could make any escape, the kid planted his hand on the door and stared at him.

"Don't you dare lie to me."

Oliver's breath hitched, caught in his throat along with the sting of bile that rose in it. He moved, taking advantage of the small gap in space between him and the much larger boy as he darted toward the stalls to avoid him.

Before he could though, Markus jerked him back and slammed him into the bathroom door and his fist crammed hard into the boy's stomach, just under his ribs.

Oliver's face twisted from fear into wild shock and he dug his nails hard into Markus's wrist to stop him from yanking on his hair. It hurt. So much and he couldn't stop his gagged up gasps for air.

"Hhh—" words stopped forming in his mind and stopped connecting to his tongue. It felt like his whole body had turned into rigid stone and jelly all at once and all of Oliver's focus stayed planted on the ground between Markus's feet.

"You put him up to it, didn't you? Tell me where my brother is *and* where that flash drive is." The way he said it was ugly and vile and Oliver grimaced with the sheer level of exertion he put into keeping the boy from pulling his hair out.

Fight back.

He couldn't get the image out of his head. Blood and glass and suffocating.

Fight back!

Markus pulled harder and Oliver winced, making some horrific little noise in an effort to keep himself from crying out in pain.

"You think I plan on going to jail over your little stunt?" He continued in Oliver's inability to answer. "Or did you grow a cock and balls over winter break?"

The senior pressed into him and his free hand dug between Oliver's skin and the fabric of his pants.

Oliver squirmed, one hand shooting down to stop him while the other clawed into Markus's wrist to ease the tension on his scalp.

He was shaking, afraid, of course. But the look of visceral loathing that flashed back at Markus the moment Oliver felt his cold fingers press into his skin hid any ounce of fear that could have been seen.

I'll kill you.

Oliver grunted, forcing down his shudder as Markus leaned in, his lips just barely grazing Oliver's ear. His voice dropped low and poison dripped from his mouth. "Yeah, I didn't think so—"

Suddenly the door shoved open and knocked Markus into him as Douglass entered the restroom.

Oliver ripped the senior off of himself and shoved him away, wrapping his hand tight around Douglass's arm.

"Oliver—"

"We're leaving." Oliver dragged Douglass out the door, his grip tightening in effort to conceal just how much he was shaking. It was too much. All at once. And he needed not to think about it right now. He needed Douglass to tie him back to the earth so he wouldn't do something stupid.

"What was that?" Douglass asked, glancing back as he heard the restroom door open and the same kid Oliver was with came out to follow them.

"It doesn't matter, just Mark—"

"Hey! Curlytop, make sure you pull her hair, she *loves* it when you pull her hair!" Markus howled after them, following up with erroneous moans.

Oliver's eyes widened and he yanked Douglass forward in an attempt to move faster. *Don't be stupid. Don't fall for it.*

"*Oh! Daddy, don't stop!*" The boy let out another loud moan and laughed, causing Oliver to halt in his tracks at his vile repetition of the words.

"Oliver he's just—" Douglass cut himself off with a slight whimper and wrenched his hand out from his friend's painfully tight grasp. He was entirely lost.

Oliver's face twisted up in visceral rage and he spun on his heel to confront that stupid, *disgusting*, piece of human shit.

"Or is he your *new* daddy," Markus remarked, blatantly ignoring the drastic shift in Oliver as he lumbered toward him, picking up pace until he seethed and frothed with a hatred so unfettered if Dindet were there to describe it, the world would have been bathed in blood.

"I'LL FUCKING KILL YOU!!" Oliver roared and the senior simply widened his ugly grin and directed his attention toward Douglass.

"You're name's Douglass, right? Did you know little Olivia over her likes to fuck her—"

Oliver's foot rammed hard into Markus's crotch and the boy let out an awful, pained squeal as he dropped down. Only to be kicked in the face again.

"Oliver! Stop!" He could hear Douglass yelling, and the sound of his shoes squeaking against the hall tiles. But Oliver's focus remained on his blind rage.

"YOU DON'T FUCKING TALK TO ME LIKE THAT!" He kicked the boy again, breaking the skin on his arms as he attempted to guard against Oliver's unbridled fury. "YOU DON'T FUCKING SAY THAT SHIT AND YOU DON'T EVER *FUCKING TOUCH ME AGAIN!*"

This is what he deserves! He deserves to be hurt!

The boy whimpered and Oliver let out a hateful scream, enraged at the possibility that this stupid, awful human being could even feel an inkling of what he felt for *years*. Enraged that he could joke about it like it was just something that made him *easy*.

"I'LL FUCKING KILL YOU!!" Oliver dropped down on top of him, cramming his fists into every possible nook and cranny to make him understand how much it really hurt. He wanted him to pay. He needed him to pay for what he'd done. For everything.

He reared back, ready to throw the hardest punch he could muster before Douglass's arms wrapped around Oliver's waist and yanked him away.

"Oliver stop!" He yelled into his ear and the boy squirmed and kicked and screamed to get loose.

"I'M GONNA KILL HIM!! I'M GONNA—"

"Oliver, *look* at him." Douglass planted his hand over his head, forcing him to look at the kid he had just turned into a bloody pulp.

That he mercilessly beat until he was lying and sputtering out blood on the ground, crying because this was likely the first time anyone had ever really hurt him.

"Look at him...*you won.*"

Oliver's eyes flickered down and around him, trying to make sense of what just happened and what he just did. And when he focused back on the boy on the ground, for a moment, all he could see was the black, splattered remains of Dindet.

You did this. You made this happen.

Douglass's grip tightened around his friend and he attempted to drag him further away from the horrific crime.

Oliver's fighting stopped, and now he shook, staring back at Markus until something awful shattered inside him and he let out a broken wail.

He crumpled, and every muscle in his body that had been balled up with adrenaline relaxed as the awful realization hit him.

You are just like him. Just like Matthew.

Douglass struggled against Oliver's now dead weight, and he dropped down on the ground, wrapping every limb available around the boy in case he would try to escape. He didn't though. Instead he simply sobbed and moaned and screamed, and the only attempts he made were weak and futile efforts to inflict as much pain on himself as possible.

Then, after that, when the teachers and the principal ran down the halls screaming obscenities at the sight in front of them. He was silent.

***

"This is out of control, they are a threat to the student body!" Principal Balboa glared at Jon, his eyes briefly flickering out the window to where Oliver sat handcuffed to the chair.

"I-I'm sure that if I just talk to him, he will tell me the rest of the story," Jon argued, "he's never acted out in such a way before, it had to have been provoked."

"Your child is a monster! A freak! It beat my boy to a fucking pulp and you think *my son* is the reason it attacked him?!" The father of Oliver's victim, Clark was his name, yelled. "It doesn't belong at this school!"

"*He* is not an *it*." Jon bit back.

"Well, *he* should be locked up." Clark sarcastically corrected. "The whole education system has gone to the shitter, allowing your transgender fucking *experiment* to roam the halls. There's a reason those things keep getting killed. They're a fucking infestation."

"You don't talk about my son that way." Jon clenched his jaw, holding back the urge to pumble the man like Oliver did his son. *With talk like that it's no hard question why he beat him up.*

"Throwing insults at one another isn't going to solve the problem," Mrs. Bradshaw interjected, pulling up a video feed tab of the hall camera. "We have to look at the facts. Dr. Jariwala's son went into the boy's restroom."

"School policy dictates that that freak is supposed to use the unisex room *my tax dollars paid for*." Clark intruded snidely. "I was at that conference."

"The restroom he has *been* using was *vandalized*." Jon did his best to force down his cruel thoughts, gesturing at the counselor to continue.

"Shortly after that, Markus went in. And then mister Furkin struggled to get the door open before Oliver and he left in haste."

"So what are you implying?" Clark scoffed, patting his son on the back with confidence. "That my boy did something?"

"With the way you talk about Oliver, I wouldn't say it's an *implication*." Jon remarked, throwing a dirty glare back at him.

"Don't forget, *your* kid is the one who beat up mine. And based on where *you* come from, It's no wonder they are so violent."

"I'll—"

"Gentleman," Jon was cut off from his biting threat by the pale, red headed therapist as she entered the office. "If I could have a word with Dr. Jariwala, I think I might be able to smooth things over and prevent any suits."

She gestured for Jon to follow her to her office, away from both Oliver and the adults contemplating his punishment.

"I— I don't understand why he would do this??" Jon's worry broke the surface tension of his rage, and the moment he and Miss

Popiviolli were out of earshot; he stumbled over his thoughts and words. "I knew things were rough, he's always had trouble getting along with people and his past— it's so unlike him to be *this* violent."

"Jon," the therapist raised her hand, "it's completely understandable. But I don't think you know Oliver as well as you imagine you do."

"What? What do you mean? He talks to me about almost everything. I'm the only one who—"

"Does he really? He's never hidden anything from you?" The woman's lips creased with the slightest of smiles, and Jon paused in thought at her response.

He hid the letter. And he hid the fact that Dindet hurt him. That he stole from me. What...Matthew has done to him....

"Let me talk to him, just for a little bit."

Amelis Behavioral Health Center

O liver stared at the floor, unable to comprehend where he was, or what exactly was going on. The only thing he could think about was what he had done.

The principal talked to him for a short while, murmuring nothing words that he couldn't understand, let alone bring himself to answer.

The boy he beat up left the office, along with the school nurse.

It wasn't until Jon squatted down in front of him that he managed to tear his eyes away from the after image of blood in his mind.

"Oliver," he said softly, placing his hands around his face and brushing his hair gently. "I'm trying to help you. I can't make this any easier if you don't talk to me."

Oliver stared at him, picking each word apart in effort to place them in the order they were supposed to go. He didn't answer.

"I need you to tell me if something happened. In the bathroom." Jon urged. "Did Markus do anything to make you want to hurt him?"

Lie. He doesn't need to know about it. He doesn't know what he did. It'll just make it worse.

"....no..." Oliver mumbled, dropping his hollow gaze back to the floor. He tried to pull inward on himself, but his hands were restrained by the metal cuffs latched around the bars of the chair.

"...I just....got mad."

Jon pulled away from him, pressing his hand into his mouth to hide the sob that threatened to break his lips.

You did this. You broke it, broke everything. You broke him, just like you broke Dindet...just like you broke Mom.

All of this is your fault.

After a while, the other boy's dad left the office too, though when he did, he kicked the chair in trite effort to startle Oliver. Not knowing he stopped existing there and would give no indication that it affected him at all.

Then Mrs. Bradshaw came out, followed by the principal. They all stared at him, as if they wanted to say something. If they did, he didn't listen.

"Ols..." Douglass's remarkably pleasant voice floated into Oliver's perception. At some point, probably after talking to the counselor about what happened, he had snuck his way to the chair next to Oliver and sat down.

"Why....*why* did you do that?" Oliver didn't have an answer for him. There wasn't an answer to give. Not one that would have justified it. His actions were the product of violence, just like he was. Deep down, he knew that.

"You didn't have to hurt him that bad. I know he said—" Douglass stopped himself, trying to wrap his mind back around what actually caused the altercation. "You...you scared me."

Oliver's eyes drifted upward, flickering back at Douglass and the awful look of worry on his face. *Don't do that. Don't be afraid. Don't be afraid of me please...I'm sorry.*

He shifted, shoving what he could of his hand into his pocket to fish out something incredibly important that he didn't deserve. Oliver unrolled his palm and brought his gaze back up to Douglass.

"Take it," he said, still not sure if the words belonged to him.

"But you said—"

"She deserves someone good to look after her." Oliver blinked and pulled his gaze back to the lockers across from him. He waited, until he felt Douglass's fingers pull the bean out of his palm.

"What is it?"

"It's Dindet."

***

Oliver sat in the back seat of his father's car. It was maybe two or three in the afternoon when he left school. He was probably suspended, for at least a week. Or worse, expelled. That could be fine though. He could start over in a different school, he figured a completely new life would wash away the disgusting ichor of the previous one.

He figured a few days at home would fix things.

Then the car turned right, pulling onto the highway and further away from the cabin.

"We aren't going home?" Oliver asked, glancing up at the rear view mirror to see the tired and broken look on Jon's face. Worry built up in his chest at it, and he searched through the window to figure out where he was taking him.

"Dad, where are we going?" Jon didn't respond. Instead, he veered down a small asphalt road on the other side of the lake. The path was covered in long dead leaves, and Oliver could see the cliff side that led around the lake and back to his home through the trees.

Eventually, his father pulled to a stop in front of a pastel yellow building. It was littered with garden beds full of bright orange and red flowers. Though Oliver's eyes remained on the sign that hung off a large mailbox.

Amelis Behavioral Health Center.

"Dad—" Oliver forced out a nervous laugh, "you're not serious....."

He smiled, because if he didn't he knew he would start crying. *Don't do this. Don't leave me here. Please.*

Jon turned around in his seat, tears streaming down his face. "Oliver, there's nothing I can do. It's the only way I could make sure you wouldn't be expelled."

"But— but I'm alright with that." Oliver laughed again.

"Oliver, you don't understand. The school— Markus's father wants to pursue legal action." Jon wiped his tears from his eyes and turned around, getting out of his seat so he could open Oliver's door.

"But I—"

"I'm trying to protect you, I really am. But my hands are tied." His father explained softly. He reached for his son and Oliver scooted to the other end of the car, the gravity of what was happening finally crashing down on him.

"I won't do it again, I swear! I'm not bad, I'm doing fine!"

His father's tired eyes stared back at him, weighted with his worry ever further until he let out a saddened sigh and crawled into the back seat next to him.

"I know you won't..." Jon said, "but they don't...and you're.. you're not well, Oliver."

Don't say that! I'm fine! I'm really...please don't just leave me here, Dad.

"Dad, *Dad*, I'm sorry! I didn't mean to hurt him, okay?" Oliver begged, growing more and more frantic despite his father's calm. "I won't— I don't want to be here, *please!*"

"Oliver." Jon stopped, forcing the boy to halt in his panicked efforts to convince him otherwise. "This isn't a punishment."

Oliver stared at him, searching for somewhere in his face that told him otherwise. *It was a mistake. I made a mistake, I can be better!*

No you can't.

"I can—"

No.

You can't.

Oliver's eyes flickered down to the floorboard of the car and he stilled, finally coming to the realization that he couldn't change his mind. *Why was there any reason to? I never made any effort really, to be better. All I did was pretend that I was and lie. It's all I ever do.*

"....I'm scared." He mumbled softly, prompting a look of abject regret from his father. Jon pulled him into a tender embrace, pressing his hand into his head and holding him tight, as if it would make it any easier to let go.

"I know… it's scary being here. I won't be able to see you, and you'll have to talk about things you don't want to." Jon paused, glancing down at his watch to make sure he wasn't late for work yet. "But this, it's going to help you. The people here are only here to *help* you."

"You won't forget about me right?" Oliver asked, clinging to his father's coat before he could slide out of the car. "You won't leave me here forever, you're not getting rid of me, right?"

"Of course not," he reassured, gently prying Oliver's fingers away from him. "I love you more than anything in the world, and I would die before I left you alone."

Jon stared at him a little longer, as if to prove how much he truly hated leaving him here. Then he stood, moved around to Oliver's door and beckoned him out.

"....It's time to go now."

***

After the fight, if it could even be called that, Douglass was made to go back to class.

His head reeled. Oliver had never done anything like that before.

"I think some time away will help him," Miss Popiviolli's voice cut through his thoughts as he reluctantly made his way back to class. She was speaking to Oliver's step-father, and Douglass paused for a brief moment to eavesdrop on their conversation.

"I don't know, he's never done well...anything like this," Jon sighed softly, "I don't think putting him in a mental hospital is going to do much...he's never taken well to therapy."

Mental hospital? Is that what's going to happen? They're just gonna lock him away?

Douglass pressed against the wall, listening closely to the therapist's words.

"I know it sounds extreme, but I'm really concerned, this behavior is— it's incredibly destructive...if not toward others, I'm certain toward himself."

"And he…he didn't mention anything to you about Markus during your sessions?" Jon asked softly, "What about his biological father? Or..his mother?"

The therapist shook her head. "Based on his history, his behavior is very reminiscent of borderline personality disorder, in combination with the previous diagnoses Dr. Aguirra had given…I know you've only just taken me on, but I would like to keep him for a while— if only to see if mood stabilizers would be beneficial. This tendency toward violence likely stems from his early home life. Rooting out those core traumas in a clinical setting like Amelis, I feel, is your safest option."

Douglass pulled in a soft breath, electing not to subject himself to further hurt from Popiviolli's psychological profiling.

The rest of the day was quiet. Abnormally so. No one in class even mentioned he'd left. Even Cassidy looked to be more preoccupied with schoolwork than the fact that Oliver had just been admitted.

Maybe it was because they expected it.

Even then, the quiet of the classroom was nothing compared to the utter silence of Douglass's walk from the bus stop to his home. He had grown so used to even just the sound of Oliver's footsteps that the lack thereof was so dissonant— he couldn't help but pull the little orange bean out of his pocket to focus on instead.

"Douglass!" His father called, and Douglass's head popped up, catching him waving from the driveway. He picked up his pace, meeting up with him as he was taking in the mail.

"You know your money from the antique shop isn't supposed to be used for bills, right?" He remarked, patting him on the back as a small thank you. Chris tilted his head, glancing around in search of Oliver. "Where's your friend?"

"What happened to our machine?" Douglass changed the subject, closing his fingers around the bean as he opened the front door. Chris stopped just behind him, hesitant to answer.

"You know, I've been noticing the stars have gotten bigger recently, and half the constellations are—"

"Dad."

Douglass glanced back at him, giving him a somewhat irritated look as he dropped his backpack on the floor.

"I told you, the conduit substance we used was unstable and it caused a short," he answered, though clearly that wasn't what his son was looking for. Douglass turned around, opening up his palm to show him the gift Oliver had bequeathed, and judging by the look of abject horror in his father's eyes, he quickly shoved it back into his pocket.

"That's not what happened...is it?"

"...no."

Douglass nodded, and retreated back to his room, intent on not continuing the conversation, even if he so dearly wanted to. He wasn't entirely sure if he would like to hear it.

Nevertheless, Chris followed him, lingering in the doorway while he restacked old movies as a way to build up his nerve.

"Did you really kill her?" It was a genuine question, and Douglass hoped that the answer would be no, but instead his father averted his eyes and kept quiet far too long for it to be anything but a 'yes'.

"Douglass, I—"

"It's okay." He cut him off solemnly, the weight of the truth dragging him down as he leaned back on his bed, staring up at the ceiling in order not to look at him.

"Did you know?" Douglass asked before his dad could answer, "I won't be mad— if you didn't know."

Chris let out a reluctant sigh and sat down on his son's bed, fiddling with the blanket while he mulled over what to say, if he could say anything at all.

"Last year..at the lab, Marie—" he hesitated, not sure if his son was quite ready to hear it. "Discovered a new type of particle. One that we studied, and learned was some kind of residual trace on an atomic level that could manipulate the vibrational rate of an object."

Douglass rolled over, facing away from him as he spoke.

"We were able to isolate it, and found out that —using the capabilities of the particle— it would allow us to send things to a theoretical parallel dimension. We *thought* it was theoretical."

"You made a portal?" Douglass questioned softly, sitting up and folding his legs up under him as he pressed back against the wall. His father nodded, wringing his hands and trying to find the best explanation he could.

"We did."

"And Dindet came through?"

"No," Chris corrected, "I had no idea your friend was one of them. But, one *did* come— I only got a glimpse. And Jon and I thought...Marie told us the jester was friendly."

Douglass lowered his gaze to the floor, "is that how it happened? The accident?"

His father nodded again, and clasped his hands together in quiet contemplation.

"I didn't believe what I saw, but Jon..." he stopped himself for a moment, "I know your mom and I never had the best relationship, but it's hard...losing someone you love...so abruptly."

Douglass brushed his fingers through his curls and rested his chin of his fist, letting his eyes trail off to the copy of Pride and Prejudice Oliver had given him. "He was trying to bring her back."

"I saw what happened...there was no way to bring her back— I didn't think he would go so far as to harbor one of them in his own home." Chris replied.

"Are you helping him?" Douglass asked, though he already knew the answer. *They were in it now, and if he really used the alien as a source of energy— if Oliver was right...then AKAN already knows.*

"I think something really bad is going to happen soon." He muttered softly, bringing out the bean again. "Oliver gave this to me...and I think...that there might be more here than just Dindet, and I don't think they are good."

Tied Hands and Pretty Flowers

Orderlies filed in and out of the office and Oliver stayed huddled up on the bed of his temporary room, staring out the open door. They moved him here and took everything away. His backpack, his sketchbook and pencils, and books, even his clothes and shoes. At least the carpet was soft.

Miss Poppy roamed in the main hall, before her attention turned back to him and she swiveled her head around to stare at him.

He drew in a small breath and immediately cornered himself against the wall as she came closer, briefly hanging in the doorway with an unnervingly gentle smile. She kept eye contact until he finally lowered his head and stared at his feet.

"I'm sorry for the wait, I had to make sure my risk staff had arrived."

…risk staff?

As if she had read his mind, the woman explained, "due to the uhm..unfortunate circumstances of your being here, I'm required to have a staff member present to chaperone you throughout the facility— it's little more than a precaution in the event there is any sort of altercation with the other staff or patients here."

Oliver stared at her, tightening his grip on himself as her words sunk under his skin and weighed him down with guilt. "Because..I'm dangerous…"

Miss Poppy's smile faltered, perfectly matching the shift in his mood and she gestured for him to stand.

"I don't think you're dangerous, Oliver, hurt? Yes, but not dangerous." She offered that same off kilter smile, patiently waiting for him to follow her direction. "Why don't we take a short tour? Before I bring you to your new room in the east wing?"

Oliver shifted, reluctant to stray from his place despite knowing he likely didn't have any actual choice in the matter. Then he stood and slowly met the therapist at the door, keeping his eyes firmly planted on the soft carpet floor his bare toes crinkled into.

They went on a set path it seemed, first the main entry, which he recognized when Jon had dropped him off a few hours earlier. It was a creamy yellow color, with large soft mustard couches and a massive hearth fireplace. Those same and strangely familiar red flowers littered nearly every vase and pot in the area, and the pollen from them was so light that it hung in the hair like an orange dust cloud. Other patients shuffled about in the dingy turquoise scrubs Oliver himself had been provided upon admission, while their prospective nurses sped around in much darker blue ones.

The building was apparently a defunct nursing home previous to its use now, and it looked it. Most of the furniture and design was left over from the old owners, and repurposed to make a mental hospital look a lot more inviting than one would typically imagine. There were still no sharp edges, or access to shoelaces and toothpicks though, and all the windows stayed locked.

Miss Poppy shifted her path from the main hall down two wings, directly across from one another.

"There are three wings in the building, south, east, and west," she said, gesturing at the open fire doors to the west wing. "West and east are the only ones in use, and are divided for patients and our on-call psychiatric staff."

"What about the south one?" Oliver questioned, his eyes drifting back to the very clearly locked doors at the back center of the hospital. He could see just barely through the grated windows in them that the hall behind it was dark, but lights were on at the last three doors.

"Oh, the south wing is just where we keep the laundry and medications. The only other thing down that way is the old morgue and the boiler room," she answered, pressing her palm into his back to keep him from looking longer. "We keep the doors locked so none of the patients have access to medications that could harm them."

"Oh."

Miss Poppy glanced up at the wall clock and her smile widened just slightly, prompting her to turn Oliver the entire opposite direction toward the east wing.

"Your chaperone should be arriving shortly, so why don't we finish our tour in your new room?" She pushed him forward, regardless of any trite objection he made, and they made their way across the main hall and down the east wing until she stopped at the room at the very end.

"Here we are." Miss Poppy grinned. Oliver stared at the small metal plaque at the top of the doorframe. *Room 224.*

It wasn't very large, but also wasn't nearly as small as he was expecting.

On the left side was an old metal framed bed, and opposite to it was a wicker chair and dresser, probably full of more turquoise scrubs, if he had to guess.

The wall on the right opened up into a doorless bathroom, with a bathtub and shower, though it likely wasn't the type of shower that came with a hose due to the whole suicide risk.

The nicest thing overall, was the relatively large window at the center of the room, overlooking the back garden and the little window sill pot of red flowers sitting just outside it.

It was calming, something Oliver didn't expect to receive in a mental hospital of all places.

On the dresser, his eyes caught a tiny cup, the kind you'd normally put ketchup in, but it was filled with something orange instead.

"What's that?" He asked, pointing at it.

Miss Poppy moved into the room and gestured for him to follow.

He obliged and she picked up the small cup and handed it to him.

"This is your medication," she answered all smiley, like it didn't turn his stomach at the idea.

Does..this mean I really am broken?

"It's just a mood stabilizer, no need to feel down about it," the therapist said, catching the look of apprehension in the boy's face. "All the patients here take a daily dose, so you're in no way singled out."

He nodded, inspecting the cup of syrupy liquid.

It smelled at least somewhat edible, and looked sort of like the orange flavored cough syrup Jon would get when he got particularly sick.

For a brief moment, he hesitated, glancing back at the doorway as he saw one of the nurses make their way towards them. Then he downed the dose, as horrific as it tasted, in one gulp.

Oliver hacked and coughed, pounding on his chest cause it felt like whatever hellacious concoction he drank had the same spice as a whole spoonful of cinnamon.

"I wish— I wish you had warned me!" He sputtered, trying to wipe the excessive amount of drool from his mouth.

"Your father left you some gifts to occupy your time," the therapist said, pulling Oliver's attention away from his coughing fit. "Though, I can't allow them in your room, you can make use of them while supervised at the craft room on Wednesdays and Fridays."

Gifts?

A small smile pulled at the boy's lips, and for an honest moment, it felt like being here wasn't going to be as awful as he had thought.

He was very, *very* wrong.

"Ah, your chaperone is here!" Miss Poppy clapped her hands together, prompting Oliver to raise his gaze up at her, but as his head lifted, he stumbled, suddenly so very disoriented by such a simple movement.

Everything turned blurry and layered on top of one another, and he struggled to focus on whichever Poppy was the real one as she backed away toward the door.

The nurse that was making his way down the hall turned sideways with the rest of the walls and as he approached, Oliver's confused look twisted downward and horror etched itself into his face.

The kid clambered forward, stumbling toward the woman as the floor felt like it swayed under him. "Wh— what'd you do to me?"

He balanced himself at the doorway, watching Miss Poppy walk off toward other patients. His skull filled up with fuzzy thoughts that felt like cushions bouncing around in his brain.

He was heavy, really heavy, and his head bobbed up and down until all sense of balance fell away and he nearly dropped to his knees, but was caught by the nurse that had at some point teleported to the door. That or his perception of time was wildly incorrect.

Oliver looked up, then down, and all around as the extra lines around Matthew's face bubbled and warbled. He tried to look at all of them at once, that pleasant and so terribly fake smile that was little more than a twitch of his father's lips as his eyes bore into Oliver.

"Olivia."

"*...no...*"

***

"Psst," Douglass poked Cassidy in the shoulder, pulling her attention away from the book she was reading.

"Mm?" She hummed, pushing her glasses up her nose as she turned. "What's up?"

"I need your help with something," he whispered, glancing around the classroom just to make sure no one was eavesdropping. She leaned forward and rested her elbows on his desk with a somewhat reluctant sigh.

"I'm not going to do your homework for you, if that's what you're asking."

"No, it's different," he corrected. Douglass paused, hesitant to actually ask what he planned on asking, but his eye caught Oliver's empty desk and it filled him with a palpable dread. "You're into weird stuff, right? Like ghosts and aliens and stuff?"

"Yeah, why?" She cocked her head, narrowing her eyes.

"If I tell you, you have to keep it a secret."

She leaned forward, even more intrigued.

"Okay?" Cassidy drew out the words, not entirely sure if he was playing some kind of joke on her. He did look quite nervous though, and kept moving his hands into his pocket while looking terribly cautious.

"I'll tell you after school, at your house?" He suggested, gauging her response. The girl sat back and folded her arms, then nodded.

"Alright, you can walk home with me."

All throughout the day, Douglass felt keenly aware of his paranoia, as though the sparkling facade of the entire town was stripped away to reveal some sinister plot that he couldn't yet wrap his head around.

It wasn't that he particularly trusted Cassidy alone, but she happened to be one of those kids that obsessed over occult things and made up theories extending from time travel to bog monsters at the bottom of the lake. So even if he *did* tell her, if she told anyone else, it would more or less just sound like another of her conspiracy theories. That, and she was the only other person willing to talk to him most of the time.

He lingered outside the school, leaning up against the flag pole while he waited for her to separate from her little troupe of friends. The girl met up with him, and before he even said anything, she dropped her bag on the ground and kicked out a skateboard.

"So, what'd you wanna talk about?" She questioned, kicking off at a significantly slower pace than he anticipated. Douglass increased his stride, struggling to not jog next to her while she swerved left and right on the sidewalk, slowing down a couple of blocks before a stop light.

"I have a theory, well, it's not actually a theory, it's the truth— I think. But it's hard to believe, so please just bear with me?" He began, stopping alongside her as they waited for the light to switch.

"What sort of theory-err, truth?" Cassidy eyed him, twisting up her tightly packed curls and tying them up in buns so they wouldn't get in her face.

Douglass averted his eyes momentarily, contemplating on whether or not now was a good time to just back out. *Except it isn't. Oliver is gone and something feels really wrong about that…and this all has something to do with the accident last year, and the one in December too, and Dindet.*

"Uh, you know Dindet? Well.." he paused, picking up pace as they crossed the street. "Well, turns out she's an alien— like from outer space."

"Oh, yeah, I already knew that! She's not actually from outer space though, she's from *interdimensional space*, which is definitely ten times cooler." Cassidy grinned a little too excitedly. She kicked her board out from under her and picked it up, opting to walk next to him instead. "I knew something was off about her, cause I looked it up and there aren't any remote cultures of people who dress like clowns, and the place she said she was from doesn't exist on any maps."

That was easy. A lot easier than I thought it was going to be.

"Also it's kind of hard to miss when she changes colors, and I saw her basically *eat* Oliver so—"

"Cassidy," Douglass interrupted, drawing her focus back to him as his voice grew lower. "She wasn't the only one here."

"Well, of course not," she remarked, "if the universe is at least thirteen billion years old, odds are there are tons of alien life in the cosmos, and that doesn't even take into account other dimensions! Oh— I wonder how many other dimensions there are, Dindet never—"

"No, I mean there are more aliens like her *in town*." He explained, "my dad met them before the accident when Oliver's mom…died."

Cassidy's smile faded and she dropped her chin, glancing back at him. "Oh…is that why he's gone?"

He nodded, swiveling his head back as a precaution just to make sure they weren't being listened to, or followed.

"I think they're here for this," he whispered, fishing the orange bean out of his pocket to show the girl.

Cassidy leaned in, inspecting every inch of it, then her whole face lit up. "Is— is that her bean??"

"I— I guess? It's Dindet's, he gave it to me before Miss Popiviolli took him to the hospital," he explained, quickly putting it back in his pocket in case any prying eyes saw.

"The hospital?" She questioned, coming to a stop in front of her old Victorian home. She opened the mailbox and shoved the letters under her arm, gesturing for him to follow.

"Some place called Amelis?" Douglass answered, peering around the front porch as Cassidy opened the door for him to enter. She dropped the letters along with her skateboard at a desk by the front entrance and pointed up the stairs toward her room.

"I've heard of that place, it's on the far south end of town, on the other side of the lake, right? So he's not that far away," she said, following him upstairs to her room and flipping her fairy lights on. Douglass, though, hung at the doorway, awkwardly picking at the cracks in the wood.

"You can come in, you know, my moms are both at work and they probably won't be home until about seven." She smirked, waving him forward before sitting on her bed and patting the mattress for him to join her. Douglass turned flush, and nodded, quickly coming in and plopping comfortably down on the bed while she leaned over and pulled a ratty box out from under it.

"We can go visit him, but I don't know what all we could do?" She sat the box in her lap and began taking out little notes and cards and crudely drawn pictures that had been clearly copied and printed from books. "I know of greys, and nordic and reptilian, but I've never heard any podcasts talk about Clowns— that's what Dindet is, like, for real. I'm pretty sure her whole species just all look like clowns."

"Well, that's the thing," Douglass murmured, looking over at the pictures she was showing, "he didn't really tell me anything? And when I asked my dad he didn't have a lot of information either...I went to Dr. Jariwala but he wasn't home."

Conspiracy Theorists

Cassidy, compiled her pictures into a small stack. Suddenly, as if a light bulb went off in her head, she dug back into her box and pulled out an entire notebook she had clearly specifically dedicated to Dindet's alien species.

"I'm a *genius!*" She chimed, adding a happy little squeal as she flipped through her notes and landed on a page chocked full of her neat handwriting and little diagrams.

"Dindet came over to my house a while back so I got to ask her basically everything I could think of— why Oliver didn't keep or make notes on an entire newly discovered alien species, I will never know, but I am *not* as careless." She scanned the notes, following with her finger until she stopped and tapped on one of the bullet points. "Right here! Their whole species is basically a bunch of single cell organisms, and the stuff we think is their body is actually a whole bunch of different molecular structures they use to move around."

Douglass blinked, most assuredly not grasping a single word she said. "So..that means..?"

Cassidy rolled her eyes and leaned forward, snatching the bean he'd taken out of his pocket.

"This." She pointed at it. "Is the real Dindet, it's like her whole body and brain, think like— the nucleus of a cell from biology last year."

Douglass nodded, prompting the girl to set the bean down and move back to her notes.

"The rest of her— the stuff that I saw that day Oliver wore the dress, or basically, what you would think is her body? All of that is like…every element on the periodic table," she explained, briefly glancing up. "She told me she was made of matter, but she also showed me she can make basically anything in the world as long as she knew what chemical structures existed in it, so I think it's safe to assume that her entire species is able to do that as well."

Douglass pressed his chin into his fist, looking very much like he was deeply contemplating this information.

"So she's a shape-shifter." He said, garnering a nearly offended look from Cassidy.

"Yeah, but also not," she replied, "they can change shape and stuff, but the way she explained it made it sound like they can do a lot more. Like…"

Cassidy paused, glancing around her room in search of something to better explain. She leaned over the side of her bed, snagging a dried up pen from her cup on the nightstand and held it up.

"She did this trick with my pen, where she took it apart, atom by atom and then remade it into a little plastic car, just using whatever was already there that made the pen." She set the pen down and cocked her head in thought. "So they can shape-shift, but they can also shape-shift other things. Which explains how she turned into that big monster and teleported Oliver o—"

"Hold up, monster? What?" Douglass held his hand up, cutting the girl off so he could actually have time to process what she was saying. "She turned into a monster? And *teleported*?? "

"Yes, can you not hear what I'm saying?" Cassidy chided sarcastically, moving on to another page of her notes. "It's an important distinction to make because it means that if they can do it to objects, then they can do it to people too."

Douglass nodded deftly, until his mind stopped dead in its tracks at a soft realization. "Do you think…that there might have been one here for a while?"

Cassidy shrugged, not really nodding or shaking her head at the idea. "Well..the only Clown I've ever met is Dindet, but I guess if your dad and the lab know about them, then they might have been here for a while?"

"No…" Douglass hummed in contemplation. "I mean like, for a really really long time. And it's what's been causing all the missing person cases? I— I know it's dumb and it's basically just a hunch, but my sister Jojo and her friends used to tell these stories about a monster in the forests. It would look and sound like someone you knew, and if you followed it, you were never seen again. But— but if you got away, it would slowly drive you crazy."

Cassidy nodded and dug through her box, pulling out a tattered article she'd printed off a few years back.

"So something like this, then?" She asked, pushing it toward him to see. The article was some backwoods internet forum looking entry with a large header that read 'MAN FINDS MYSTERIOUS GOO IN PUHUNKY ILLINOIS'

"Uh...I guess?"

"It's a really interesting read. This guy, Richard Asne, was out fishing when out of nowhere, this black goop that 'looked like the night sky' just started bleeding out of thin air! The biological research center collected samples and said it was a type of fungus, but this picture here," she pulled out a printed photo of the spot the man supposedly found the goop and pointed to a dark patch on the grass, "shows some kind of weird light refraction, see?"

Douglass leaned in closer, trying to see what she was supposedly pointing at.

"Richard reported that the slime turned into something humanoid and then just flashed out of existence, but he was later admitted to a mental hospital after a nervous breakdown." She set the picture down in the bottom of the box. "He said whatever it was, got in his head and made him relive the war, over and over again and about two years after he was…"

She trailed off, eventually looking up at her friend. "He was reported missing."

Douglass's eyes were glued to the photo, and his thoughts returned to Oliver and the way he completely fell apart just before Miss Popiviolli took him away.

"We have to get him out of there." He breathed, glancing up at Cassidy and hoping with every thought that she agreed.

"Douglass—"

"No, I mean it," he insisted, "I think this thing, in your story— I think it might be Miss Popiviolli, and I think she's going to hurt him."

"You don't know that—"

"Cassidy." Douglass's voice raised ever so slightly, causing her to jump from his sudden earnest, and he quickly closed back in on himself. "I saw him, he looked really messed up, Cas, I've never seen Oliver look...like that...before."

The girl glanced down at her box, then back at Douglass, contemplating the gravity of what he was implying. Did he seriously think they could just show up and break Oliver out? Without any sort of repercussions?

Odds were, if she were honest with herself, he was there for a reason.

Still, the idea of performing a top secret heist of one whole person, against a slew of potentially dangerous aliens conspiring to do— whatever it was they were planning to do was really, really cool.

"..okay," she finally said, setting the box back down on the floor and turning to face him. "What's your plan?"

Douglass blinked.

"I figured you would do that," he answered dumbly, watching her furrow her brow and huff in small noncompliance.

"You're the one who wants to get him out, you have to come up with the plan." She narrowed her eyes at him and pursed her lips expectantly. "Or are you just in it to drag me along so you can look like a big hero, rescuing your crush?"

"Wh-what?" he stammered, raising his hands in objection, but he still turned bright red at the implication.

"No, no," he cleared his throat in an effort to assert himself just a little more, "no, it's not for that, I just— I'm worried about him is all."

"I'm just joking!" Cassidy lolled her head with a laugh and poked him hard in the shoulder, lowering her voice to a near whisper, "I know you're too chicken to ask him out anyways."

"What'd you just say?"

"Nothing!" She giggled, dropping down to the floor to reach under her bed for something else, "nothing at all."

She tugged out a whole new and barely used journal, flipping it over to a fresh page. "First, we can't go rushing in without any idea of if we're right. We have to be absolutely, totally, no doubts whatsoever sure that Popiviolli is a Clown, or at the very least has something to do with all the missing people, right?"

"How do we do that?"

She drew little X's as bullet points for a list, "get evidence, duh. I print off the missing person's posters for the classrooms, so I have a list of everyone that's disappeared in the last year, right? So I just need a list from her..probably like, her patient files? Which I'm pretty sure she keeps in her office at the school."

Douglass slipped down to the floor next to her, still somewhat reeling from the fact that she was so comfortable just helping him.

"You know this is illegal, right?" He questioned, prompting her to bob her head.

"Yeah, but I don't ever get to do anything like this because the other girls think it's weird," She remarked. "Also, I kind of really want to do just one badass thing before summer."

Douglass nodded half mindedly, until what she said actually registered in his head. "Wait, so you don't actually believe me?"

"Well, not really about Miss Popiviolli, No, but I definitely believe you about the aliens," she corrected, "I was pretty sure they were messing with some weird stuff at the lab before the explosion, but when Dindet showed up to class I knew she wasn't a regular person."

She sat back, pulling out her phone to show off a few pictures she'd taken of the alien, "I caught these on the second day of school, see?"

Douglass leaned in to get a better look, sure enough, it was

Oliver and Dindet in the classroom just after the day ended, except the clown was half melted into the ground.

"Didn't help that he never let me ask her anything." Cassidy flipped away from the photos and to her search engine, quickly searching up the facility Douglass had spoken of.

***

Oliver's eyes fluttered open and the moment full cognizance returned to him, he groaned, wracked with a horrid and burning throbbing at the base of his spine that spread down his arms and legs. It felt like his skin had been pulled and stretched in ways it wasn't supposed to be and he sputtered out some hiss of a curse as he sat up and all that pain radiated straight into his skull like a vice grip locked around his brain.

He was in his bed, or rather, the bed of the room Miss Poppy had brought him to just before he was drugged. He was sure that was something that really happened.

Everything after, on the other hand, he couldn't make a lick of sense.

Matthew.

Oliver drew in an unconscious gasp and threw the covers off, inspecting his bed and body for anything that could denote what his father had done to him. It was pristine though, not a stain nor garment out of place. The strangest part was that he didn't hurt—not in the way he expected to, at least.

The boy shifted, gingerly throwing his legs over the side of the bed and readying himself to stand, though any attempt at doing so was a sore mistake because the moment he lurched forward, his legs failed to do the one and only job they had, and Oliver promptly crumpled to the floor in a painful heap of stifled and very angry sobs.

Serves you right. God, I'm such an idiot to have ever thought he wouldn't—

Oliver stopped himself, prevented from his spiral into self loathing by some other quiet and lingering thought.

Jon. I can call him. I can call him and tell him and he will take me out of here! Matthew will go to prison for breaking the court order and I'll never have to see him again.

He smiled, despite how much it hurt his face to do so, and struggled his way upright with the help of the dresser acting as much needed support. Oliver stumbled, still reeling from whatever Matthew had drugged him with and haphazardly made his way into the bathroom to see if there were any noticeable marks that could indicate what he couldn't confidently remember.

"Holy—" Oliver cut himself off, leaning over the counter to balance his weight as he tilted his head up and to the side, staring in dumbfounded awe and confusion at the strange and incredibly thin bruises that spidered around his cheeks, just ending at the bags under his tired eyes. They looked like veins, thick near the splits and thinner, almost invisible at their ends, and they trailed all the way down toward the nape of his neck, prompting the boy to try and twist around to see his back.

Oliver pulled the hem of his shirt up, wincing as the fabric grazed along his tender skin— it didn't help that the way he had to lean against the sink put an agonizing amount of pressure on the exact spot he hurt most.

His back was so much worse, a massive bruise that turned his skin purplish black trailed up the center of his spine, branching off like cracks of lighting that spread around his ribs and waist, up his shoulders and halfway down his arms.

He's never…done anything like this before.

"Oh thank you, the next shipment should be available within the fortnight," Miss Poppy's voice made him jump and Oliver quickly pulled down his shirt and stumbled to his door, pulling it open just enough to peek through the crack.

The woman stood at the other end of the east wing, checking things off on a clipboard as delivery men dollied in several boxes. Nurses roamed behind her and other patients milled about the main hall like ghosts.

Oliver scanned every passing face in search of Matthew's, though not a single nurse matched his gruff look.

He was here. I saw him..

Oliver opted for a second scan, certain that this time he could pick the man out in a crowd. His thoughts turned over in his head, trying to pull up memories from after he'd been taken to his room, after he drank that nasty medicine.

She said the nurse was here..and it was him..right? The picture is blurry but I know his face. I know it was him. What happened after that?

Oliver pressed forward, before his toes caught on his heel and he stumbled through the door, losing what little balance he had before he smacked hard into the carpet with a startled yelp.

Miss Poppy's head swiveled back to stare at him and she said something to the delivery man and handed him her clipboard, already making her way down the hall to Oliver while he struggled to get his feet back under him.

"You really took a dive there," she mused, pressing her hand into his back. "You're a bit of a clumsy kid— this is the second time I've seen you faceplant."

Oliver hissed out a nothing word and arched his back to escape her touch. "Matthew hurt me, he's here."

"Your biological father?" The woman's voice was kind, but had some layered other descriptor Oliver couldn't focus on at the moment.

He pulled up his shirt to show off the massive bruise. "He did something after you left— you let him trick you."

The therapist's lips pursed and her face shifted into pensive confusion. "Love, you must have bumped your head. I know the first dose can be a bit of a knockout but I can assure you, my facility would never allow someone like Matthew inside. I took extra precautions to ensure he knew nothing of your whereabouts — should he return to town, Dr. Jariwala and I *both* would know about it."

Playing Detective

Oliver stared at himself in the mirror, lifting his shirt and twisting around over and over again to try and wrap his mind around how his massive bruises had just simply...vanished.

It didn't make any sense, he could clearly remember seeing them, feeling them, the strange burning sensation that had crawled from the base of his spine all the way up to his head and down to his toes.

Something like that doesn't just disappear.

Miss Poppy stood outside of the bathroom, leaning against the door and he could hear her idly tossing her stress ball as she waited for him to come to grips with the honest reality that he was just *wrong*.

The boy poked his head out from the doorway. "You're certain he's not here? He didn't get like— hired on under a fake name? He didn't put anything in the medicine?"

The woman raised her gaze and caught her ball, setting it back into her pocket.

"Absolutely certain, Oliver." Her chin lifted with further confidence. "It's normal to be wary— I know you've never been to a hospital like this before, and Dr. Aguirra handed me the reins to this facility before she retired, but I do my absolute best to make my patients feel safe and secure. I guarantee your paranoia has no justification within these walls."

Wow, that definitely instills confidence.

The woman's smile twitched, and as much as she hid it well, Oliver's head leveled and he stared at her for what he knew was an uncomfortably long time.

It's like she can—

"I'm sorry to cut our conversation short," Miss Poppy broke through his thought, removing herself from the door frame. "Unfortunately, I have alternating shifts in Pineton's school district, so I won't be available Mondays, Wednesdays and Fridays."

Oliver nodded curtly, pulling out of the bathroom to follow her into the main hall.

"My risk staff alternates shifts as well," she continued, checking her wrist watch, "nurse Surlat— your evening supervisor won't be arriving until after 5pm, so for the time being, nurse Carpenter will be the one escorting you to and from sessions."

She stopped at the edge of the east wing, met by a very exhausted looking larger woman in deep blue scrubs, who offered probably the most vacant smile Oliver had ever seen.

"Hi! You must be mister Jariwala, Oliver, right?" The nurse's cheery voice didn't match her zombified look, but she jutted her hand out for him to shake regardless. "Nurse Carpenter, but you can call me Kaylee if you like?"

Oliver eyed her over, his gaze flickering back at Miss Poppy's also vacant smile before he hesitantly reached out and shook the woman's hand.

She promptly gripped him, tighter than he was prepared for and began tugging him off to the sitting area on the other side of the fireplace hearth. "Your session won't begin until after noon, so why don't we go ahead and introduce you to everyone else? Maybe you can make some friends!"

Oliver resisted her urgency, keeping his eyes trained back on Miss Poppy as she finished up with her deliveries, or he resisted until nurse Kaylee jerked him forward a couple of steps and forced his attention away.

She slammed to a stop just on the other side of a large love seat and pushed him into a small circle of other patients, all who seemed just about as interested in introductions as Oliver was.

"Okay everyone, I'm sure you all noticed the newcomer, why don't you introduce yourself?" Kaylee said, gesturing broadly at the small circle of patients and ending with Oliver, singling him out with her placid smile and almost robotic movements.

The boy shifted uncomfortably, immediately dropping his gaze to the vase of flowers that sat on the small coffee table before him.

"Uh…h—hi.."

"Go on, don't be shy!" The nurse cheered, making him infinitely more reluctant to draw attention to himself.

Oliver opened his mouth, then closed it, and then tried to make words come out a third time.

"I…hh..am…" he glanced up, only to see if anyone were actually even listening to him and to his absolute dismay, he was met by the eyes of almost every single person in his six foot radius.

Almost immediately upon that realization, his throat closed up and he just stood there, for several minutes, wringing the hem of his shirt like an idiot while he struggled to make noise at all— let alone intelligible words.

***

"So?" Douglass caught up with Cassidy as she strolled the halls well before the first bell rang. "What's the plan?"

The girl dug into her tote and pulled out a sizeable ream of paper, handing him half of it. "I always go to the front office to make posters for the missing students first thing in the morning, I figured just letting Mrs. Deauxtree know you're there to 'help' will get us in. Then, I'll just sneak into Popiviolli's office and you can keep guard by the printer, it's like right down the hall."

"And I can shoot you a text if I see anyone coming your way," he added with a nod. "Do you by any chance know Miss Popiviolli's schedule? Like if she has any early morning sessions or anything?"

Cassidy's lips pursed in thought for a moment and she shook her head. "I don't, but I know she only shows up every other day around 7 a.m., outside of that, she usually keeps her office locked."

The two came to a soft stop just before the front office doors, hesitation preventing them from entering.

Cassidy muttered under her breath a string of French so fast Douglass barely even registered them as words, then they shared a look.

"We're really doing this," She said, reaching for the door with a solid gulp of breath. Douglass's lips turned down in an apprehensive frown but he nodded, and the girl opened the door.

"Bon matin," Cassidy put on a bright smile, prompting Mrs. Deauxtree to briefly pull her gaze away from her computer. "Douglass wanted to help me make new posters, if that's okay?"

The secretary's eyes flitted from the girl to Douglass and back and she gave a kind smile in return. "Of course he can, you know where the printer is, oh— and we had a staff meeting this morning so feel free to take some of the leftover donuts in the breakroom, goodness knows *I* don't need them!"

Cassidy gave a wave of acknowledgement and led Douglass around the front desk, beckoning him to the hallway of offices and meeting rooms.

She stopped at the printer and plopped down her half of the ream, then pointed to a door at the very end of the hall.

"That's her office, if she's here today, it'll be unlocked," she whispered, drawing Douglass's attention from the printer to the door. It had a small grated window, but no light on inside, from what he could see.

"Right, I'll stay here, printing posters and if anyone asks, I'll say you had to run to the bathroom, kay?" He pulled out his phone, making sure he had her number at the ready. "If I see Popiviolli, I'll shoot you a message, idk, something quick and easy cause it's not a super far walk."

Cassidy nodded in agreement and dropped her bag down on the ground, scuttling down the hall to jiggle the doorknob to see if it was locked.

She glanced back at Douglass and gave a thumbs up before opening the door and stepping inside.

***

Oliver busied himself, picking the petals off one of the familiar flowers that littered the entire facility, while Kaylee stood behind him trying to figure out how to make him talk again after her absolute failure to read the room.

"I know it's probably a lot, being here," she said in her robotic and way too happy voice. "But I promise, after your session with Miss Poppy, you'll really start to love it."

He raised his gaze to stare at her, utterly confounded by the prospect. *Why would anyone enjoy being in a mental hospital? Involuntarily?*

The poor nurse waited for him to respond, as he just watched her smile fade over the course of his increasingly long silence until it was gone and he could focus his attention back on his dumb flower.

The forced ring of introductions sucked. Shortly after it was made apparent that he wasn't going to cooperate, and made an absolute fool of himself in the process of trying to, the few other patients in the circle all introduced themselves.

A woman in her early twenties, who struggled with Bulimia was the first, she was nice and smiley, and she was by far the most talkative one in the whole building.

The next three were people with depression, two of which Oliver could see the failed attempts on their lives in the scars on their arms. He figured he looked quite similar to them, with his gauze hiding Dindet's claw marks.

The other two were so little interested in making friends that they simply left to do anything even mildly more interesting about half way through the woman's spoken life essay.

Oliver tore the last petal from his flower, inspecting it closely as he saw tiny droplets of plant juice seep from the three pistil it had. He looked closer, recognition flickering over his face as his eyes widened.

These are from the Peace Zone.

The flowers were familiar, he knew that, but the ones he'd been given from the tournament had dried up and darkened after about a month without water. These ones were bright and red, shaped weird, sort of like an orchid with those orange dusty spores that shot into the air at the slightest touch.

How did she…

Oliver's eyes drifted up, searching around the main hall for other evidence, finally resting on one of the delivery men dollying Poppy's supplies into the south wing. He looked normal, albeit occupied with trying not to let any of his boxes fall, but Oliver's attention rested on the most innocuous little sticker on the boxes. Just a logo. A very familiar logo.

Randy's Dimensitech Outpost.

He almost started up, but forced himself to stay seated, instead turning his attention back at his nurse, who by now had gone incredibly quiet and sat in the big mustard colored chair next to him.

Oliver swiveled his head around to look at the door of the south wing, then back at the nurse.

She looked like she hadn't slept in weeks, and she sank further into her chair, eyes drooping.

Just a little longer.

He glanced back at the door, watching the delivery man cart his dolly back into the main foyer for his last few boxes as urgency made him more fidgety the longer he waited for Kaylee to fall asleep completely.

Oliver watched her eyes dull and finally shut, and the moment they did, he quietly hopped up and snuck his way to the south wing, catching the door before it shut.

***

Cassidy flipped the light on, doing a quick once over of the office.

It was a typical office, probably one that used to be used for storage, because there was a clutter of posters and boxes in the far corner, and a large mirror that had a good decade worth of dust covering it.

Popiviolli had a small desk right next to the clutter corner, a chair directly in front of it, and a slightly larger couch directly across from it. It definitely gave off 'new teacher' vibes.

Cassidy rounded the desk, setting her phone on it before she began digging through the drawers for files, a vast majority of which were just school employee paperwork and some consent forms. She moved from the left side of the desk to the right, which had deeper drawers a whole lot more conducive to holding student patient files.

Bingo.

She pulled the bottom drawer open further upon seeing those familiar manilla colored tabs and began thumbing through them, referencing the list of missing persons she'd made with Douglass the night previous.

At least, until her phone buzzed.

The Mime

Oliver slid into the shadows of the south wing, the only light in the hall emanating from two rooms at its far end, but the most perplexing thing upon his discrete entrance was the horrific odor of the wing.

Like a rotting corpse.

It was faint near the entrance doors, likely sealed off by them because no such rancid smell touched the rest of the building. It came from somewhere far at the back, where he couldn't see past the shadows that were split by the two lit rooms.

He treaded lightly and carefully at first, keeping to the walls with his shirt over his nose and a scowl on his face from the stench of the place, as he moved closer.

He listened too, for any staff or delivery men that still lingered, until Oliver was certain he was the only one in the hall and his pace picked up slightly, headed straight for the lit rooms.

Then he stopped, forced by a flash of movement somewhere behind one of the defunct patient rooms.

Oliver stared through the small window from the other side of the hall, searching in the darkness and hoping his eyes had adjusted enough to see inside.

Nothing.

He crept closer, rising up on his toes just enough that he could peek through to get a good glimpse.

In the dark, the shadows morphed and his eyes adjusted, picking out the same decor from his own room, and a person on the bed. A staff member, it seemed, from the particularly dark hue of their clothing.

Well…I guess that makes sense? It was a hospital after all, with 24 hour staff, which gave some modicum of sense to why his risk staff member looked like she'd have keeled over from exhaustion.

It still doesn't explain the Peace Zone stuff…

Oliver backed away from the door, turning his attention to the lit rooms once again and continued his way down the hall, his eyes watering with how horrifically *worse* the smell of rotten death became the closer he got.

***

Cassidy ripped her phone from the desk, opening the message she got.

God I hate that.

She blew a breath of relief and frustration from her lips and promptly deleted the stupid spam text, continuing her file stealing with slightly renewed confidence.

A vast majority of the missing people in town were adults, and most definitely not in any of Popiviolli's files as Cassidy had surmised, thankfully she had the forethought to only write down those who she knew attended Pineton's schools. She glided through names, pulling out the folders for every student that matched the name of a missing person, which only consisted of two or three students.

I'll have to match their pictures too to make any solid connection.

She paused, hovering over Oliver's file, the tips of her fingers just barely grazing the edges of it in a deep desire to open it.

He's not missing…I really shouldn't.

Cassidy's gaze flickered up at her phone, then the door and its little window into the hallway. *Douglass hasn't sent me anything, so I'm still good.*

The girl bit her lip in tender moral conflict, before stealing the folder out of its place and opening it.

Patient full legal name: Olivia Annere Tarsul Jariwala

Psychiatrist: Dr. Debra Aguirra, CCTP, Amelis Behavioral Health Centers, LTD.

Diagnosis: C-PTSD comorbid with Depersonalization-derealization Disorder and Selective Mutism.

Notes on Admission: Patient of 11 years admitted into care following hospital release. Medical records display no previous history of care. Admitted to emergency care with severe physical injuries. Parent declined SANE examination of patient.

Patient admitted into care for the following:

•Withdrawn, will not speak or engage in any verbal communication.

•Aggression, typically physical destruction both to external people/property and to self.

•Disordered sleep patterns, most often night terrors and sleep paralysis.

•Severe panic reactions of a varying sort, most common being extended bouts of catatonia, fight and flight responses.

Initial Summary of Observation: patient shows signs of severe trauma, including but not limited to physical abuse and neglect as well as psychological abuse, with a strong likelihood of—

Cassidy cut herself short, forced from reading by the second dread inducing buzz of her phone. Quickly, she closed the file and slipped it in with the rest of the ones she'd taken, then grabbed her phone. It was Douglass with a singular emoji as his warning.

Immediately the girl began to scramble, gathering all the files and tucking them under her arm as she frantically searched for a place to hide.

***

Oliver drew closer to the first lit room, slowing down as he listened closely for the sound of any movement inside.

He filed himself against the wall when he reached the frame, and peeked into the doorway.

Oh.

It was just a laundry room, as Miss Poppy had mentioned the previous day. Scrubs sat in fat piles on top of several washers and dryers on the right side, and were neatly folded on the bar counter on the left. A couple washers and dryers were on, rolling over the clothes inside with a soft tumbling hum.

There was no one inside and nothing of particular intrigue about the room, so he moved on.

Oliver trotted across the light of the doorway and halted safely in the shadows once again, his nerves settling somewhat at the thought of his own paranoia being the cause of his suspicion.

He leaned over to stare into the next room, expecting it to be nothing more than a closet full of prescription medications.

Oh…oh no.

The boy took a quiet step into the light, scanning the empty laboratory with confusion and soft dread.

It was a much larger room that looked like a repurposed industrial kitchen, stainless steel counters and sinks covered by test tubes and glass vials on hotplates. The delivery boxes all sat stacked by the door, only one or two torn open to show the shipment of even more red flowers.

Oliver moved slowly, picking up the stray flowers to inspect them and their relation to whatever Poppy was doing with them. Many had been cut open and stripped of their petals, strained until they were little more than dried husks, and on stands they dripped into a small glass cylinder bright orange and syrupy liquid.

The stench of death was even more foul here, and Oliver followed the long trail of winding tubes and heating elements that extracted and combined the sap from the flowers with other equally bright chemicals down the counter until he reached its end.

In several stacks were bottles, just regular plastic ones with labels on them in a language he couldn't decipher, and next to the bottles were small cases of the same paper cups used to dispense medication to the patients of the hospital.

Oliver picked up one of the bottles, turning it over and watching that orange liquid slosh about slowly, then tried his best to read the tiny translation on the bottle.

Tellarin Viugaal Orchid no.2247? She's using the flowers to make her drugs…

Oliver set the bottle down, this time moving his attention to something else in effort to figure out just what Poppy was doing in her mental hospital.

There was no doubt that she was from another dimension now, and no doubt that she had lied to him about the medication.

Oliver's eye caught a glass cabinet refrigerator, and the several cannisters of what looked like slime or jelly hermetically sealed by thick metal caps on both ends. They were sorted into colors, bright reds and greens, oranges, yellows, purples and pinks, and one pitch black near the far right side. They were labeled as well, in a script that bore no translation, only symbols and markings that vaguely resembled Wingdings.

The boy pulled at the latch of the refrigerator, but it was firmly locked, causing a small grimace to form on Oliver's face when he realized he couldn't inspect it further.

So instead, he moved back to the other side of the room to a part of the counter that had been cleared of equipment and littered with paperwork and notes.

They were written in the same Wingdings style symbology as the jars in the refrigerator, scribbled notes in ink with diagrams of the Peace Zone flowers both dissected and not. Oliver thumbed through the pages briefly, trying to put together the calculations on their own without his ability to read any of the actual notes.

Those flowers make you feel really good— like a high…but whatever she made with them knocked me out for hours, and I don't— I don't remember what happened after…

Oliver scanned the page, finding nothing and turning it over for the next one. Then he stopped.

It was another diagram, of a different looking plant, tiny notes scrawled all around it with even more equations and calculations.

It looked like another flower, with wide petals, a fat cone in the center and several long vines and tendrils sprouting out from it. Not anything like he'd seen around the hospital.

What is that?

Oliver's brow furrowed in confusion at the indecipherable notes on the page, picking out English words littered few and far between the symbols. All were names.

He flipped the page and pulled a smaller notepad in the corner of the desk closer, perusing that as well in search of some kind of connection. He stopped at a list, all in English, every last bullet was a name.

Asne, Richard – Peace Zone quadrant 684
Finn, Karl – Peace Zone quadrant 235
Hyun, Nicole – Dead Zone quadrant 6
Thakur, Bo Paul – Peace Zone quadrant 1
Hernandez, Maya – Dead Zone quadrant 9
Mull—

Oliver's blood ran cold as he stared at the last name on the list. *Mulligan-Higgs, Cody – Peace Zone…quadrant 481*

***

Cassidy heard the latch of the office door turn and huddled herself into a crevice between the desk and the boxes, taking just barely enough time to pull one in front of her to shield herself from the mirror that, if Miss Popiviolli looked long enough at, would have given her away.

Quickly, she turned her phone on silent and cupped her hand over her mouth to stifle the sound of her frantic breathing. *Calm down…I got what I needed, I can just wait for her to leave and sneak out behind her.*

She forced down a steady breath and kept her gaze locked on the mirror, wincing as the light flipped on and flooded the room with sudden brightness. Poppy stood by the door, only half of her visible in the mirror with a bored and somewhat distracted look on her face as she stared into the room.

The therapist blinked and her gaze shifted off to a corner Cassidy couldn't see and she stepped inside, setting something on the couch before she began cleaning and rearranging the contents of the small cabinet by the entrance. Then she closed the door of the office and turned, pausing in front of the desk with a look that set Cassidy so on edge, she half thought the woman could taste her panic.

Poppy stared at the mirror, though it didn't seem like she was looking at herself, or anything for that matter. Cassidy blinked and breathlessly pushed her glasses up her nose to focus on the woman.

She just stood there, for an incomparably long time it felt, staring at nothing until she pulled something small and blue and round from her pocket and a strange shudder rippled through her and Cassidy's eyes widened in silent, horrific realization.

She's a Clown.

In half a blink, the woman's appearance morphed, her pale skin bleaching until it was paper white and three long black and thin triangle markings bled down from her eyes. The color of her bare arms striped black and white and her fingers lengthened into pointed claws as she took the appearance of a monochrome mime, retaining her cherry red hair under her pitch black beret.

Cassidy waited with baited breath, expecting the alien to see her the instant her eyes flickered down to the base of the mirror. But she didn't, and instead Poppy rolled the ball in her palm pensively, as if she wasn't even present in the room.

Her face looked focused on something entirely outside of where she actually stood, and she made no note or even minor reaction to Cassidy's presence, hiding corralled between boxes stacked high around her.

What..what is she doing? Can't she see me? Taste…me?

Cassidy's thoughts built up in strengthened anxiety at the alien's stillness. Half of her thought she didn't exist inside her body at all.

Then Poppy's eyes widened with shock and rage, her flat expression twisting with a frown as a breath of a whisper escaped her lips.

"I see you."

Venus Flytrap

liver flipped further through the catalog of names, people on a list that he understood with increasing horror led to no positive outcome.

The dread of his bones seeping up through his skin made it crawl with prickling goosebumps and he felt that spike of terror one feels when they sense eyes boring into their back. Like a million watchers stood just behind him, crying out in abject silence.

Then he heard a noise.

Oliver swiveled around, met by the man's still frame in the doorway, hand plastered against the wall.

Short, inconceivable seconds passed in his recognition, the way Matthew stared back at him with shock that so quickly and so terribly twisted into rage as he registered Oliver's presence.

Then the man moved and Oliver scrambled, darting to the other side of the lab to evade his lumbering attack and find some lasting protection behind the island counter as he broke for the only exit.

His biological father twisted around, wielding a fist full of Poppy's flowers in one hand and lunging to grab the boy from over the counter, to which Oliver ducked and ran to the other side in his effort to escape.

Before he could react, Matthew's hand tore at the back of Oliver's head, jerking him off balance as his father shoved him into the island and slammed his skull against the metal.

"NO!!" Oliver kicked and clawed at his father's grappling hands, kneeing him hard in the groin and gaining the avenue he needed for freedom. The boy jolted out from the side, sending glass cups and bottles to the floor in a cacophonous crash as he clambered up the island and over the man's back, kicking off of him and forcing Matthew's head to make the same impact on steel that his had.

His father grunted, swiveling around with a hand that shot out and wrapped around his child's leg, ripping Oliver from his brief flight and yanking him down into the tiles where he wretched and grappled with the air that was forced out of his lungs.

Matthew's hulking frame dropped down, dragging Oliver back a foot or two and wrapping muscular and tensed arms around him, forcing the boy to claw at his face and wrists for escape.

"GET OFF!!" He shrieked, only for two fingers to shove into his mouth in attempt to force it open. Oliver felt his jaw click with the strain of fighting to bite them, and Matthew's legs wrapped around his waist, trapping him down with his weight.

He felt his blood under his nails that dug into his skin, tearing it and leaving nasty claw marks on the man's arms.

Fight back! Fight back! Don't let him—

Oliver's thoughts scattered as his father's hand forced his mouth open wide and several of those bright red flowers were shoved down his throat, causing the boy to hack and cough and choke on them.

A hideous, gut-wrenching howl erupted from the child and his frantic flailing turned into desperate clawing, shrieking and begging as he dug and squirmed to free himself from under his father.

Oliver bit down hard on the fingers in his mouth, flooding it with that thick metallic flavor of blood until he felt the bones crack and he instinctively swallowed, choking down blood and petals and gagging on its noxious mixture until the man yanked them out with a pained look on his face.

Matthew lifted his leg and the boy shot out from underneath him like some tortured, screaming, wild animal, intent on making his escape.

Every part of him shook and trembled, and he couldn't think.

He couldn't look at anything other than the hard white tiles in front of him. They had become fuzzy from the concussion he no doubt had.

Oliver staggered to his feet, hoisting himself up with the countertop as the lines of things around him bulged and bent. *Th— the flowers.*

He'd swallowed them, and as soon as the realization hit, his pounding and reeling head lulled and he reached out and up, or down. He stopped being able to tell. Stopped being able to feel anything at all.

Oliver's hand collided with glass, he only knew because the sound of it shattering against the floor made his dizzy gaze drift back to where his soaked hand spread around the shards on the counter.

Leave. Run. Move! Do something or he's going to— going to…

"You..whh…." Oliver buckled, turning his attention backwards and upside down to Matthew as he moved to his feet, fingers still dripping kaleidoscopic blood on the ground. The boy trembled, numb and unable to tell if he even stood anymore. When he tried to take a step, he simply dropped down into a pile on the ground.

I can't…I can't run. I can't feel my body at all.

Oliver blinked, desperate to rearrange his bones, get them going like he wanted to, but he could only meekly and haphazardly press them into his father's chest as he dropped down and pushed him up against the island cabinets.

"Don't…please.." They were little more than half formed mutterings and Oliver could only stare at all the blurry colors and warbling lines and edges as he watched Matthew hastily pull his clothes off and hoist him up into his arms.

***

Cassidy stared at the alien through the mirror, watching her rage filled face settle before she shifted back into her much more human disguise and swiveled around to leave in clear haste. The moment the door closed, she shoved the box out from in front of her and crawled out of her hiding place, taking all the files she'd stolen in her arms before quickly exiting the office altogether.

"She was in there for a really long time, I tried to warn you but—"

"We need to talk, somewhere else. Alone." Cassidy cut Douglass off, waving him forward and wiping the sweat from her brow so she could put on her bright smile for Mrs. Deauxtree.

She paused at the breakroom, running in and grabbing about six of the leftover donuts the secretary had offered before jetting out the front office with Douglass tailing confusedly behind her.

"Did you get the files?"

"Yes."

"Did Popiviolli see you?"

"No."

"What was she doing in there—"

"Douglass!" Cassidy turned on her heel, shooting him a quick glare before she nodded toward the broken janitor closet. "I'll tell you but we really have to be careful from now on."

The boy's mouth clamped shut and he nodded, following her to the janitorial closet so they could speak somewhat more privately.

Once inside, Cassidy spread out the files she'd taken from the office and pulled out the list of missing persons.

"I only found three matches for names in her drawers, cause most of the people don't go to school anymore, and only a couple go to Pineton High," she explained, opening them up to show the student pictures. "You printed off those posters, right? If any of the names and faces match, then we know she's the one taking people."

"I thought you said it would just be a connection?" Douglass questioned, dumping his tote full of freshly printed posters on the floor. Cassidy shrugged and her lips parted in an uncomfortable grimace.

"That was before I knew she was a Clown."

Douglass stopped, setting down the poster in his hand as his gaze raised to meet the girl's. "You're certain?"

Cassidy nodded. "I wasn't before, because it seemed a little out there, but I saw her, Douglass. I saw her change color and ripple the same way Dindet did. And she held this like..this ball? It was blue, so it's probably her bean— like Dindet's but shaped differently. It's round, not an oval. And she wasn't colorful and didn't really look like a clown. Or at least— she didn't look like one the way Dindet did…more like a mime."

For a flicker of a moment, the girl's eyes brightened with realization and she ripped her alien notes out of her bag to scribble down her discovery. "That means there's probably different kinds of Clowns. If Dindet was a regular one, and Popiviolli is a mime one, then there's likely other types too."

Douglass's forehead creased with worry at the notion and he quietly tried to continue sifting through his posters for matches.

"What would that have to do with anything?" He asked, already dreading the answer his friend might have.

"Well," Cassidy moved from her notes back to the files, marking off names on her list. "Dindet told me that her species changes color based on what they eat, and they eat feelings, right? Well she said that different feelings have different colors, the worse the feeling is, the darker it is in the spectrum."

"Okay?" Douglass responded, clearly not grasping where she was going.

"So far, both Dindet and Miss Poppy have super white base colors. But Dindet had a bunch of other colors like purple and orange, greens and blues and stuff. Mimes are black and white, meaning, she eats the worst feelings anyone could make." Cassidy looked up. "Like a monster that makes you relive your worst experiences. A monster like Richard Asne's."

The intensity of her stare faded as Douglass's eyes flitted down to the file she'd conveniently failed to set out in their collective pile, and his lip twitched with agitation.

"That's Oliver's." The quiet anger in his voice was only marginally subdued by his lilt of concern. "We know where he is…why'd you take it?"

The girl's look of shocked guilt shifted into embarrassment at his tone and she tugged the file out. "I figured there might..be a correlation between him and the other missing people."

It was a bold faced lie. She knew that, and did her absolute best to hide it from Douglass. In truth, Theo, Dindet, the accident at the lab and Oliver's own evasion had piqued her interest to the point that she was desperate to know what he was hiding. If not an alien clown, then something else. What she was able to glean from the file in the short time she'd read it, only further drove that interest.

"I only read a little—"

"You read his file?" Douglass interrupted, his judgment causing the girl to shrink back slightly. "That's like, personal medical information and stuff! You can't just go looking in it."

"I didn't read all of it!" She shot back, "Besides, what do you think we're doing right now? Picking daisies? If there's something in there that has to do with Poppy kidnapping people, then shouldn't we be obligated to check? Wouldn't he want you to know anyways?"

At that Douglass's chin dropped and he sat back on his knees with a small huff. "If he wanted me to know everything, he would have told me on his own."

"Has he?"

Douglass averted his gaze, trying to return his attention back to the posters.

"Douglass."

"No. Why do you even care?" He muttered, far more frustrated that Oliver continuously lied and hid things from him than Cassidy's prying. "You're not really his friend, you mostly only hung out with Dindet anyways. Why do you all the sudden care about Oliver?"

"I'd like to be." The girl's demeanor shifted and she spoke a lot softer, continuing to sift through paperwork. "His friend, I mean. We were in the same class back in middle school, whenever he first started going? I'd just moved here and he still looked like..well, you know."

She paused briefly, capping her pen and beginning to clean the mess of paper she made on the floor. "I come on a bit strong, I know people see me as the girl who adopts all the new kids, even if I wouldn't normally get along with them. I...wasn't really popular back then, and people thought I was weird because I talked differently and didn't act like the other black girls here, wasn't in the regular classes like everyone else."

Her solemn tone prompted Douglass's soft scowl to loosen in sympathy. It was a thing he couldn't relate to, having lived here his whole life, knowing the same people, the same places.

"Oliver was in my class though," she continued, "and we were the only two uhm..girls..at the time, and both in Accommodations. I really wanted a friend, so badly because the other girls were so mean, and he was new too. But I messed up really bad, I think. And I want to try and fix it, if I can?"

Cassidy sighed softly and set the files into her tote bag, all except Oliver's, which she held out for Douglass to take. "But…you're right, I really shouldn't be reading personal stuff like this. You should take it, you know him a lot better than I do."

Douglass stared at her for a moment, specifically the sincere apology on her face as she waited patiently for him to take the folder. "Okay."

He grabbed it and carefully put it into his backpack and turned back to the girl with active and dire seriousness. "Now that we know what we know…how do we get him out?"

***

Oliver drifted in and out of consciousness, he still couldn't feel, and the wavering of his surroundings spread out like a fan, colliding with other duplicates of walls and doors and blinking lights that moved in opposite directions. Matthew hadn't hurt him, not in any of the ways he had expected him to.

Instead, his father carried him, cradled in his arms down the south wing hall toward that rank odor of death. Oliver closed his eyes, and when he opened them again, they had entered a different room altogether.

This one was less dark, and much more rancid. There were machines, bright buttons and computer screens that flickered and morphed in his vision, making little beeping noises that drew Oliver's attention before Matthew stopped at the edge of a big white line on the floor. It could have been three lines though, they performed osmosis on the ground every time Oliver's eyes drifted down to look at them.

His father bent down, gently dropping the boy on the ground and shoving him just to the other side of the line to lay in his drugged and paralyzed, naked stupor.

What…what is he doing?

Oliver opened his mouth to speak, only for a slathering of drool to sputter out and no intelligible words. The extra lines and pictures started moving closer, slowly, and he felt the beginnings of sensation as his skin and muscles tightened with pins and needles and the cold of the cement floor.

Try to move. Oliver stared at his hand, placing incredible focus and intent on the tips of his fingers as he willed it to bend, extend, anything.

Come on. Please! Just move!

As if it were a miracle, his pointer twitched, and he tried again, managing to make it curl and extend in stilted and disjointed movements. His attention drifted to in front of him, where Matthew stood at the enormous computer, inputting data or doing something with it that made whatever thing behind Oliver groan loudly and release a burst of that reeking smell.

Something dripped, a heavy platt on the cement and if he were able, Oliver would have turned his head to look.

His father glided from the machine to behind him, not even acknowledging Oliver's existence as he pulled on something, his tough grunts quickly drowned out by the hideous sound of something wet and gross splattering onto the floor.

He didn't know what it was and didn't want to, and as Oliver watched his father haul another naked boy back from the shadows his desperation burgeoned in his chest and his bones burned for freedom.

Oliver reached out, tears stinging his eyes and further blurring what he could already barely see. One arm, then the other. *That's all I need. Move..just move..please.*

The boy picked his hand up and with great effort, slapped it palm down on the ground, praying that his sweat and skin and strength alone would be enough to drag himself forward.

Desperate and hopeless endeavors, because the door was ten or twenty feet away from where he lay. But he still tried.

Oliver rolled, managing a few inches while Matthew was distracted with the other victim of whatever heinous crimes he committed here in the dark. The boy kicked, or tried to, feeling that burn of static increase in his toes when they bent on the ground and gave him traction. *A couple more inches.*

Then, some wretched and loud buzzer went off and Oliver halted, stiffened by the horror of not knowing what it meant.

Matthew turned around, moving to the other side of the room, to another machine that spat out some kind of liquid into jars. He seemed to inspect them closely for a bit, before setting the cylinders down on a trolley and grabbing a syringe.

Then, he turned, his dark eyes meeting Oliver's as he stepped closer, dropping down to his knees and methodically moving the boy's limbs back and close to his body so he stayed just behind the line.

Oliver's eyes gained focus, just enough to see the man's face and strangely, the profuse tears streaming down his cheeks, unable to cease, despite Matthew's intense and unfeeling stare.

His father cupped his hand under the boy's cheek, lifting his head so that his neck was easily accessed, and plunged the sharp needle of the syringe into Oliver's numb skin.

It burnt, slightly, and he could feel how quickly the ice cold liquid coursed his veins and shut down the static of his slow returning senses. His vision blurred further and that familiar high of the flowers made him struggle once again to move or feel at all, to stay conscious.

Matthew stood, staring down at Oliver as he exercised one last ditch effort to plea.

The boy's fingers twitched again, and he lifted his head, lifted his arm, reaching for someone he knew would never grant him safety.

"...daddy..." Oliver begged, though the word was nothing but a hoarse whisper, and all it did was cause Matthew to take a heart-rending step back.

Oliver felt himself be pulled, the remnant of sensation already dying as something long and dark and snakelike wrapped around his outstretched arm. He was low, on the ground at first. He knew that because that was where Matthew had laid him.

But now, somehow, he was above him, being lifted and pulled, held up as his biological father watched him safely from behind that white line that still performed osmosis in rhythmic patterns on the ground. And then, it was very, very dark.

The Plan

Jon pushed through the front entrance of the school, swiveling his head left and right as he searched for the Counselors office and made a B-line for the room.

"Is this about the charges?" He asked the moment he stepped through the threshold of the door. Mrs. Bradshaw turned her attention away from Markus and stood up at her desk, her eyes briefly flickering to Douglass, who sat in the chair on the opposite wall, before they rested on the scientist with a sorry look.

"My son is being taken care of," Jon continued in earnest, keeping his eyes on Douglass as his face shifted into a look of confusion. "I promise, he won't be able to cause anyone any—"

"That's well and good, Dr. Jariwala," the counselor interrupted, holding up her hand. She shot a look at the boy Oliver had beaten before continuing. "That's not why I've called you here though. Markus, your phone please."

The senior looked positively mortified, sitting and shaking in his seat. He leaned back and childishly shook his head, keeping his palm firmly planted on his pocket. For a second or two his gaze flickered up to Jon, causing the man to furrow his brow at the look of absolute terror in his eyes.

"Douglass," Jon asked, prompting the boy to sit up in his seat, almost at attention. "What's going on here?"

"I— well," Douglass dropped his eyes off and away, clearly struggling to form words. "When Oliver beat up Markus..he said some stuff. I just— I forgot to mention it to the principal or anything, so I came in to tell Mrs. Bradshaw about it. They want to...open an investigation..."

Jon's face stoned immediately and he shot a wild glare at Markus before he forced himself into a calmer demeanor. "What *kind* of investigation?"

Mrs. Bradshaw circled around her desk, gesturing for him to follow her out into the hall for a more private conversation.

"Recently," she said softly, closing the door behind her. "The teachers had been taking notice of a few rumors about your child, Dr. Jariwala...and with the vandalization of the bathroom and the still as of yet, unknown cause of this fight, I've asked Principal Balboa and the Superintendent to open an investigation surrounding some...potential allegations."

Jon dipped his head in silent contemplation, the way she spoke, avoiding saying things, made his skin crawl at whatever unspoken allegations she could be alluding to. But he held soft and spoke quietly. "What sort of rumors? What are these allegations?"

The woman's whole face scrunched with apprehension and she looked away, back through the window at where Douglass spoke to Markus inside her office.

"They are...of a sexual nature," she paused, hesitant to continue with the way Jon visibly sank into himself, how he let out a terribly shaky breath— like he knew what she was about to say next. "Jon, I know you care about him more than anything in the world and would never—"

"That *bastard*." He cut in coldly. Jon pulled away from her, pacing around in a little circle in the hall as he gathered his thoughts around himself and tried so very hard to keep his nerve.

"Please, calm down—"

"How can I be calm, Patricia?! You *know* what he's been through, you *know* how bad it was." Jon spat. He brushed his fingers through his hair and down his face in order to push down his rage.

"Am I under investigation now? For protecting *my child*?!"

"No," Mrs. Bradshaw affirmed, allowing the man to settle in the relief of the statement. "I testified on behalf of you and Oliver and I would do that again in a *heartbeat*. You know that."

Jon nodded, slowly at first, and then faster as her words registered. "I know, I just— I know…"

Some small silence fell between them, prompting the woman to glance back once more at her office window. "The allegations..are against Markus."

Jon blinked, his expression moving from disbelief to shock, to pure unadulterated rage. "Elaborate."

Mrs. Bradshaw drew in an uncomfortable breath and slowly drew her eyes back to Jon, focusing on the way his fingers balled tightly into fists, waiting for her to explain.

"Young mister Furkin came to me the other day, to tell me that..while Oliver was—" She avoided the word, "he was yelling about Markus..touching him. I went back over the video feed of the incident and it's evident that whatever occurred in the bathroom was suspicious enough to warrant a closer look and…"

"And?"

"With his father's permission, I was able to confiscate Markus's phone." Mrs. Bradshaw pulled her gaze away from Jon's increasingly whitening knuckles, drawing his attention from the floor and to her face. "The two of them had been in contact with each other for several weeks leading up, there are some...photos..and unsavory things."

Jon forced out a slow exhale at the woman's words, drinking them in and letting them ruminate in his brain between her uncomfortable pause.

"Based on their conversations," she continued in earnest, gently nudging the man away from the door. It was clear his thoughts were turning to violence. "Based on their conversations, it was mutual, but as of late December, Markus's texts became much more hostile."

"That's what that money was for.." Jon breathed, his eyes flickering from the door back to Mrs. Bradshaw.

"Oliver had stolen around eight hundred dollars from my wallet before he left for India," He clarified, "was he being extorted this entire time?"

Mrs. Bradshaw stared at him and he watched as the crease of her lips turned down in a sad, honest frown as she nodded. "It seems Mulligan-Higgs found out about the custody case—"

Before she could finish, Jon threw her office door open and charged into the room, shoving aside the desk as he gripped Markus by the shirt and yanked him out of his seat. Douglass immediately stood and darted to the corner to evade his rage, staring in shock at just how terrifying the seemingly endlessly kind scientist had become.

"*What* did you do to my son?" He asked in a low growl, glaring daggers into the terrified boy's eyes. Markus blubbered and stuttered with nothing words, struggling to find an answer in his shock and fear. "WHAT DID YOU DO TO HIM?!"

"I'm sorry!" Markus cried, "don't put me in jail! I don't— I can't, please, I didn't mean to, I swear! She said it was fine, she wanted to— I swear!"

Jon shook him and he let out a pitiful cry, holding up his hands as if to bar any potential attack. He was just a child, after all. A wretched, abhorrent child that needed to be taught a lesson. *I want to teach him a lesson.*

Jon's lips curled up in an ugly snarl at the thought. How easily he could pumble him far worse than Oliver had. But as he glared at this shaken boy, all he could see was his own child's fear. *It won't fix things. Let go.*

The scientist unfurled his fingers from the collar of the boy's shirt and stepped back, far enough that he stood several feet from him as he watched Markus scramble behind Mrs. Bradshaw in the corner of the room. Jon's gaze flickered so briefly back to Douglass and the way the poor kid stared at him, dumbfounded and bewildered by such an outburst.

"Are you planning to press charges?"

"Oliver won't testify." Jon said coldly, moving his gaze back to the Counselor.

"He'd be subpoenaed," Mrs. Bradshaw added, keeping her gaze on Markus. "Douglass...thank you for your time."

At her words, Douglass dropped out of his stupor to stare at the Counselor. She tilted her head toward the door with a gentle smile and he gave a short nod, quickly sliding around Jon and out of the room. Markus moved as well, slowly and cautiously from behind the desk.

"Not you." Mrs. Bradshaw stopped him, holding out an arm that forced him back.

"Jon," she continued once Markus sat back down in his seat, "Judge Oxford was lenient last time because he was in the hospital and there was enough evidence on top of my testimony to not require him there..but *this* is different. You've had two brushes with CPS already, Oliver *has* to testify if you plan to take anyone to court."

Jon nodded curtly at her words, mulling them over and trying so hard to come up with an answer, a solution. *He won't do it. He didn't even tell me about this. There is absolutely no way he'd be willing to testify in front of a jury. He will just lie. Even under oath. There's....*

There's nothing I can do.

"Give me some time, I—" Jon's phone rang, interrupting his words, "I'll see if I can—"

It rang again and he promptly pulled it out of his pocket to turn it off but paused. *Director Miles.*

"I— I need to take this," he said defeatedly, glancing back at the woman as he backed toward the door. "I'll talk to him. I'll figure something out. This isn't over."

***

Douglass ducked out into the hall, still trying to shake off the residual shock of seeing Oliver's father so angry. He'd never gotten that angry before.

Maybe I shouldn't have—

"So, did it work? Is he gonna get him out of Amelis?" Cassidy's voice crashed through his skull and he doubled back to catch her snooping around the fire exit.

"I-I don't know," he answered as she caught up with him. "He was really mad, I don't think I've ever seen him so mad before…"

"But it worked, right?" *Is that all you care about?* Douglass gave her a bewildered look and the girl pushed her glasses up her nose as she took a faster stride.

"I asked my mom after you left, and she said that if something really happened, then Oliver would have to be there to prove it did, cause he's fifteen," she said, "so that would get him out of the hospital and away from the aliens—"

"Keep it *down!*" Douglass chided softly, "we don't know how many are here, someone could hear you and—"

He paused, trying to get his thoughts to settle on what Cassidy was so hopeful of.

"Oliver isn't…really the kind of person who likes to *talk* about things, even if something did happen…" The boy grew silent, his whole heart turning over in his chest at the idea. At how full of rage Jon was…*what did Mrs. Bradshaw tell him?* "What…what do you think happened in the bathroom?"

"I don't know? *You* were the one who was there. Did you not see anything?" Cassidy glanced back at him and he shook his head.

"I mean, I was just trying to get in the door, I guess someone was blocking it? And we left so fast— mostly I just remember—" *the way Oliver beat up that guy.*

"Well, I guess statistically, *something* was bound to happen, since he's trans and all. I was reading this news article the other day about a kid in Ontarica that was made to pull down their…" Cassidy trailed off, finally registering the look of absolute horror on Douglass's face. "I mean, I don't think our school is as bad as *that*. I— I'm sure it wasn't anything like that. If— if anything, with everything we know, Markus could be one of the alien's and Oliver caught onto him."

Douglass made a small noise and looked away from her, following up with an even more emphatic sigh. "I just..I wish he would tell me things, you know? It gets so frustrating trying to figure out what the hell is going on in his head, or, or if he's even okay."

"You really like him, don't you?" Cassidy's tone shifted and she gave the boy a gentle smile. "You've been friends since he started school, right? Back when he didn't talk."

Douglass offered a meager nod.

"We live right across from each other, and I had met him before then, sort of. Most of the time he just goes home and ignores me." He explained, growing more disenchanted at the thought. "Sometimes he gives me his old books, or little pictures and sculptures he makes. But we kind of...stopped being friends after the accident. We hung out a bit over break but...I think he just wanted a distraction. All we did was watch movies and play games."

Cassidy stared at Douglass for a solid second and half, thoroughly reading his self dismissal and turning her focus back to the path in front of her. "Oh, he definitely likes you."

Douglass gave an incredulous little laugh. "Yeah, *sure.*"

"No really," Cassidy countered rather objectively. "You *just said* he gives you his art and stuff. Even little sculptures and books? How much time do you think he spends on that? How often do you think he finishes a book and says 'I think Douglass would like this'? And you spend time together— and I don't mean just time alone. I *always* see you two together."

The boy blinked, trying to wrap his mind around such a notion. It sounded lovely. And also hardly even believable at the same time. "He just does that because *he* doesn't want them anymore. And he spent just as much time with Dindet."

"I still only ever see him with you. It only doesn't look it, cause he's not *saying* it," Cassidy added, "but he's still going out of his way to do stuff with you or give you things, it means he thinks you're worth giving those things to. It's not like he goes around giving just *anyone* stuff that's probably really important to him."

"Yeah, but even then, half of it's unfinished."

"Cause he probably thinks you'll still value it, even if it never got finished." Cassidy retorted happily. "*Boy. He likes you.*"

The girl brushed her curls over her shoulder with a confident nod and offered a wide, encouraging grin that Douglass only met with a dejected hum and a downward gaze.

"He shouldn't," he muttered, "I already ruined it because *I* was the idiot who asked him to be my girlfriend...right before his mom died..right before he...started being a boy."

Cassidy's smile faded and she readjusted her glasses once more as they neared their classroom.

"I get that," she said, much more calmly. "But you gotta think...how does that feel for him? Knowing you like him, but probably thinking it's because you see him as the wrong thing?"

She paused, hoping for Douglass to fill the silence, but he didn't.

"*Or* you could just ask him when we go visit the hospital tomorrow." Cassidy continued. She grabbed the classroom door handle and glanced back at Douglass, gauging his confused expression.

"Wait— we're going over there? H-how?"

"In your car, duh." She answered, a big wide smile slipping across her face as she swung the door open.

The poor boy sputtered nonsense words while he tried to process how quickly she'd come to that solution. "But— but I've never even *been* on that side of town!"

"You'll figure it out!" Cassidy countered, failing to hide her cheeky grin as she slipped into the room before Douglass so much as had the opportunity to object.

Visiting Hours

"Hurry up! You have visitors." The sound of Matthew's voice through the doorway made him jump. Oliver quickly scrambled to his feet, wincing as he reached up to turn off the bath water. Huge welts covered his torso, it turned his skin an ugly purplish yellow, and his head still throbbed from being smacked against a steel countertop.

The spidery bruise that ran up his spine and branched around his back was still faintly visible and his stomach turned at the thought of whatever thing in the dark had caused it.

Oliver peeked out into his room. The door was still closed, but he could hear Matthew shuffling from the other side of it. He glanced around in search of a fresh pair of clothes.

He rifled through the drawers, digging through old bedsheets until he managed to pull out a pair of scrubs that were at least a size too big for him.

"Come on," Matthew slammed his fist against the door, causing the kid to immediately drop to his knees in shock. "Your friends are here to talk to you."

"Jus— just a second, I'm not dressed!" he stammered back, throwing on the clothes as quickly as possible until his eye caught something bright and red on the window sill. *Matthew's cigarettes. He must be staying in the room while— while...I'm unconscious.*

Oliver stopped and stared at them for a second as a tiny plan began to concoct itself in his head. He glanced back at the door. *Still closed.*

The kid grabbed the pack of cigarettes. It was a long shot, but there was a chance, albeit miniscule, that it would work.

Oliver paced around his room, his panic slowly growing, until his sight rested on the large basket on the outside of the window. It was barely open, but his fingers were small enough to fit through that little crack and pull one of the flowers loose.

"Alright, times up." Matthew barged into the room, prompting the kid to spin on his heel and shove the cigarette into the bulb of the flower, completely soaking the tip of it.

"I— I'm coming, sorry," Oliver pushed the cigarette back into the box behind his back.

Matthew stared at him, just long enough that the boy began to sweat under his gaze. The man's hand reached up and Oliver grit his teeth, preparing for some kind of brutal assault. But he instead caressed his face, sliding his fingers between the locks of his hair.

His father stared at him, for an uncomfortably long time that Oliver was wont to evade his touch. But he didn't, and simply stood there, studying the ambiguous look etched across the man's face, like he was having some secret conversation in his mind.

After his silence doubled in length, Oliver noticed something particularly peculiar. He was crying.

Not in the sense that his father's face had screwed up into a sob, but rather it was completely still, and his eyes watered to the point that a tear rolled down his cheek as he stared at him.

Matthew's grip tightened around his son's hair, pulling it taught enough that it stung and made the ebb of his already pounding head stronger.

"Where's Kaylee?" Oliver asked, defiance in his tone despite his trembling. He resisted the urge to drop his gaze.

"She's out sick." *Liar.*

"I'm watching you today, to make sure you behave." Matthew continued, blinking the tears from his eyes. "You feel *better.*"

"...I.." Oliver hesitated, long enough that it prompted Matthew to further tighten his grip on him. "I do, I feel better."

"But you're not ready to leave." Matthew's voice grew stern and quiet, like a low growl that made his child look at him with the smallest of pleas.

A shudder ran through the boy and his eyes flickered past his father to the doorway. Douglass and Cassidy sat in the foyer, idly waiting at a table for him to come out.

"....I'm not— I'm not ready to leave... just yet."

"Good girl," Matthew smiled and let go of him, patting him gently on the head before pushing him toward the door. "Now go have fun with your friends, okay? They've come all this way just to see you."

***

"I'm telling you, I don't think this place is legit, it looks like an old nursing home, not a mental hospital. Look at that lady over there." Douglass pointed toward a young nurse, who for some reason kept repeating the same action. Cleaning one spot of the window in a daze, as if she were being mind controlled.

"Everyone here is either super smiley and happy, or basically totally empty, it has to be a sham." He continued, keeping his voice low as he glanced around the area.

Cassidy nodded. "I don't see any other patients with visitors either, there's gotta be at least fifty people here, but we're the only ones who came to visit anyone."

"H-hey, guys." Oliver offered a meager fake smile, but stood well enough away from the two of them. "It's really cool that you showed up."

"Oliver!" Douglass practically leaped from his seat, causing the kid to stumble back at the sudden movement. "How are you doing? What's been going on? Are you safe?!"

Douglass rounded the table, expecting some kind of answer, but his friend's attention had already moved toward the nurse that stood down the hall, intently watching the three of them.

"Ols?" He reached for the boy's hand, and Oliver instinctively snatched it away, swiveling a startled glance back at him.

"Oh, yeah," he smiled, "I'm perfectly fine. A-actually— things have really calmed down, I don't know what it is with the flowers, but they have a way of..of..of..."

"Of what?" Cassidy questioned with a subtle and strange gesture. Oliver stared at her for a moment or two, trying to recognize the familiarity of the movement.

"I— I forget, sorry," he shook his head, offering another lie of a smile as he sat down at their table and prompted Douglass to do the same. "The medication is kind of intense."

"What kind of medication do they have you on?" Cassidy asked, though her gaze had shifted toward the same nurse Oliver kept looking back at. She rested her hands plainly on the table, loud enough that it drew the boy's attention down to the distinct placement of her fingers.

"I know a few that are anti-psychotics, I figured that's what they would give you." She continued, subtly and silently changing through letters in the sign language alphabet. **Do.**

"Something like that." Oliver replied slowly, keeping his gaze on her upside down letters. **You.**

"So Cas tells me," Douglass elbowed the girl lightly, pulling her attention away from the nurse and back to the conversation. **Need.** "That this place is uh, what did you say?"

"Oh, I heard that they work really well with people in *unsafe* situations?" She replied. **Help?** "So, uh, Ols, did they say anything about that?"

Oliver's gaze flickered up from Cassidy's hand and the two met eyes for a solid second or two. He lowered his head and rested his arms on the table, finally allowing himself to relax just enough that he hoped no one noticed.

"Yeah, they try to make sure everyone here feels...*safe*," he answered, praying he could remember enough of the sign language he was made to learn in his sixth grade accommodations class.

"Right, uh," Douglass struggled, "are they treating you okay?"

"Of course! I feel a lot better now," he answered, loud enough that his father could hear. "It's actually been pretty great, I haven't—"

Oliver stopped himself, and for a brief moment, his face twisted up with terror.

"*Don't* turn around." He breathed, reaching out to grab both Douglass and Cassidy's hands. Poppy stood behind them, though it didn't look like she was paying any attention to their conversation. Her focus was on the nurse that had managed to clean the window so well, she had rubbed a crack into the glass.

Douglass hesitated, resisting the urge to look at whatever it was that scared Oliver to the point of silence. But instead, his attention was caught by his personal nurse. A burly man in his late forties that had quietly moved behind where Oliver sat.

"So, when are you planning on getting out?"

Oliver's forced smile faltered, and he kept himself from sucking in a gasp as his father rested a massive hand over the back of his chair.

"Everything going alright?" The nurse casually asked, offering a gentle smile. "Can I get you guys anything? Snacks, drinks?"

Oliver sat uncomfortably straight in his seat, his throat closed by the intrusion of their conversation and Matthew's swift theft of their safety.

"No, we're good, thank you though." Cassidy's eyes darted toward the nurse, but she kept her poker face, patient for an answer.

Oliver squirmed slightly, prompting Matthew to crouch down behind him. The boy's gaze dropped away from his friends and he slowly retracted his hands, dragging them along the table until the very last second, when he rested one palm over the other in the briefest of pleas. **HELP.**

Cassidy's eyes flickered to Douglass and back to Oliver, breaking that perfect poker face just long enough that the nurse behind him met her with stern, narrowed eyes.

"It's time for your next session," Matthew whispered to his son, loud enough for the two guests to hear. "Say goodbye to your friends."

Oliver nodded silently, attempting to pull his arms back to his lap before his father's palm rested over his wrist and pressed the boy's hand into the cool of the table. "It's probably gonna be a while...before I'm ready to leave..."

"But—"

"Guys, I'm doing fine. Besides...visiting hours are over."

A Villain at Rest

Oliver watched as the two kids got up from their table and made their way to the exit, every step further prompted more pressure on his arm from his father. Until the front door finally closed and Matthew forced him up from his seat.

"What was that?" He almost growled the question, twisting the skin on the boy's wrist until he winced at the burn of it.

"Don't break it—"

"What were you doing just then? With your hands? You think I'm an idiot?!" Matthew jostled him enough to force Oliver into a pointless cower.

"Mr. Tarsul," Miss Poppy's ice cold voice made the grown man freeze, immediately dropping his grip on Oliver and letting him scramble to temporary safety behind the therapist. She placed a somewhat comforting hand on his back and smiled, bringing tears back to Matthew's eyes. "I would appreciate it if you were less forceful with our patients. We like to uphold a *positive* image here at Amelis."

His father grumbled some idle grievances, boring a glare down at his child in the moments before he huffed and nodded. "I understand."

He…he's doing as she asks?

The woman cocked her head, her smile widening just slightly at his obedience. "Thank you, and...I do believe nurse Carpenter should be ready to begin her shift in a few hours, if you could escort Oliver to his room for the time being, as he has no sessions today. And he's late on his medications."

The man glowered back at Poppy like he were three seconds from attempting to rip her head off, but he shortly nodded and stuck his hand out for Oliver to take.

It's like she owns him.

"I know the way." The boy narrowed his eyes. Quietly, Oliver stepped forward, dignified in the little protection whatever Poppy's end goal offered him, even if it was going to be short lived. He knew he held some type of value and thus Matthew couldn't touch him, probably.

He followed his father back to his very pretty prison cell and the moment the door closed and he was locked inside with him, all pleasantries fell and he whipped around with the most hateful glare he could muster.

"Why are you here? What are you doing?" Oliver spat, disregarding the danger his tone brought.

Instead of answering, Matthew simply sat down in the wicker chair, sinking into it with visible exhaustion and pressing his bandaged fingers to his temple with a groan.

Oliver moved back from him, sitting on his bed so he maintained a good three feet of safety. "What do you want? To take me back?"

"I forgive you." Was all Matthew responded with, lifting his fingers to show off the damage Oliver had done in their altercation. It filled the boy with such a palpable rage he wanted to break every last bone his father had.

"I'm *not* sorry." He retorted, fully aware that in any other situation the words would have led to far more pain than they would here. "*Answer my question.*"

Matthew rolled his eyes and sat forward, and the movement made Oliver shift away from him, expecting him to do much more than just that. "I'm not here to take you with me, or whatever idea you've concocted in your head. I'm here because *I can't leave.* "

Oliver's rage wavered for a moment, cold realization drifting over him at the idea. Matthew did what he wanted, when he wanted, where he wanted. He was always in control. *Never* the one being controlled.

What did she do?

"Wh— why not?" He asked dumbly, not entirely sure how to approach this new and ugly sympathy he felt for someone he hated so much.

"You have no idea what you've gotten yourself into, baby girl," Matthew replied through his tired sigh, "That woman is *not* like your friend."

So she's a Clown... Oliver's face screwed with indignation and he changed the subject.

"You deserve it," he grumbled, "whatever she does to you. You deserve *all* of it."

Matthew groaned, dropping his hands from his face to shoot his child a sarcastic look. "I think it's time to take your medicine, Olivia."

"That is *not* my name." Oliver corrected, letting the words drip like poison from his mouth. They were powerful, at least to him.

Matthew muttered and stood, and it'd be a lie to say Oliver didn't force himself to hide his quick flinch at the movement.

He watched his father step into the bathroom and unlock the cabinet full of what he could only assume were more of that awful drug.

"You've grown quite a mouth on you," Matthew drawled from the bathroom, returning with that little paper cup. His eyes leveled in a dead stare at his son. "You get that from your momma."

Oliver bit back his snarl at the remark.

"I'm not taking that," he stated, half of him trembling at his gall for defiance. Matthew took a step closer, his imposing frame strengthening that unconscious tremor Oliver choked down with every fiber of his being.

His gaze flickered down to his father's bandaged fingers, still fresh with blood.

Part of him relished in the sight and the strength and

confidence— no matter how temporary it was— that was provided by Poppy's dominance over the man.

It made Matthew human again. A thing that could be hurt and broken. Something that *he* could make bleed, even.

"Don't make this harder than it needs to be, Liv." Matthew's bloody fingers twitched, prompting the boy to raise his gaze once more. "I'm not going to ask you again."

He raised the cup of liquid, presenting it for Oliver to take, and if he had any bone left in his body subject to satisfy his father's demand, he would have taken it. Done exactly as he was told because that is what a good kid did. That is what kept you from being hit.

Except it didn't.

It wouldn't.

All it did was delay the inevitable. And right now, all Oliver wanted to do was get it over with. Make it predictable.

Right now, it was the only thing he had some modicum of control over.

So he raised his hand and promptly smacked that little paper cup down on the ground, taking brief and wonderful reprieve in such a blatant act of insubordination.

Even the look on Matthew's face was priceless. That shock, mirrored only by Oliver's own expression at what he'd just done.

Matthew stared at him, in a period so short and so long that Oliver couldn't tell exactly what he would do in response.

"I—" His father's hand raised and Oliver cut himself short, cowering in preparation for whatever violence Matthew would dole out.

But it didn't come.

Instead, Matthew's raised hand clenched into a fist and then relaxed. He let out a beleaguered sigh and dropped down to pick up the small paper cup.

What?

Oliver watched as his father tossed the cup into a small trash bin, utterly dumbfounded by his deliberate refusal to hurt him. It was strange. Unnerving. Wrong in a way he couldn't understand.

"Why do you make things so hard for me, Liv?" Matthew grumbled, taking a step back toward the wicker chair to start on a fresh cigarette.

Oliver couldn't comprehend what had just happened, let alone form words in his mouth. So he simply sat stupidly on his bed, staring at his father as he drew in a drag.

"I worked so hard to get you back, you know. I planned a life for us. Planned a life for you. A good one too," Matthew said. "I could have paid for your schooling, gotten you everything you could ever need. No dingy apartment in bumfuck mountains. A nice place, with a nice kitchen…but no. You had to ruin it for me. For us."

It took a few seconds for the words to register in Oliver's brain, though he was still hanging in the violence that never came. *This isn't right. He's not— he's not acting right.*

"I…no, you—"

"Did you think I wouldn't find out?" Matthew cut in, flicking his gaze up at the boy's confused face.

"Wh— what?"

At his dumbfounded expression, Matthew stood, prompting Oliver to pull himself further back onto the bed. The man drew closer, looming over Oliver as he spread his arms over the boy like a cage.

He leaned in, forcing Oliver to press himself into the wall, scrunched up and confused and so taut with tension and apprehension that his breath lay locked in his lungs.

"You cheated." Matthew spoke in such a low voice that it sounded closer to a growl than words. All Oliver could focus on was the look in his eyes, like he wanted to hurt him. But he simply pulled back and stood straight, casting his gaze out the window as he took another drag from his cigarette.

Oliver kept himself close though, refusing to relax until he was certain— if he could be— that Matthew wouldn't hurt him. Or that he at least knew when it would happen.

"I should have expected as much," the man muttered in lieu of Oliver's silence. "You are your mothers daughter, aren't you?"

***

"What were you doing with your hands?" Douglass asked, prompting Cassidy to pause their prison break planning.

The two of them sat on the floor in her room, printed off papers and old images of Amelis all around as they mapped out the best way to get inside.

"You were being weird, I didn't wanna say anything cause I figured it was supposed to stay a secret."

"Oh, that was sign language," she answered, "My mom, Jen, went deaf so when I moved to the country, I was put in an accommodations class. Oliver was in the same class like way back in middle school, and they taught us ASL."

Douglass blinked. "Huh. Learn something new every day, I guess…did he say anything back?"

"He said help." Cassidy mimicked the sign to provide an example. "But I have no idea how to make for certain that we can even get him out. Dindet didn't exactly tell me her species' weaknesses, you know."

"Actually…I think there might be a way," Douglass returned, "my dad had these samples, I think it was part of Dindet, but he was using them in his machine to test their conductivity— and, when the voltage gets too high, it makes the sample all spiky and then it burns up."

Cassidy glanced at him, "so if they are all made of the same stuff, then a shock would probably hurt them? that…actually makes a lot of sense. Clowns are made of well, everything, and that includes super conductive materials, so they're probably really susceptible to any electrical current."

"Exactly."

"I think I have the perfect thing!" Cassidy dropped her phone and stood up, turning around to dig in her closet for something. She returned with a small colorful box, opening it up to show off some party gags.

"Toys?" Douglass cocked his head, eyeing her as she let out a sarcastic sigh.

"No, these." She plopped back down on the floor and dug out

two little jelly buzzers. "They are small, easy to hide, and shock the ever loving crap out of anyone who shakes your hand."

Douglass picked one of the buzzers out of her hand and inspected it closely, "I guess it works, I was just gonna grab my dad's taser."

"Oh, no, definitely bring that too."

He stood up, dropping the toy into his pocket for the time being and glanced out the window. *It's getting late.*

"I should probably go before the extra curricular bus leaves, I have a shift at the antique shop tonight," he said. Cassidy nodded and stood up, grabbing the door for him to head out.

"I thought you got your license?" She asked as she followed the kid downstairs. He shook his head though, and somewhat anxiously glanced out the window before stepping on to the porch.

"I only got a permit, so I have to have an adult with me after like, 6pm. I don't really wanna risk getting caught after curfew without one." Douglass answered, the girl nodded and her eyes flickered from side to side as she lowered her head in secrecy.

"Can I ask you something?"

"Okay?" Douglass nodded, watching the girl shift in her increasing reluctance to speak. She played with the hem of her shirt for a moment, opening and closing her mouth in hesitation.

"Do you— know what Oliver's dad looks like?"

The boy blinked. "Well, yeah, he's kind of tall? Like 7 feet I think? Dark hair, beard, sort of brownish skin? Dark eyes—"

"I don't mean his step-dad," Cassidy clarified softly, pulling Douglass's thoughts down into a much darker topic. "I mean like, his *dad* dad."

The girl kept her gaze on the floorboards, though she could sense the tensity in Douglass's shoulders as he straightened up. "I only ask, cause...that nurse at the hospital seemed really off and I don't know, it looked like Oliver knew him, or maybe— maybe they knew each other? I don't know, I'm probably being paranoid right?"

Douglass failed to respond.

"I mean, it's probably nothing to be honest—"

"It's okay," the boy cut in, much more calmly than Cassidy anticipated. He offered a sad, almost hollow smile in effort to ease her nerves. "I know what you mean, but...I've never met Matthew before. And Oliver never talks about him. I don't think he even has any pictures from before..then."

"You're certain?" Cassidy urged, finally looking up from the ground. "You've never seen him at all? Or seen Oliver with him?"

Douglass shrugged. "Sorry, I only ever saw his truck."

"What about when he first moved next door? Or when he came to school? I remember he used to get pulled out of class alot—"

"That was because of the divorce, I'm pretty sure." Douglass interjected.

Cassidy heaved a small sigh and opened her front door to let him leave.

But before he did, she stopped him one last time. "Would Theo know? I know they used to be neighbors so..would you ask her maybe? Just to..make sure I'm wrong."

"Yeah, uh, I'll try."

Quiet Suggestions

It had been hours. Oliver sat curled up and into himself on his bed, waiting for Matthew to do something, anything.

The raw tension of his lack of action made the boy's anticipation wring knots into his muscles until they ached and he couldn't stop himself from shaking.

Matthew sat in the wicker chair, emmassing a pile of ashes at his feet from his smoking.

Every movement he made, from the tilt of his head to twitch of the muscles in his arms, set Oliver on edge. He would hurt him. At some point.

He didn't know when, or how, but he knew it would happen, and the soft terror of that knowledge made Oliver's bones rot and a vile pit open up in his stomach every time his gaze happened to flicker over in his father's direction.

"Why are you acting so scared?"

Oliver flinched and his head lifted to dart eyes back at his father. Matthew leaned back in his chair, flitting ash on the floor. "I thought you said you were a man."

They writhed like maggots burrowed under his skin, his father's words. Oliver stared back at the man, unable to come up with a response.

It prompted a nasty smirk to twist at Matthew's lips.

"So I guess you're only one when it suits you, huh?" He said, leaning forward to rest his elbows on wide spread legs. He flicked more ash on the floor. "Like when you beat that boy bloody."

Immediately Oliver averted his gaze away from the man. "I…I shouldn't have done—"

"No," Matthew cut in, shifting in his seat as he took a drag from his cigarette. "I think you should have. God knows since you're gonna keep playing dress up, you ought to play the part well, right?"

No…I don't— I don't want to be that. Be like you. Oliver shifted uncomfortably, trying to press himself even further into the corner of the wall. "It was wrong.."

Matthew laughed at the statement. "Right. But it felt good, didn't it? Bet you felt nice and strong, a real *big boy.*"

The boy winced at the thought, how wretched it was that Matthew was right. That it *did* feel good. Deserved, even. That he wanted Markus dead for what he'd done. Oliver's fingers dug into his arms at the idea. How he echoed the same words his father said with his hands wrapped tight around his neck and glass between his fingers.

I'm not..like you. I'm not like that…right? I can be better…right?

His thoughts were stirred by Matthew leaning forward, trapping the boy in a deadlocked stare. He was relaxed, and it was wrong.

"I'm proud of you…Oliver."

If he were alone, he'd have cried, probably shrieked and wailed and clawed enough to rip his skin off. That most cruel validation made him want nothing more than to shed himself of everything that made his person. Instead Oliver just sat, staring at his father and the way he smiled at him.

He watched as Matthew fumbled with his pack of cigarettes. The four times he attempted to catch a flame with his lighter before he drew in a drag and the soft, white film of smoke invaded Oliver's peripheral.

Matthew coughed and he flinched again, moving his eyes to his toes and how they were turning purple from the cold.

His father coughed again, this one a violent, ugly hack before he muttered some nasty curse and Oliver dared to flick his gaze toward him.

"The fuck—" the man lurched toward him, uneven and staggered steps as Oliver registered what was happening.

The cigarettes…I— I drugged his cigarettes.

The boy's eyes widened and Oliver shifted, rolling just out of reach of his father as Matthew dropped to his knees and clambered for the bed, cursing and spitting before his pupils dilated and a slathering of drool dropped out of his agape mouth. Then he hit the floor.

It took several seconds for it to process in his mind, and in that time, all Oliver could really do was sit there on the edge of the bed, reeling at the miracle that had just presented itself in front of him. A perfect escape that he had completely forgotten he had the forethought to plan.

His gaze flickered over to the door, the darkness underneath it. *I can leave.*

Just as quickly as the thought occurred to him, Oliver scrambled in a rush of adrenaline as he reached for the door.

He halted.

I have to be careful. I can't be seen…

Quietly, and with the utmost dexterity, Oliver stepped over his incapacitated father and creaked the door open.

The entire hallway was dark and all the rooms were closed, their patients inside after the sun had set.

Never more than now had he ever thought to step so lightly, so discreetly, even when he had snuck under the kitchen cabinets to visit Theo's apartment, he was less cognizant of every single sound he made.

He walked, slowly at first, his pace only quickening when he neared the edge of the east wing, where it opened into the foyer and office. Then he stopped to scan every inch of it.

The lights are still on in the south wing.

Oliver drew in some soft and precious breath, his attention moving toward the possible avenues of escape before him.

The south wing was off limits, despite it being attached to the morgue, which likely had a direct exit to the parking lot.

There was a fire exit in the foyer, it had been briefly propped open when Poppy had her deliveries made.

It'll set off an alarm if I open it. That leaves…the front entrance.

Oliver stiffened himself, forcing down every jerk and jolt of energy and even more so the aching of his body in order to get his feet to move. He crossed the foyer in the fastest, quietest pace he had ever done, holding his breath in anticipation of reaching the darkened front office.

He jiggled the knob and quietly slipped inside.

The office was somewhat cluttered, and the moonlight had been dispersed by several walls and windows, making it harder to find a key to the front doors. Oliver paused though, his gaze caught by his backpack and things, a massive block of the highest quality marble he had ever seen, and an even more precious rotary tool. *Dad's…gifts.*

He stared at them for some soft moment, hoping he would have the chance to use them. Then it dawned on him.

My phone!

Oliver dropped down on his knees and dug through his backpack, immediately dialing his father.

"Oliver?" Jon's groggy voice answered over the static.

"Dad—"

"Oliver! It's so good to hear you, I'm— I'm so sorry I haven't been able to visit, I promise I'll be there soon," Jon cut him off in earnest.

"Dad, it's really fine..can you, can you—" Oliver's blood ran cold at the soft click of the door behind him. His whole body stiffened as his step-father rambled on about how much he missed him.

Quietly, Oliver turned, dread blooming in his bones and making it so much harder to breathe.

Kaylee stared down at him, filling the doorway with her silhouette in the shadows of the room.

The boy froze, far too hesitant to look up at the woman's face and the rage it might have held.

"I've missed you so much," Jon rambled into his ear. "I was able to talk to the principal and Patricia has started an investigation with the incident in the bathroom, Oliver I can get you—"

"I— It's okay…Dad," Oliver murmured softly, the lie barely escaping his lips without the terrified quiver in his voice. "I was just trying to…I just wanted— for you to visit me…soon, please?"

"Of course, of course, of course, Oliver, are— are you sure you don't want to leave?"

Oliver bit his lip, holding down the sob that ached in his throat as he held Kaylee's gaze. "I..just wanted to talk to you…before bed. I— I have to go now."

"Oh, I…I understand." Jon's voice was so raw with hurt that it made his son's heart bleed as he quietly pulled the phone away from his face. He ended the call, prepared for whatever punishment the nurse would provide.

"I'm sorry, I really was just—"

"Shhh" the woman cut him off, holding her finger up as she listened. Oliver held himself as still as possible, his focus turning over as he heard the sound of steps enter into the foyer. Hushed speaking.

"Please inform Smile that there's been a minor breach of confidence." Poppy's voice was soft, far away and she spoke to someone else, though neither of them knew who.

"Yes, it's still under my supervision," Poppy said. "The other humans are all contained. I'm stretching myself thin though. Seventy-two implants on top of my scheduled shipments— and having to go organic is taking more energy than I have available to consume. The father has been useful in keeping the human child under control, but I am expecting a divergence soon."

Poppy's voice faded as she moved out of earshot, leaving Oliver stunned and staring back at Kaylee's sad and too tired face.

"They want you." She whispered, gesturing for him to come closer, despite Oliver's terror keeping him locked in place.

Smile…is here?

The memory flashed in his mind, the look of abject horror on

Dindet's face when she spoke of them. Her fear of them. And Poppy was here, working for them. Doing *something*.

"It's not safe to try right now." Kaylee interrupted, prompting Oliver to raise his gaze. Her eyes darted to the south wing and the shadow that passed over the light at its end.

"Wh— what?"

"She's awake." The nurse pulled him away from the door, placing her hands over the boy's shoulders. She didn't move so robotically as the first time he'd met her, and acted much more like an actual nurse would.

In Oliver's failure to move, Kaylee stepped forward, rounding the office desk as she quietly engulfed him in a soft and warm embrace. At first, he jerked. Taken aback by the sudden comfort of her mushy body wrapping around him.

"I know you want to leave…but you can't, she won't let you." There was something in her voice that made the statement raw, like it hurt to even say. But her embrace was so gentle and honest.

He gave in to it, some absolute and loving grace provided by a stranger in the dark.

An ugly moan grew up from the boy and his whole face contorted in an attempt to stop his tears.

"Shh, shhh, it's okay, baby...come here, come with me." Kaylee murmured, gently tugging him out of the office and toward the foyer couches. He sat down and Kaylee sat next to him, rubbing his back like a mother did to her own child. Maybe she was a mother.

He hadn't thought about it until now.

The idea twisted in his chest and made his heart ache. Her comfort was so needed. It felt real. Like Jon's.

Oliver's sobs grew into anguished and pointless gasps at the thought. It would have been a happy, happy thing, Jon coming to visit…if he'd not already known better. *Poppy won't let me leave, even if he came to take me home…*

Oliver drew in a ragged breath, the exhale just as shaky as he came to the conclusion. *Matthew was right.*

"I'm trapped here," he said, hesitant in the words as though if spoken, they were now cemented into reality. He shifted in her hold, looking up at the nurse's tired and shadowed eyes. "We all are…aren't we?"

Kaylee's face crinkled with empathy and she pressed her soft hand over his knee to draw his attention.

Oliver held his breath up, forcing his focus onto the woman and noticing her eyes flicker back to the south wing as quiet fear drifted across her face before it settled in determination.

"In your bathroom there's a window, it hasn't been replaced yet…" Kaylee's eyes darted back at Oliver. "The condensation from a hot shower makes the old caulking weaker."

Loud Silence

"Theo, there's some old dresses in the back room Douglass needs some help with, could you please run back there a moment? I can take over the counter." Theo's grandmother called from the back office, waddling up in her fuzzy slippers as the girl finished handing a customer her change.

"Ci, Abuela," she called in reply, quickly nodding and waving the customer off as she slid around her much shorter, fatter grandma.

"Oh I love it when you call me that, dearie," the elderly woman chimed, mostly to herself as Theo left.

The girl trotted into the back storage area where Douglass stood grappling with two too many boxes full of donations while simultaneously trying to climb his way up a short ladder to the top shelves.

"My god, you're gonna kill yourself, I swear." She rolled her eyes, quickly stepping underneath him to pluck his second box away and set it somewhere that hopefully wouldn't create a trip hazard.

"Here," Theo held her arms up, gesturing impatiently for the dumb boy to drop his overfilled box into her hands so she could properly sort the clothes. Douglass did as she directed and promptly stepped down from his step ladder.

"Sorry." The boy rubbed his neck in embarrassment. "I thought maybe I could get both of them up at the same time and then be able to move on to the picture frames."

Douglass gestured back behind him at a very poorly stacked pile of large and ornate picture frames, causing Theo's mouth to drop open with an annoyed scoff.

"You can't put the clothes on the top shelf because those are always what sells first, you have to start with the frames, and then use the space inside them to keep the boxes secure. That's like, stocking 101."

"Sorry."

"Stop apologizing," she chided, "you sound like Olivi— er."

Douglass visibly cringed at her remark, then deliberately turned his attention to the boxes she was sorting through and reorganizing. He was quiet then, and for a while. Until the silence became unbearably awkward and she shot a look back at the boy.

"It was an accident, stop moping about it." She remarked, assuming his demeanor had turned all poopy because she'd failed to uphold the secret don't-deadname-the-trans-person rule that nobody even told her was a rule in the first place. *It's not like he's even here. He's been at a freaking crazy house for like, a week.*

"Actually," Douglass said with hesitation, "I wanted to ask you a question, about Oliver, I mean."

Theo stopped folding the dress she held and narrowed her eyes at him. "What kind of question?"

Douglass bobbed his head, sort of like he didn't even want to ask her at all. It made the girl ten times more suspicious at his followed silence.

"Well?"

"Do you remember what Matthew looks like?" He finally asked, throwing the girl for a loop and causing a whole storm of conflicting feelings to send a shudder down her spine.

Theo promptly averted her gaze with a nasty snarl. "Like I would tell you. Why do you even want to know? I thought he was gone after the custody case?"

"You knew about that?"

"No *dur*," she retorted, "Oliver hates dresses, he only ever wore them because that's all his dumb parents would buy. His mom is dead so that only leaves one other option."

"Oh.." Douglass responded with that disenchanted, spacey look as he continued to sort the donations. "I was just wondering if you had ever seen him in person. I know you guys used to be friends before he moved."

Theo sputtered and quickly shoved her box away from the boy, opting to face the exact opposite direction he was located so she didn't have to keep talking to him.

He's only asking because he has the fattest crush in the whole freaking world. What an idiot.

"He's never gonna say yes, you know," She said after a minute. "You can ask over and over and I guarantee it'll just be a waste of time."

The boy made a noise, something settled right between melancholy and frustration and it almost made Theo's heart sing at the thought. *You don't even know him really, cause you weren't there.*

"You don't know that," Douglass argued gently, gaining a meaningful dagger stare back from the girl. "Also that wasn't even why I was asking."

"Well, then." Theo twisted around to look at him this time. "Why are you asking?"

"Cassidy and I went to visit him and we think Matthew might have come back."

At that the girl froze, the look of soft terror visible on her face just long enough that Douglass took note and scooted closer, prompting her to evade.

"You *do* know what he looks like." He leaned in and Theo got to her feet, scooping up the clothes in her arms to take to the laundry.

"Ugh, no, Olivia— Oliver and I aren't even friends anymore. I may have seen his dad like, once or twice but that was basically when we were, I dunno, eight?? He probably looks different now anyways." She huffed, turning on her heel to leave the conversation as quickly as possible. Mostly to hide the rash of goosebumps that ran up her arms at the thought of him being back.

Again? I thought he was gone for good? And she's older now so why would he even want to have anything to do with her if he lost the custody case? I saw those marks. Olivia can't be…okay with it again if he hit her like that. No— it's fine. I'm getting worked up over nothing!

She dropped the box of clothes in the laundry machine and drew in a staggered breath at the thought.

"Theo—"

"JESUS CHRIST!!" She yelped, startled by Douglass's sudden intrusion on her moment of much needed and unfortunately very brief solitude. "Don't just— sneak up on people like that, what are you a ninja?! Christ!"

The boy's brow furrowed at her remark. "Uhm. Unnecessary."

"Sorry." She huffed with a gracious eye roll to boot. "You're like a freaking ghost, seriously."

"You will let me know if you remember though, right? It's kind of important." He urged, regardless.

"Yeah. Fine," Theo muttered, "I'll like, send you a text or whatever."

After their shifts ended, and Douglass carted Theo from the antique shop home, he stopped at the turn-in to the apartments she lived in, unlocking the door to let the girl out.

"You will let me know, right?" He requested once more. All he got in response was another eye-roll and some grumbles before Theo grabbed her school bags and basketball and promptly scooted herself out of his car.

***

The drive to his house was easy enough, Douglass didn't have much to think about aside from the fact that his best friend was trapped in a fake mental hospital, probably being tortured by an alien for god knows why. Granted, that was sort of already a lot to think about.

And it consumed him, almost completely, that he didn't even notice his dad was talking to him.

"Douglass, what's going on?" he asked, planting his hand on top of his head and tousling his hair to snap him out of his daze.

"Huh-what?" Douglass's head dipped and he glanced down at

the half eaten dinner on his plate. Then, he looked up at his dad, who looked ten times more exhausted than usual. And also concerned.

"You've barely eaten, did something happen? With your friend?" His tone turned ever so slightly more grave and his eyes flitted toward the window view of Jon's cabin.

Douglass shook his head, resting it on his palm as he continued to play with his food, reluctant to tell him anything.

"Why did they take him?" He asked instead, murmuring it soft enough that his dad had to lean forward to hear him. Chris tapped his fingers on the table uncomfortably, and leaned back in his chair until the legs lifted off the floor, then he let out a sigh.

"Because..." he hesitated, trying to find the best way to word things, if he could. "AKAN made an arrangement, with Jon and I, to complete a project in a specific amount of time and to find...the Clown—"

"Dindet."

"Yes, Dindet," he corrected himself softly, "they don't want any distractions, and they felt they had to...motivate us."

Douglass perked his head up and immediately his eyes narrowed, putting two and two together quickly enough, "so they threatened you."

"Not me." his father took a nervous sip of his drink. "Not me, yet, but Jon is in a much more vulnerable state than we are. They are under the impression that you and I didn't know about Dindet— which we didn't— but...Jon and Oliver were harboring her in their home, for months."

"They're gonna arrest him..." *and put Oliver in a home, or worse, send him back with Matthew.* Douglass stood up from his seat and promptly tossed the last of his food in the trash before setting the plate in the sink.

"Can't you do something about it?" He spun back around, not expecting the words to come out as angry and violent as they did. His dad dropped his head, averting his eyes before standing up from his meal as well.

"Douglass, if I could I would..but you're at risk too now." He raised a hand, attempting to catch him as he pushed passed toward the hall.

"So what? That means you're perfectly fine just working for them?" He retorted, "you can't just let them do whatever they want, it's not fair."

"Douglass—"

"Dad." Douglass shot a glare at him, ignoring the verifiable guilt in his eyes. "Just leave me alone."

It was absurd. Absurd in absolutely every way imaginable. *No one wants to do anything! You don't just let the bad guys win like that!*

Douglass screwed around with a hoberman sphere, opening and closing it in silent frustration while his thoughts whirled up in a tornado in his head. *If no one else is going to do anything, me and Cas would have to. And if she's right—*

Douglass paused in his thoughts, lingering on the idea that Cassidy had presented just before he left. *If Matthew really is that nurse...*

He hated the idea of it. Specifically that Oliver was trapped with such a monster like his father. Douglass couldn't know what the Clowns could do, but he did know what people could be capable of.

***

Theo sat at the dinner table, pointlessly pushing around her peas while she waited for her mother and father to settle her younger brother in his high chair to eat their dinner.

Her thoughts stayed planted on Douglass's request. *He can't be back again. Right? They moved out years ago.*

"Theo, por favor siéntate, es hora de la gracia, mija." Her mother drew her attention from her pea pushing as she set down her brother's smaller, less prone to spilling plate of Salisbury steak.

Her father joined them, or tried to before her mom swatted at his shoulder and pointed out the massive grease stain on his coveralls.

"Honestly, Phillip, you can't even take the time to wash up? You're going to get grease stains all over the tablecloth," she chided, though the smile in her voice betrayed her annoyance. "Instead of gravy it'll be motor oil in our mashed potatoes."

"It's not my fault Johnny lost his grip on the oil pan today," he grumbled in reply, still taking a moment to reach for the nearest wet wipe and clean off what he could of the stain. "He's fresh out of school and I swear, Theo could do a better job without getting half as dirty— am I right, hun?"

He gestured at his daughter and she hummed some distracted noise.

"Hey, you remember the Tarsul's, right?" She changed the subject softly, hoping to avoid several minutes of uninterrupted prayer she had almost no interest in partaking in. "They used to live next to us in 809."

Phillip shared a look with her mother before he completely evaded the question by focusing on his son, Micah, who had managed to slather potato all over his high chair.

"The couple who argued all the time?" Her mother questioned in lieu of his silence. "They split up a few years ago, and a good thing too. That poor woman looked so exhausted every time I saw her."

Theo nodded, keeping herself from glancing back at the kitchen that she knew sat directly against the apartment next door. "Do you remember their daughter?"

At that her mother shook her head, chewing through her food as she flicked her fork in Theo's direction. "Oh no, mija, they never had any kids."

"Yeah they did," Theo corrected, rolling her eyes at the absurdity of such a statement. "We used to hang out together, she's the—"

"Oh," Phillip interrupted, popping a slice of steak into his mouth. "You're still going on about that? The imaginary friend you had in the wall? What was her name— Olivia?"

Theo's face screwed up with anger and she set her utensils down. "She wasn't *imaginary,* she literally goes to school with me, you *enrolled her in my class, Mom.*"

"The transgendered one? That's her niece." Her mother

corrected matter-of-factly. "Didn't I tell you? Micah stop throwing your peas— Miss Marie told me she got her divorce from that nasty man after her sister passed so she could take custody of her little girl about four years ago."

What?

"That's not—"

"Poor thing…I heard about the accident at the lab," her father cut in through his chews. "Lost her aunt and her mom in the last few years. Kid needs real help, not whatever that gender bullshit is—"

"Phillip!" Theo's mother smacked him on the shoulder. "You can't talk about her that way, now isn't the time."

Are you serious? It's not even why I asked about it and you're already—

"Well when is a good time?" Phillip dropped his silverware and gestured at the air. "All these kids out there, thinking they're something they aren't, betraying God's will and all— that one ain't any different."

"Ugh," Theo slumped in her seat, loathing the turn in the conversation. "I'm not even talking about her, I was going to ask—"

"But it's just sad, you know?" Her father cut her off again, waving his fork as he paused for thought. "It didn't used to be this way. We were all right. Boy's were boys, girls were girls, men married women and then that stupid president got elected and now all of them think it's completely fine to flaunt that shit out in public. It's disgusting—"

"It's not disgusting," his wife interjected, turning her gaze back at Theo, who sat uncomfortably quiet in her seat, resuming her pea pushing. "They can't help the way they are. We love the sinner, hate the sin. Mija, don't listen to your father."

Theo kept her eyes on her plate. *This was a royal waste of my time.*

"I think I'm done with my dinner," she said, standing up and grabbing her plate. "I have homework I still have to do."

Pulling Strings

"Good morning, Oliver." Poppy's voice drifted quietly over the boy, waking him up and sending a sharp stab of dread down his spine. He jerked from his place on the couch.

Where's—

"Nurse Carpenter is taking her break," Poppy interrupted the thought, drawing Oliver's gaze back to her. She sat by his legs, trapping him where he lay.

"There was an unfortunate incident with Mr. Tarsul last night. It seems as though he ingested some of your medication. While he's recovering, I'll be acting as your risk staff today," she said.

Then, right in front of him, she morphed. Losing all semblance of color as the alien bulged and bubbled.

Poppy reformed as what he imagined she preferred to look like. Her disguise was little more than a fresh and very white color pallet. Her bright red locs curled up around the base of her chin, perfectly coiffed. And her cheeks now bore three thin triangles that peaked at the crease where— if she had human lips, they would have been.

"Oh *no*, you've figured it out," she mocked his brief look of disbelief. "What am I going to do now that my secret has been discovered?"

Oliver glared at the alien, despite the fact that her casual reveal made him shake with apprehension. "What do you want from me? Are you gonna eat me?"

"Oh, I've been eating you." Poppy answered, flicking something out from under her long, white claws. "You should be worried about what *we* are going to do."

Oliver drew in a soft breath and pulled himself further up on the couch at the simple response.

She let out a huff and rolled her eyes at him, "relax, if all goes according to plan, you'll finally get to see your mother. That's what you want, isn't it?"

That's not reassuring in the slightest.

"What plan?"

The alien pulled out what he could only assume was her bean. The familiar round blue ball she kept on her at all times. She bounced it in her palm for a moment, as if contemplating how she might answer him.

"We need your friend."

Dindet?

"Yes."

"She's gone." Oliver's eyes flickered up to meet the alien's unfazed gaze. "She...she died."

"Ohh," Poppy deadpanned, "that's too bad. Unfortunately that means I'll have to use you as bait."

Bait?

The boy drew in a soft, unconscious gasp at the thought. "..she's bigger.."

"Yes, and she is very much alive. Just not *all* here." She continued casually, "she won't bring all her matter into this dimension unless you're in danger, so…"

Poppy opened her palm, some small black thing growing from it until it sat in her hand.

Oliver's eyes widened in horror at the innocuous little device that held such awful things on it. And what it meant.

Markus's flashdrive.

"I've had to..what do your people call it? Pull a few strings." The mime smiled. She closed her palm, stealing away the evidence of her manipulation. "Having young mister Mulligan to keep track of you and using Markus to lure you into my care has been my most fruitful idea yet, I believe. Though I am quite proud of my forethought in keeping Mr. Tarsul."

"You…you…" Oliver barely breathed the words.

"I— I—" the alien laughed at his inane attempt to speak. "Yes, I did all of this."

She turned, gesturing broadly at the room and hospital. "I found your father after he'd been admitted to my ward for care. I manipulated the school system into hiring sweet Miss Pamela Popiviolli to find you and that *abomination* of a Clown, used Cody to spy on his brother and ensure that both of you were in the right place at the right time."

She chuckled lightly, her black pupils flickering back at Oliver as she clearly relished in the accomplishment. "I even made sure that Dr. Aguirra was out of the way so I could take my place as your personal therapist."

"Wh— what are you going to do with me?"

"Nothing," she answered, standing and directing him toward the east wing and his room. "Right now, so long as you don't attempt to escape, I won't be made to punish you."

That's hard to believe…considering.

The alien opened his door and gestured for him to enter before she crossed the room to the window.

"You've seen these before, haven't you?" Poppy asked, twirling the bright red flower in her fingers. She began tearing the leaves and petals off, releasing little puffs of spores into the air that mingled and floated with the dust.

Oliver drew his attention away from the door, how open and wide it was and how he couldn't so much as take a step toward it. He was held there. By her. But he didn't know how.

"The Peace Zone," he muttered, dropping his eyes the moment hers flickered back to him. She nodded and looked back at the bulb she had successfully stripped of petals.

"They're native to that dimension, the spores release a pheromone that makes most organic beings euphoric," She explained, "which is why they use them as a consolation prize for the combatants in their tournaments. The spores make you euphoric, but the water inside the plant— if modified can induce total paralysis, as I'm sure you've realized."

"You use them to sedate people," he remarked, turning back to look at her. she crushed the bulb of the flower and a viscous orange juice seeped between her fingers.

"What a smart little human you are," she lilted sarcastically.

"What are you going to do?" Oliver closed further in on himself, glancing back at the door as his arms shook, begging him to make a break for it. "To make me bring her back?"

"I told you, nothing." She repeated, "I'm not permitted to kill you. Your stay here was an arrangement made by our Court Jester while Dr. Jariwala completes the molecular transporter. My purpose is to make sure the timeline of events play out exactly as planned— to the best of my ability."

"That doesn't make any sense," Oliver straightened himself, glaring at her while he racked his brain to understand what exactly the gain was in this situation. "It's not like I even know where she is, I was the one who told her to leave, *why* would she come back for me at all?"

Poppy's eyes lifted, meeting his gaze.

"Because she always comes back for you, Oliver. This is a time loop."

"I don't believe you." Oliver watched as Poppy opened his window just slightly to let in some fresh air.

"Oh *do*." She returned, pressing her hand into his head, a subtle laugh rumbled through his mind as she read his thoughts. "It always goes the same way, Dindet shows up, you have your little fun, and then you die. And she puts the entire universe in reverse just to bring you back."

Poppy made a soft, thoughtful hum. "Like clockwork."

"....I'll...." Oliver couldn't finish the sentence. *That's not true. This isn't true. She's lying, don't believe her.*

The alien laughed lightly, leaning in close over his shoulder and causing a small, painful shiver to ripple through him as she spoke. "I've always wanted to be the one to tell you."

Her fingers inched around his back, dragging on his skin as she threatened to wrap her claws around his neck and squeeze.

But she didn't.

Instead, she stepped away from him, moving to the window again.

"I've existed in this dimension longer than your civilization has existed at all— at first I had no idea about the loop." She explained, staring through the window at the sky. "The first time I came across you two was a fluke, a happy coincidence."

Oliver tried to blink, or think, to wrap his mind around what she was talking about. *Dindet never...she never said anything. Did she even know?*

"No," Poppy answered his thoughts, "most often, no one knows until key events occur. Triggering memories of previous loops...but that's only if you're connected to the loop itself."

"You're lying...you just, you're just trying to get in my head." Oliver stuttered stupidly, forcing himself to shoot a hateful glare at the alien. She simply turned and sighed, as if bothering to explain was a nuisance to her.

"I'm already in your head, Oliver." She answered blandly. "Your *friend* is the amalgamate that killed me. And she has continued to kill me in every iteration. Every divergence after that."

"She wouldn't do that." Oliver argued, "She wouldn't hurt anyone like that. Not on purpose."

Poppy cackled at his weak argument. "You have no idea what that *thing* is capable of."

The mime's face turned down and her smile splintered across her face as she combed through his thoughts. "You assume I have anything left to gain from this situation. That I might believe there's some miniscule chance that things will change, that I will survive."

Poppy drew closer, and parts of her flickered, wavered and bubbled in her quiet and bridled fury. She bent down, uncomfortably close as her black eyes stared through him and into his very core. "Let me make this glaringly clear for you. I am going to die, and you are going to die, this whole universe *is going to die*. And your friend? She will be the reason why."

The mime stood straight, though her eyes never strayed. "There is no little fix, no way to change it. It *will* happen. Accept your fate, I've accepted mine."

Oliver gulped dryly, the unsettling realization of what real danger existed here. *She doesn't care. At all.*

Poppy was entirely apathetic to the concept of her own demise, to the point that any attempt to convince her otherwise had already been made null.

And Oliver was nothing more than a tool to be used. Something that could be manipulated and thrown away just to reach the end goal.

Poppy's dreadful stare contorted into a soft, almost pained smile. "It's fine though. Your universe is going to collapse, and when it does, it will envelop every adjacent universe in itself. Entangling all of us in a lateral trans-dimensional black hole....or at least, all of *you*. The Cornucopia exists outside of the loop."

Col..lapse...?

"Yes." Poppy answered, as though the thought itself warmed her heart. "In the *correct* version of this timeline, AKAN laboratory will recreate the molecular transporter your mother designed and tear a hole in the space time continuum. The hole will eat away at the matter in this universe, and pull in matter from the ones closest."

Dad lied....that's why he's been so busy with the lab. That's what they're working on, and if—

"There are Clowns...at AKAN..." Oliver mumbled, the realization creeping over him. *She did this to separate us...so they could trap him there and use me to...does he even know? Is that why he's been so worried??*

"You're not going to hurt him..right? You're not going to hurt my dad he's—" *he's all I have left.*

Poppy smirked, "I have no idea. I've never lived long enough to see that outcome."

The alien's chin dipped and she took a step back from him. "Oh I forgot, you have visitors."

The mime turned, shrinking as her matter morphed and sloshed, molding into a perfect mirror of Oliver's face, staring right back at him with the ugliest of smiles.

"Your step-father is here to see you."

Your Ultimatum

Jon stood outside the Amelis doors, mentally preparing himself to step foot inside them and see his son after at least a week. Nothing could sate his desire, let alone that gnawing guilt at his innards that made his stomach twist over into loops that refused to digest any food.

I have to bring up Markus. I can't leave without an answer....God, he's gonna hate me for it..

"Doctor." A desk secretary pushed the door wide open with a gracious smile. "It's so good you found time in your schedule to come visit. I know our visiting hours are a little inconvenient, but I'm sure Oliver will be absolutely thrilled to know you're here."

"It's the least I could do," Jon gave a tired smile, one weighed down with his worry, compounded by long, exhausting work. "I would be here everyday if it weren't for....other complications right now. I can only hope he understands."

The woman nodded, holding the door for him as he entered, that placid smile fading the moment he passed. She quickly wiped a tear from her eye. "He's in the west wing lobby."

The scientist gave a short nod and immediately turned on his heel toward the lobby.

The hallway entrance opened up into a large room, decorated with warm peaches and pinks and yellows. Creamy spring colors that blended together in the background against the bright red flowers littering every table and countertop and the dull, bluish gray scrubs of the patients.

They all mingled like programmed characters, just enough interaction that Jon wouldn't be able to tell the difference.

And at that particular moment, he couldn't care.

His mind stayed wholly focused on his son, who he found curled up in the couch, picking the petals off of one of the flowers he'd plucked from the vase in front of him.

"Oliver!" Jon's voice lifted his gaze. Then, like the sun had finally risen, his whole demeanor shifted and the boy promptly shot off the couch and slammed into his father with the tightest hug he could physically muster.

"Dad!" Oliver shoved his face into Jon's stomach, muffling the unabashed joy in his voice. "You're here!"

Oliver dipped his head, tightening that precious hold just slightly before he pulled back and gave the biggest, brightest, so-clearly-not-suffering smile he could give.

They met gazes, briefly, but it didn't last long, because Jon was already gently directing him back to the couch, going on and on with profuse apologies that, at this moment, meant nothing.

"I know I haven't been able to see you, and I know that's been hard, lots— a lot of stuff has been going on with work, and I just, I *had* to see you. To make sure you were doing alright," he said, plopping down into the recliner across from Oliver.

The boy gave a soft smile.

"It's alright, I know you'd started getting busy with your..eels and all," he replied, prompting an uncomfortable look from the man. They both knew there was a lie between them. Unfortunately, only Oliver was the one with the full picture of that deception.

"So." Jon gestured at the air, glancing around the room as he changed the subject. "How are things? You're eating right? It looks like you lost some weight, so— so I brought you some snacks. I had Manpreet ship a wholesale box of those veggie bars you like. It- it's in my car. I can go get it right now—"

"Dad, it's alright." Oliver chuckled at his father's enthusiasm. "I've been eating fine…the medication is a little intense but everything is really okay. I'm okay."

Jon's smile faltered slightly. *It's okay…if you're not okay, son.*

"I just…I'm worried, I worry about you, Oliver…" Jon rubbed his face, all but dropping that excitement for something that sagged his shoulders down and made his heart pace up in his chest.

"I know you lie to me."

The boy quietly drew his legs onto the seat, folding up in preparation for whatever would next fall out his father's mouth.

Oliver watched as Jon pulled out his phone, briefly checking the time before he scrolled through messages and photos, each passing swipe sinking the man's stomach further into itself as he grappled with how to approach the subject.

"Pamela confiscated that— Markus's phone…after you beat him up," he murmured, stopping at a photo that made him close his eyes and set the phone face down on the arm of the chair. "Is that why you stole the money? To make him leave you alone?"

Oliver averted his gaze. He nodded. A stilted, broken movement that only served to spur that guilt and shame further into Jon's chest. He let out a soft sigh, it wasn't meant to sound frustrated. Angry. But that was all Oliver likely got from it.

"I'm sorry—"

"It's not—" Jon stopped himself, reworking the words in his mind. "I wish you had told me. I could have done something— I want to protect you, Oliver. But I can't do that when you *don't* talk to me—"

"I talk…"

"You know that's not what I mean."

Oliver pressed back against the couch. It hurt, more than Jon had expected it to.

"I…might have found a way to fix it," he continued, much softer, "and I can take you home today…if you agree to it."

Oliver's gaze lifted and he inched closer to the edge of the couch in anticipation. Jon nodded, moving closer to match his son's interest.

"I have enough to press charges, and make sure that boy never sees you ever again..." he hesitated, just long enough for him to notice the way his son's anticipation began to bleed into horror as he understood what Jon meant by taking him home.

"Everyone will know," he breathed, finding his place sunk back into the couch.

Jon shook his head, as if he could prevent Oliver's logic from burrowing deep inside his bones. *I knew this would happen...it wouldn't work.*

"Not everyone, just— it'll be just the court. Not everyone."

"Lawyers, the jury, the judge, anyone who shows up to watch it— watch me...they will all see it...Douglass was there...he would testify..." Oliver trailed off, his eyes shifted, from his father who waited patiently for an answer, to the hall where his room was.

"I can't..." the boy answered softly, dropping his gaze away from his father.

"You're sure?" Jon leaned further forward, pressing his palms into the cold wood of the coffee table. "I know it'll be hard, I know— I know it will be the first time—"

"I can't do it...Dad...*please*. Don't make me do it. I'm— I'm not ready...I need more time." Oliver pleaded, this time raising his eyes to meet his father's gaze.

The man shifted in his seat, combing his fingers through his beard in an abject attempt to quell his stress. His face weighed down, twisting from his frustration into understanding and a sadness that made Oliver look thoroughly uncomfortable when he saw it.

"I—"

"It's alright, son," Jon interrupted, raising his hand for pause as he sifted through his work bag. "I knew it was a lot to ask...and ultimately, it's up to you in how you want to move forward...and, if you need more time..."

Jon pulled out an object, wrapped in cloth to prevent it from breaking on the ride here, and handed it out for his son to take. "Careful, he's fragile."

***

Oliver stood in his room shaking. He shook furiously at every agonizing attempt he made to move. To take a single step forward toward that wide open door where just down the hall he could see his father holding that monstrous creature in his arms with compassion that didn't belong to her.

He couldn't even yell to get his attention.

If anything were far worse torture than what Matthew offered, it was the cruelty of Poppy dangling safe haven right in front of him and snatching it away just before he could grab it.

The boy watched his doppelganger as she waved his best means of escape away and turned one knowing look back at him, dropping her false smile the same way she dropped her intangible grip on his bones, letting him crumple to the floor in a crying heap.

"Oh come now, it only hurts when you try to fight it," she said, still wearing his face and using his voice as she stepped through the threshold of the door.

Oliver winced and dragged in a staggered breath.

"You're a monster." Was all he could manage in between his attempts to force himself back up.

The mime only laughed in response, tossing something heavy and thick sounding between her hands as Oliver regained his footing. "I wonder what that makes you, then?"

Oliver shot her the nastiest glare he could muster, despite how much it hurt to keep himself standing. "I don't hurt people to get what I want."

At that, his reflection scoffed, stopping her tossing of whatever Jon had given her. "You don't? It looks like you hurt everyone you seem to care about...just to get what you want. Or...am I mistaken?"

"That's different." Oliver spat, attempting a step toward her that she easily evaded.

"Is it?" The alien mused, casually unwrapping the cloth around the gift she'd stolen. "You hurt your father because you want to hide from the truth. You hurt your friends because you want them to see you a certain way."

"I'm not hurting them—"

"And you hurt Dindet *very badly* just because you want your mother back." Poppy cut him short, unraveling the rest of the cloth the same way she unraveled Oliver's mind.

He paused, his gaze resting on the precious thing in her hands. *Ugly Ganesh.*

At his thought, the alien turned the murti over to inspect.

"I wonder what kind of mother she must be, that you are so willing to risk everyone you love or care about to reach her," she said, "must be a good one."

Poppy held up the statue, pulling it just out of Oliver's reach the moment he moved for it.

"Don't drop him!" Oliver pleaded, the shock of his desperation at the thought making the mime ripple. Her eyes widened, then narrowed.

"Oh, is this important to you?" She mused, taking obvious glee in his hesitancy to answer.

"You humans and your little toys are so *cute*. What is it? Some kind of.." Poppy paused, looking over the idol with scrutiny. "..paperweight?"

"It's a murti," Oliver answered quietly, hoping dearly that the soft thought of shattering the fragile stone wouldn't enter the alien's mind. "We..made it."

"An idol.." Poppy repeated softly, turning the statue over. "An object of religious value…and a representation of you and your step-father's loving relationship…how *sweet*."

She held it up like a trophy of her conquest over him. A blasphemous and monstrous display that only served to make Oliver's tired heart ache in his chest.

"Please—"

"Oops!"

Oliver scrambled to catch the precious thing before he was forced to halt. Forced to watch it shatter on the tile of his room.

And every hope he had of Jon saving him from this hellish hospital shattered along with it.

***

Jon waved goodbye to his son one last time, his heart twisting in his chest at the thought of him being away for any longer. *He's safe..that's all that matters.*

He checked his watch, then his phone. *Director Miles called…*

As quickly as he could manage, the scientist walked across the lot to his car, throwing the door open and sliding in with barely a thought before he was stopped by the reflection in the rear view mirror.

"Dr. Jariwala, I'm so glad you were able to find time to visit your…child." Director Miles spoke from behind him, their long and pale fingers filed between each other and resting pleasantly on their crossed legs. Almost as if to spite the unsettling nature of their appearance.

Jon's grip on the mirror tightened just briefly, some millisecond of a moment before the urge to escape forced him to move. He reached for the door and the locks clicked on their own, trapping him before he realized just what horror sat behind him.

"It's always important to show those we care so deeply for that we are there for them, I feel." Miles continued, through the scientist's increasingly frantic effort to escape.

He kicked the brakes and gas, only for a burst of black and starry sludge to flood the floorboards of his compact car and slog down his efforts as it pooled around his ankles, rising higher with every passing second.

It felt slow, almost. That dawn of realization that blinded him and made the man move so much slower until he finally stopped, hands gripping the steering wheel until his knuckles lightened with the tension.

"You." Jon breathed. *The video of Marie. The explosion…the creature in captivity at AKAN…all of this was orchestrated.*

"Being a parent is so much of a struggle, I've come to believe," the Director spoke softly, almost melodically as a smile draped across their face. "I know that I struggle trying to keep my children under control. We want so much for them, but they seem to self-destruct at a moment's notice. I understand the need to put them away for their own good…but I can't help but imagine how that could lead to so much more suffering."

Director Miles' head leveled and they stared back at Jon through the mirror as matter rose to his knee, and then waist level. It bled from the confines of the vehicle, a trap that was laid the moment the scientist dared to escape.

"I'm sorry, Jon. But I can't let you interfere."

What Makes You

"I'm telling you, it's him. He looked the same way Hailey described that time I hit her," Theo overheard Cassidy's frankly, very loud whispering to Douglass as the two kids settled into their seats for first period.

"Did she say anything to you about it?" The girl continued, piquing Theo's interest as the conversation tilted toward her. She sat up in her desk, making a point to dig out a book and pretend she was reading while she eavesdropped on the conversation.

"Well, no, not really," Douglass answered. "She mostly got angry about it and said it's not something I need to know…it's like she *wants* him dead."

I don't want him— God. Whatever. Theo twisted around in her seat to face them, her mouth dropping open before she managed to get a full thought out.

"How was your visit to the psych ward?" She drawled, despite the nominal effort she made to not sound as nasty as she did. "Is Oliver in a straightjacket hopped up on drugs?? I bet he feels right at home, huh?"

"It's not any of your business Theo," Cassidy chided, glaring at her from over her glasses.

"It is when his dumb friend with a savior complex drags me into it," Theo countered, eyeing off Douglass and just how red his face got at her call out. The boy shifted in his seat under her gaze before his eyes flickered down to his bag.

Theo followed, noticing the Manila folder sticking out of it. And noticing even more that Oliver's name was printed on the sticker on its tab. Immediately her face screwed up with intrigue and frustration and she reached for it, snatching it up before either Douglass or Cassidy could counter.

"What's this?" She flaunted it, waving it in front of the two of them and quickly jumping out of her desk before they could manage to steal it back.

"Don't that's—"

"It's Oliver's, is what it is," Theo cut in, taking another solid step away from them. She inspected the cover of the file for a moment, some nasty rumble of laughter rippling up from her chest. *A school file? Oh, that's rich!*

"You *stole* his school papers?" Theo cast a look back at Cassidy. "Wow Cas, didn't think it was in your programming to break rules."

"Those are classified and you can't just take them—"

"Hypocrite," Theo sing-songed, holding the folder as high as she could to keep them from taking it back. "I bet it has juicy stuff, if the world's best bootlicker and comrade crossplay thought to *steal* from the school's office!"

The girl back-stepped toward the classroom door, opening the file and licking her finger as she scanned the papers with vindictive glee. Then she stopped and her bones shuddered at the words on the paper. *This is…*

Theo's eyes flickered up at the two kids and the look of confusion on their faces at her sudden horror.

"Why…do you have this?" She asked, the creak of anxiety in her voice wrought.

Douglass took a step forward, his hand raised in apology already. "We haven't looked at it, we just needed to—"

"Needed to what?" Theo cut in, far angrier than she thought she was. It burned in her chest and made her fingers tingle at the thought of them. Of anyone knowing. "These don't belong to you. They're hers— his."

Cassidy took a step forward, her voice soft and riddled with near petrifying concern. "Theo…what do you know?"

Theo's eyes flitted to the door, still open before the morning bell rang. Students were still roaming among the halls. *My locker.*

Her head tilted and her gaze shifted for some half second as she registered how close Douglass and Cassidy already were. She bolted.

"Theo wait!" She heard Douglass call from behind her, but she was fast and already flying past the other students, her long legs carrying her in quick steps down the hall before she skidded and heel-turned for the gymnasium where her sports locker was.

Douglass was on her tail, albeit a lot slower than she was, and Cassidy was just behind him, apologizing as she shoved other kids out of the way to catch up.

Theo scrambled down the stairs, taking them two, even three steps at a time before she crashed into the gym doors and slipped in among the crowd of volleyball girls leaving their morning practice.

"Made it!" She panted, searching the immediate vicinity for the familiar pink dial padlock she had for her locker. The girl promptly sat down on her knees, tucking the file under them for safe keeping as she unlocked the locker and shoved her personal practice basketball and uniform aside for a space to hide the file. At least before Cassidy's voice sounded and Douglass's hands tried to rip it out of her grasp.

"Stop!"

"We need that, to make sure we can help him get out—" Douglass grunted, fighting the girl's mortifying strength to gain access to the folder. Theo elbowed him hard in the groin, sending him down for the count with a pitiful whimper before she shoved the files in, slammed the door shut and successfully locked them inside.

Cassidy caught up shortly after, out of breath with shock on her face at just how fast Theo had made it all the way across the school, as well as Douglass rolling on the ground crying.

"My god, Douglass are you okay?!" She dropped down on her

knees, hovering over the boy while he slowly pulled himself up and sat against the bench with a tired and pained sigh.

"She elbowed me in the dick," he said, casting an obligatory glare in Theo's direction. She returned with a flippant middle finger between her own breathless huffs.

Cassidy sighed with compassion and plopped down next to the boy, even out of breath and sweaty, she looked perfect. Theo averted her gaze.

"Why did you do that?" The girl asked, prompting Theo to roll her eyes at such an inane question.

"Why does anyone do anything?" She retorted.

"But why?" Cassidy repeated, sounding a lot more forlorn over Theo's plan foiling than she'd expected.

Theo grunted and sat up, letting the cold metal of the lockers chill the blood rush of her adrenaline. "Because it's wrong to go snooping into people's personal lives— especially their medical records. Like, why are you even mad at me? *You* were the ones who stole it."

At that Douglass raised his head. "You stole it from us. You're not any better."

"Yeah but—" Theo stopped herself and dropped her gaze. "I stole it for a better reason."

"Better reason?" Cassidy repeated, the sneer in her voice almost tangible. "We took it because we are trying to *help* Oliver. You don't even know what's really going on, and even if you did, I don't think you would care because you're just a big bully."

"Bully?" Theo scoffed, despite how Cassidy's words stung her skin. "At least I don't go around flaunting how *great an ally* I am for being in the same class as the trans kid."

Cassidy's jaw dropped at her remark and she sat forward. "I do not *flaunt!*"

"Seriously?" Theo's eyes practically rolled to the back of her head at the notion. "You act so high and mighty because your dumb moms are gay and that makes you think you can steamroller anyone who isn't being *supportive enough*. Have you ever noticed how Oliver avoids you like the freaking plague?"

"Ugh," Cassidy scoffed. "He doesn't avoid me, he's my friend! And I don't *steamroller* anyone! I just think that because he's so quiet and won't correct anyone about his name or pronouns that well, *someone* has to? But I don't figure you have the capacity to imagine how hard it probably is for him to bring it up, considering *you're* the one who shits on him more than anyone else!"

"At least I don't treat him like some weird exotic *thing* that I think is cool but don't actually care about!" Theo shot back, causing Cassidy's face to twist into a rage filled scowl. "Maybe if you knew anything *about* him, you'd know that he doesn't think it's worth the effort to police everyone about stupid stuff like that!

Cause if you *really* cared as much as you say you do, you'd be trying to get the school to let him do sports or *use the freaking bathrooms*. But you don't.

You're good with every teacher in the whole school, *and* the office, *and* the principal, and you can't even take the time to learn about the petition *I started* to let him back in the school—"

"Would you both just SHUT *UP!!*" Douglass cut in, grabbing his head in sheer frustration at the insanity of such a *stupid* argument about a person who wasn't even present to speak on it. He got to his feet, pacing in a little circle as he grappled for words.

"Neither of you are helping!" He finally said. He pointed an accusatory finger at Cassidy. "You're only helping because it makes you feel good to help someone you think is *less* than you, and for some dumb adrenaline rush because your life is apparently so boring! You didn't even *think* about what put Oliver in the hospital in the first place! You called it a *statistical probability!!*"

Theo chuckled at his statement and Douglass promptly swiveled around to glare at her. "And *you?* You've been cruel to him for no reason since he started going to school! You can't act like just because you do nice stuff behind the scenes that it fixes how mean you really are to him! You said his mom *killed herself* just to get away from him! And you're literally making everything harder just because you think it's funny, when it's not! And— and you of all people are the one who should know better because *you were there!!*"

Theo clamped her mouth shut and averted her gaze, prompting Douglass to let out an exasperated and incredibly frustrated groan.

"Right now, my *best friend* is in a mental hospital being run by a psychopathic alien *clown*, probably being tortured as we speak, and you guys are complaining about freaking identity politics?! Matthew could be there, hurting him! And all you care about is whether or not you're being a better ally. *It doesn't matter and you're not helping!*" He threw his hands down and drew in a tired breath. "I need a break."

And with that, Douglass swiveled on his heel and left.

"Well…that was…I don't really flaunt?" Cassidy remarked after a moment of terrifying quiet.

Theo was far more focused on Douglass's words though. They hung in her brain, swaying back and forth like flesh on a chain. *Matthew could…be there?*

Quietly, she moved to her feet, prompting Cassidy to stir from her self reflection.

"Where are you going?"

"It doesn't matter."

***

Douglass collapsed against the retracted gym bleachers, his face hot and his head aching and *god* everything was falling apart around him. *If he's hurt…I can't lose him. I can't do that again.*

His mind wandered, softly. To a memory he kept locked away with his grief.

It was one of those kind of memories that hurt because it was both happy, and also so very sad.

Josephine

She was older than him by six or so years, and he could almost hear the heart moniter's quiet beeping in between his sister's words. The cancer had spread, and he had known it. They both had known for a very long time that there was..so little time left.

'There's a girl in the room next to me,' she'd told him, her frail hand holding his with barely any strength left in it. He remembered how green and pale her skin was. She'd stopped wearing her wigs when they'd gotten the news…and his mom left. 'She's all alone over there, got moved up…from the emergency room.'

'But I don't want to leave you.' It hurt so much more because he knew there wasn't a choice in the matter.

Josephine had smiled, in this way, he remembered how there was almost a laugh in it. She had always had a morbid sense of humor.

She had looked up. At the fluorescent lights that buzzed above them, then back at him. 'It's okay, I don't mind being alone for a bit. Her, on the other hand…I think she needs a good friend.'

'But I don't want to be her friend!'

'Alright then, I'll just die knowing my dweeb little bro will be *totally* friendless without me,' she had made this face, that sly, joking kind right before her eyes crossed and she stuck out her tongue and she'd popped off the pulse monitor on her finger. Not long enough that it had alerted the nurses, only enough for Douglass to panic and make her laugh. 'Seriously though, I think you'd really like her. She reads those schlocky period romances you like and everything.'

Douglass's face broke at the memory, and he failed to hold down that ugly and twisted sob that rose from his chest and made his eyes sting with fresh tears. He quickly wiped them away in an effort to regain control over his heart.

He barely even noticed Theo fall in, sliding down to sit beside him in silence.

"What do you want?" He croaked softly.

"He has..brown hair…and eyes." She answered, almost coldly. It prompted him to draw his gaze away from the floor to her. Theo's fingers gripped the hem of her jacket sleeves. "He usually wears it slicked back. There's a cut on his chin that healed over. And he's tall. But not as tall as his new dad."

Douglass drank in the description, slowly matching it to the nurse that attended Oliver at the hospital. It fit, almost to a tee, if it hadn't been four years.

"If you find him," Theo added, much softer before she turned to face him, absolute hatred in her eyes as she spoke.

"Beat the fucking shit out him for me."

Escape

Oliver threw a hand out, attempting to balance himself on the lip of the bathtub as he tried to reach the tiny rectangular window just above him. It was small, but he figured if he sucked it in hard enough, he could fit. Once he was out, he could get his phone from the office and call his dad, or 911, but he doubted that would really work in his favor.

The entire bathroom had become particularly slippery as condensation from the shower grew on just about every surface. But the noise helped cover up his attempts.

He reached up, planting his fingers right at the seam of the window and began pushing as hard as he possibly could, hoping that the water had seeped into the caulk enough that it became weak and would give way. Oliver stretched, trying to balance himself and simultaneously put the right amount of pressure on the window when his foot slipped and he tumbled backwards, smacking his head hard on the plexiglass tub.

The kid drew in a ragged breath, and then a couple more, and immediately grabbed his head, curling up with a silent little wail at the stinging pain.

He wanted to stop, just give up, honestly. But this was probably the only real chance he had, so he sat up and struggled to regain his balance on top of the bathtub.

A little more. Just one last push was all he needed to get that stupid window to budge.

Once it did, he scrambled up the wall, hoisting himself half way into the frame and clawing his way out the other side.

Oliver tumbled, crashing into the flower bed below him and causing a puff of spores to release in the air.

And then he ran.

All the way across the yard to the road, veering off into the forest to lose anyone who could possibly follow on foot or in a car.

Eventually he slowed down, exhausted and his bare feet burned from the frost covered grass. He came to a stop and leaned up against a tree, slowly dropping down to the ground so he could rest and catch his breath.

He closed his eyes a moment, sucking in a heavy inhale as tears burned his already hot face. His lungs ached from the cold air.

I'm free—

"Oliver?"

The familiar voice forced him to look up, and he swiveled his head around in search of her.

"Dindet?" He breathed, stumbling back to his feet. He spun around, his head reeling as his thoughts consumed him.

You're back?

Then he saw her, standing only a few feet away, looking so dumb and so lost and so *alive* and every ounce of his fear and confusion drained away at the sight of her. He crashed into Dindet and dragged her back a few steps as he spun around her, engulfing the alien in a hug so tight he was sure he would accidentally vivisect her.

"You're okay!" He cried, gripping her tight in his arms and pressing his forehead into hers with a terribly broken laugh. "You're okay..I'm so sorry, I'm *so sorry* I made you go, I—"

"Oliver," her hands reached up, wrapping around his arms tight and only growing tighter as her eyes met his. "You are so *gullible.*"

The kid yanked back, digging his heels into the ground as the imposter morphed, and Poppy's sinister smile spread across her lips.

"L-let go!" he pulled harder, feeling his scars burn at her touch.

The alien grew larger, black, ugly fire billowing off of her as she pressed her claws into him. She forced him down to the ground and let out a horrific, metallic screech that made his head feel like it was going to explode.

He drew in a gasp and clenched his eyes shut just as she thrust him back into the hospital room and slammed the door shut behind her.

Oliver hit the ground with a painful thud and scrambled under the bed, or tried to, but her tendrils wrapped themselves around his foot and yanked him back out from under it, tossing him into his bed as she grew against the walls and windows, preventing any form of escape.

"I have *tried* to be accommodating!" Poppy shrieked, losing whatever calm that existed in her. The alien's voice turned from one to a million, and screeched like a thousand knives on glass plates.

"I have *tried* to be reasonable!"

Oliver grappled with the walls, but they reached out and twisted far too many limbs around his arms and legs, stapling him to themselves and wrenching away his mobility. Poppy towered over him, digging her claws into his bed and staining it black with her matter.

"But you are so *stubborn*, you insolent, human BRAT!" The beast reared back, letting out another vile screech, spitting her bile on him in her rage and twisting up into some ungodly mess that opened its maw over his head.

"I'm sorry!" Oliver cried, shaking horribly as she closed in, pressing her claws into his chest. He buckled, forcing out the last of his breath as he felt the weight of her push and pull his lungs and begin to crush him. "I'm sorry, I'm sorry, I'm sorry, I— I won't do it again, I swear!"

The monster dug her talons deeper, bleeding under his skin and turning it black as the liquid burned in his blood and forced a visceral, horrified shriek to erupt from the child. His skin lit on fire and he was certain she was going to kill him. Poppy accompanied his agonized howling, tearing her claws out of him, ready to devour him completely, before all that rage turned to an icy calm.

She retracted, bringing herself back together and composing herself once more into her disguise while Oliver trembled silently on the bed.

"Get up."

Oliver stared at her, bewildered by the demand. "Wh—"

"I said get up." The mime's cold voice repeated. She moved to the doorway, opening it to reveal Matthew with Kaylee by his side.

The man trudged forward, grabbing Oliver by the arm and yanking him off the bed.

"What are you doing?" It was a stupid question, he already knew the answer. They were going to punish him. He just didn't know how yet.

Poppy led them toward the south wing.

"No! No don't! I'm sorry, I won't do it again, I promise!" Oliver kicked his feet out, forcing his father to struggle to maintain a grip on him. In reply, Matthew socked him in the gut and dragged the retching child onward.

Kaylee walked stiffly beside them, a couple paces back and Oliver could see tears streaming down her face, leaving trails of mascara along her cheeks.

They continued down the hall, toward that stench of rotting death in the dark until Poppy reached a large fire door and effortlessly pushed it open, allowing that horrific smell to burst into the hall and cause the boy to gag.

Inside was a familiar room, large machines on either side blinking and beeping and printing off little sheets of data. Dread grew in the pit of Oliver's stomach as he recognized it, and the large white line twenty feet from the door, the darkness shrouding that *thing* Matthew had laid him out for and its rank odor just behind it.

"You can drop him, he can't go anywhere," Poppy muttered, turning to face the two of them. Matthew obliged and let his son go.

Immediately, Oliver bolted for the door, only for him to come screeching to a halt.

Without his want, or permission, Oliver's trembling stopped and every muscle in his body contracted all at once, forcing the child to gradually turn himself around.

He drew in a ragged breath. Every movement burned and ached, and it all stemmed from a terrible clawing of his brain that made him grit his teeth in agony.

"S-sstop," He begged, inching ever closer.

"Relax," Poppy mused, "it makes it easier for me to move you. You'll die faster if you keep fighting back."

Tears streamed down the boy's face, and every part of him resisted against whatever monstrous control the alien had over him.

"If— if you're gonna k-kill me just do it!" Oliver sputtered. Poppy's smile dropped a second, and she burst into laughter at the statement.

"Kill you?" Her eyes flickered back toward Kaylee's frozen body for a brief second. She thrust her claws into the woman's chest. "Believe me, I can do much *worse* than just kill you."

Oliver's clenched jaw dropped in horror, watching as she poured herself into the poor nurse, staining her veins a crude black.

"You see, it takes a lot of energy to create and destroy things. You put enough of yourself into it though, and you can mold anything into what you want."

The alien retracted its claws, leaving a gaping black and bloody hole in Kaylee's chest. The nurse buckled, and dropped to her knees, her face turned up in anguish as she stared confused and afraid at the beast that just revealed itself.

"But what I do requires *finesse*," she continued, directing her gaze back at Oliver. "A fine tuning of any organic being's cerebral cortex takes time, *effort*."

The boy's eyes widened, and he felt the full velocity of what this thing was. What it could do.

"I don't think you're familiar with our species." She added with a chuckle. "We don't *kill* our prey. It's against our rules. Besides, how would I be able to harvest so much if I went around slaughtering everything I ate?"

Her gaze turned down toward Kaylee, and her brief interlude of vindictive joy ceased. "No, that's considered *'inhumane'*. We do something entirely different."

The woman wretched and groaned, dropping to her hands as she let out a guttural cry, her fingers clawing into the dirt and rubble as she grappled with a terrible burning that grew and enveloped her.

"With enough matter, you can completely rework the entire composition of an organic being. Rendering them functionally incapable." Poppy stated it so casually, like it was nothing close to death. Like it didn't even hurt them. All while Kaylee cried out and tore at herself in shrieking agony.

She bled and begged, her skin and muscles slowly melting together as her organs twisted and turned, forcing her to vomit up a disgusting black bile that reeked of putrid human remains.

"Stop it!" Oliver pleaded, wrenching his head away from the awful sight, only for Poppy to force him back to watch as that precious human life wasted away in front of him. As she turned into some awful, reviled mess on the floor. A sack of flesh and meat that cried and whimpered in guttural noises indecipherable to the human ear.

"STOP!!" For a split second, the hold the entity had on him ceased, and Oliver crashed into the floor, heaving and retching at the rank odor that emanated from what used to be a human woman. A person with a life, a family.

Poppy turned to him, and crouched down, placing her hand so gently on his back that the child jerked away. He stared bewildered at her cold, dead eyes.

"Why would you do that?! She didn't do anything to deserve that!! She didn't—" Oliver stopped, and brought his hands to his face, covering his eyes from the horror. *This is your fault. She... is this..this thing, because you tried to escape. She helped you and it led to this. You did this.*

"Let this be a lesson," Poppy said, placing her fingers under the boy's chin as she pulled him to face her.

"I can do far *worse* things than you could ever imagine."

Oliver trembled under the alien's gaze, unable to form words as she traced long claws across his cheek and her focus moved to just behind him.

She stood and with a mere flick of her finger, Oliver was made to stand as well, taking burning steps backward, one agonizing step after the other until he stood, his toes just behind that white line.

Then, she released her hold on him, letting him drop to the floor with a howl of pain.

"You have five seconds to run."

Caught

Oliver blinked, registering her words all too slowly as he scrambled to his feet and made a break for it, zooming past Poppy and her bored face as he sprinted for the exit.

He was maybe five feet away from it, gaining if he could, before something long and disgustingly sticky lassoed around his ankle and yanked him back, smacking the boy's chin hard on the cement floor.

Oliver twisted around, catching a good look at the vine coated in small sticky hairs that wrapped tight around his ankle, dragging him back toward the nightmare it was undoubtedly attached to.

His first thought was to kick at it, but the moment his bare foot touched its surface, it stuck to it like a rat to a glue trap and he instinctively yanked back, yowling at the tearing of his skin.

"What—" he cut himself off as another vine shot out from the dark, lacing up his wrist with the same sticky tendrils that ripped the hair off his arms when he pulled at it.

The boy shot an anguished look at Poppy, knowing she would never aid in his efforts, as it only prompted her to make a somewhat pleased face.

Frantically, he grappled with the vines, managing to loose his arm and leg and return stumbling to his feet to try and reach the exit before a third vine attacked, this one wrapping tight around his throat and knocking him back hard on the floor with a dizzying concussion.

Oliver gasped, digging his nails into the plant before another one tangled in his arm, forcing it up and away.

"The more you struggle, the harder it's going to try to catch you," Poppy remarked, the pleasure in her voice palpable. "Normally I drug my stock before handing it over to the Tellarin Ralflaesia, but I figured I might let it play with it's food this time."

Oliver shot a wild, terrified look at the alien, kicking his legs out in effort to force himself up onto his feet. He yanked the vine from his arm with a hideous cry and turned his attention back to the one around his neck, managing to twist himself painfully out of its grasp and gain a couple staggered steps before four vines whipped out.

They coiled up his legs, forcing them apart as the alien plant jerked him upside down to fight against the other two vines that threatened to restrain what little mobility he had left.

Poppy took a step closer, just at the edge of the white line Oliver hung over.

"It's a plant native to a planet in the Peace Zone, the same planet I get my shipments of orchids from, actually," she said, the calm of her voice dissonant against the boy's yelps and grunts. "A carnivorous parasitic fungus that senses prey within a fifty foot radius through vibrations in the ground."

Oliver gripped one of the vines tight in his hand, hoisting himself upright in effort to gain some kind of control over it. All he managed to do was allow the creature to reverse the direction the vine moved and lace up his arm, tacking itself to his skin and clothes until it reached the pit of his arm, yanking it almost hard enough that it pulled the joint from its socket. He let out a guttural wail, now down to just his left arm free to combat the awful alien plant.

He flashed one last horrified look backward at the darkness the vines erupted from, catching movement of something much larger lashing out toward him.

It fanned like an ornate split tongue of a serpent, coated with the same sticky mucus the other thinner vines produced.

But when it opened up, a long and terrifyingly sharp pointed barb bobbed inside it like the stinger of a wasp.

"It's quite a unique species, you see," Poppy continued, "it expends a significant amount of energy catching its prey, then feeds off of it for several weeks, slowly dissolving the flesh until there is nothing left."

Oliver swatted at the much larger tendril, swaying and swinging against the strength of the plant and gravity that threatened to drop him twenty feet onto hard cement should he break free. Another vine twisted up his last free arm, yanking and turning him over until his back faced the fanned stinger.

He struggled ceaselessly, even as the thick and sticky leaves folded around his shoulders, waist and hips, clinging to any skin uncovered by his clothes. It was like a tongue, pulsing against him, constricting until the barbed stinger shot out in one quick and agonizing jolt.

A shriek ripped through Oliver's throat and his desperation to escape amplified with jerking, frantic movements against an awful, burning, crawling sensation that bulged under his skin, branching out from his spine, over his back and down his arms and legs, like thousands of tiny tentacles just beneath his flesh.

"Once it has restrained its prey, it releases a branched proboscis that attaches to the animal's nervous system," Poppy's lips curled up with a small smile as she explained just what Oliver felt. "After that, it uses the prey's own nervous system to render the animal immobile. The process is quite painful, as I'm sure you've noticed. Which is why I prefer to drug those I intend to farm."

Oliver retched, coughing as his stomach churned and forced its contents up, making him vomit and hack before the monstrous plant took control of the rest of his organs. It burned, so fiercely he could do little more than shriek and cry and howl like a dumb animal until his even his vocal chords were frozen over and he simply hung there, unable to move, to blink, to scream. Oh how badly he wanted to scream.

He could feel, somewhat, that pulsing of the plant's tendrils under his skin, like veins he was forced to harbor in his body.

The vines lowered, relaxed slightly, bringing him down to the ground so it could freely drag him backward.

Poppy stepped over the white line, some horrifically casual pace as she met his wide, terrified and frozen eyes, unable to even look in her direction as she pressed her fingers into his chin, lifted and turned his head.

"Don't worry, it's not going to kill you," she comforted, as if it gave any meaning to the word. "This is a genus of my own creation, unable to dissolve the prey it catches, instead, it's going to make you feel a lot of very different things. Think of it like…emotional regulation."

She let go of him and took a step back, allowing the plant to continue its slow pull back to its center.

"If you're good, I might even let you out before it destroys your mind."

No…no! Please…

Oliver pleaded, prayed, begged and tried so very hard to make a noise, a sound, to move at all. It hurt though, even to think, as the plant pulled him up its rank petals and toward a soft and pulpy center.

A thick, semi transparent lip undulated around him, stretching and growing as he was dropped into a puddle of stinging slime, it pooled higher, as the opening grew and closed at its top. The stench of the flower would have made him gag, or cry, if he had any control over his own body. Any basic function that hadn't already been overridden by Poppy's horrid science experiment.

He dreaded the choking mucus as it seeped into his mouth, the plant forcing him to breathe it in, turning off his ability to cough and hack, to reject it at all.

He was half submerged already by the time Poppy had turned to the massive computer on the wall. She pressed buttons and pulled levers, put codes that made it whir and scream and in turn, the plant it was connected to lifted Oliver up, constricting on his bones until it made his body react against his will.

Rapturous joy flooded into him so suddenly he hadn't any idea how to process it, some drastic and terrifying increase in dopamine that took over his system and warped his thoughts. It was fine now.

Being here..trapped..was fine.

A Measured Response

Douglass paced outside on his neighbor's porch, he wanted so badly to barge in and yell and scream at Jon for letting Oliver be taken away to that awful place. For allowing him near Matthew at all.

He rang the doorbell. Once, twice, then repeatedly in frustration until he lost his patience and trudged around to the sliding door in the back that he knew Oliver always forgot to lock.

Just as he thought, the sliding glass door was still unlatched and Douglass promptly shoved it open, unprepared for the absolute wreckage of the home inside. He stood there, slack-jawed and baffled as he registered the upturned chairs and tables. All the drawers and cabinets in the kitchen were thrown open and papers strewn all over the floor.

What…happened?

His thought was interrupted by a cranky meow from one of Oliver's cats that hopped down from the stairs and sauntered into the living area. If he recalled, it was Pancake. An orange tabby Oliver had snuck home from the dumpster outside the middle school. She had gotten particularly fat from the last time Douglass saw her.

The cat immediately wove itself between Douglass's legs, purring and mewing for food, despite his struggle to focus on whatever happened to the cabin. So, to save himself the effort, he just picked up Pancake and carted her around with him. He could put her back outside once he figured out what was going on.

Douglass moved from the living room into the kitchen, taking note of the groceries left out on the island. The greens had gone bad already— having never been put in the fridge. On the floor was a trail of paper, stamped with thick black ink that Pancake had left footprints with going into the master bedroom.

Douglass followed her trail, inspecting the room and how every last place of storage had been tossed out, files and paperwork and lockboxes on the bed and floor. *They were looking for something?....who?*

Then the idle concept struck him hard like a brick to the face. *They took him. MY DAD'S AT THE LAB!*

Douglass dropped the cat and ripped his phone out of his pocket to dial his father, praying that he would pick up. *I need to warn him, I need to make sure he knows what they did, that the aliens— the Clowns are there.*

"Douglass? I'm a bit busy—"

"Dad! Dr. Jariwala, he, they took him! I think— I think it was the Clowns. I came to the cabin to tell him Matthew was at the hospital with Oliver and he— it's really bad, I checked, I looked for him but it's empty, Dad, the whole house is empty!" Douglass rambled, he could feel himself shaking and trembling, but he tried hard to focus on the sound of machinery in the background of his father's line.

He heard talking, voices that he didn't recognize from his father's coworkers. Then the line dropped and all he heard was the dial tone.

***

Jon woke with an awful groan, his body ached and he struggled to sit up, not realizing he'd been restrained to the top of a large desk.

"It's truly a shame I had to intervene, Dr. Jariwala."

His dizzy head swiveled around. Director Miles stood at his side, far enough away that he could see the person as they circled around him in what he recognized was the basement of the lab.

Slowly, Jon picked out his environment. It was a containment room, built for highly dangerous and lethal substances, but all the separate pieces and parts of the molecular transporter had been hauled into the back of it, every mechanism had been tripled in size, though it still sat unfinished.

"My son!" Was the first thing he said, followed by futile jerking and writhing to free himself from what was most assuredly cuffs composed of the same substance Dindet was.

"Yes," Miles nodded, a brief look of contemplation on their face before an ugly and uncanny smile spread across their lips. "I'm sorry I had to do this, but I couldn't let you interfere. The divergences in the timeline have gotten too far out of hand....but if you like, I can swear to you your child will be safe and secure."

"You *fucking bastard,* you fucking monster! You lay one god damned hand on my boy and I will kill you myself!" Jon spat, though he knew the threat was idle. The director merely cocked their head as if they were entirely unconcerned by his words.

"You needn't worry about that," they replied, slinking around the room to inspect the unfinished machine parts. "There was an attempted escape that Poppy was able to thwart. Your child will be held until the proceedings are complete and our court has placed them accordingly."

"Court?! What are you doing to him?! What do you want? My machine? My blueprints?! You can fucking have them just give me back my son, let me see him! I need to see him!" Jon kicked and jerked wildly, despite how much it hurt to move. He struggled to recall how he got here. *The car— I was going to get Oliver.*

Director Miles filed their fingers together and turned back to him, sauntering around him like this was a casual conversation. "I'm afraid I can't do that. There's already an agreement in standing— I need your child to uphold my end of the bargain. And I really don't want to have to do this again."

"What bargain?! He's just a kid! You want the clown girl? You want Dindet? He doesn't—"

"Dr. Jariwala," Miles hushed him with a brush of their fingers on his hand, instantly filling his head with more information than he could comprehend. A vast array of knowledge, experience and memories that all collided into one singular thought.

Marie.

Jon shot him a wild glare, his eyes so wide they looked like they could have bulged out his sockets with rage.

"Your child will be safe in the Cornucopia," the Director continued, "provided you continue to cooperate."

"*You.*" The word fell out of the man's mouth vile and discordant, filled with his loathing of the creature in front of him. "You were the one who took her. You took my wife! You took Marie and you're taking my son! I WON'T LET YOU! I'LL STOP YOU!! I'LL—"

Jon was cut off by the abrupt jabbing of the alien's fingers through his skull, they burned and melted into his skin, slowly, making him drop his mouth open in a horrendous shriek that filled the room. He writhed in agony for what felt like hours but was only a few seconds before the Director released their hold on his brain and pulled away, leaving him shaking in his stupor.

"You know that's not going to happen, Jon," The alien answered, bending down to look him in his wild and terrified eyes. The scientist sputtered and wheezed, but he stopped trying to fight out of his restraints. Instead he stared at him, tears pooling and streaming down his face at what he was forced to witness— to feel.

The scattering of his bones, breaking away, turning to dust and crinkling, twisting of all his muscles, his very cells into nothingness.

"You don't want that to happen to Oliver, do you?" Miles smiled, a look of eerie understanding creeping across their face. "Your precious family?"

He couldn't answer, couldn't bring himself to speak at all. The memory burned into his skull, laced around every thought he had and every effort he made to move or say a word was lost in the indefinite scattering. That horrific shrieking.

Miles bent closer, their lips nearly touching his ear as they whispered, "Neither does your wife."

The Director stood back when Jon jerked and moved around him, trailing their hand along the desk and over his legs as they circled. Their gaze had moved away though, planted off in the distance.

"It looks just the way I remember it," Miles murmured, more to themselves than to their captive. "I do say, I applaud your species for your intellect. Humans discovering our elementary particles is quite common...but finding a way to reverse engineer them? That is a miraculous feat of scientific discovery. It's only happened once before...though that was quite a long time ago."

They paused, glancing back at Jon and his dumbfounded trembling. "It's a shame you keep destroying yourselves with it."

***

Chris snuck through the AKAN halls, avoiding BERC agents in his swift and discrete mission to escape. He hadn't seen Jon in the workroom and after Douglass's frantic phone call, he had an undeniable sense of urgency to escape. So he quietly moved through the server room to the file directory— knowing full well he would have to stop existing to get away.

"Yeah, so I told him 'dude, my bean is out of my control, I'm not gonna move it cause it looks weird— at least mine isn't as big as Bozo! Right?" He stopped, overhearing one of the aliens in disguise in the break room across the way.

"Yeah, and you know, these human skins are *so* uncomfortable," another added, "I don't know how Smile does it all day! And they left that proxy in the containment unit? I'm just ready for the court— I wanna see the amalgamate get Nowhere'd."

Two of them. They will probably know I'm human if they see me— I need another way to the files. Chris doubled back, heading toward the supercollider to make a trek around the building and hopefully avoid them.

BERC agents littered the lab, but most stayed contained near the refurbished wing. Chris had caught on quite quickly that the entirety of this supposed hand of the government was infiltrated.

There was no telling just how invasive the Clowns had been in their secret takeover.

He was safest making an exit by the nuclear reactors further up the mountain.

Find Douglass, get the hell out of here at the first opportunity—

"Ah, Mr. Furkin," the familiar voice cut off Chris's thoughts and he froze in front of the new Head Director. "I've been looking for you."

Chris forced a nervous smile, "I'm sorry, I was just heading to check the reactors— my turn for duty and all."

Director Miles stared at him, he couldn't tell if they were able to read his thoughts from here, to see the fear burgeoning in his chest as his heart began to race between their uncomfortable pause.

They looked to be deliberating something, then they blinked slowly and offered a discomfortingly sweet smile.

"I appreciate your enthusiasm, but your engineering expertise is required in the transporter room."

Shit.

"I, uh, yeah—" he fumbled, taking a small step back from the beast. "About that, have you seen Jon? I can't—"

"Dr. Jariwala is currently being tasked with the micro-engineering aspects of the project. He won't be able to assist in any further development." Miles cut in briskly, stepping past him in order to force Chris to follow them back the way he came.

"You have a child as well, correct?" Director Miles questioned, talking as if it were a casual conversation despite both of them knowing full well that it wasn't.

"I— I do, yeah." *They're threatening me.*

"It seems most of the employees here have children..." there was a noticeable shift in the Director's voice. It caught the scientist off guard.

Is this still a threat?

"You're quite fond of them I can see, though I imagine being a parent to be a hassle."

What are you getting at? What sort of ploy are you making?

"Well, they're kids. It's just as hard being a kid as it is being a parent," he answered, hoping he strung the words together in a comprehensible manner.

The Director hummed softly in response. "I imagine that would be true. Based on my observations your— *our* kind goes to great lengths to protect our own. And destroy them."

Poppy's People Farm

"Okay, what all did you bring?" Cassidy dropped her backpack down on the bench outside the student parking area and plopped down next to Douglass while he sifted through his school bag for not particularly school related things.

"I took my dad's taser, and I got some tools too, a wrench, some screwdrivers— Phillips and flathead, your buzzer thing, oh, and also some snacks for the drive there…I get hungry when I'm anxious." He pulled out each item, showing it off before finishing with a granola bar, which he promptly opened to start on.

"Cool, I got this night stick from my mom's closet, a map of the building, a rope— just in case— and some cash in case we need to get a bus back." Cassidy twirled her weapon, a little more enthusiastically than Douglass expected. "It's four now, and the drive is only about thirty minutes, so we should get there around four thirty, so you won't miss your driving curfew."

Douglass grunted softly, standing up. Cassidy nodded and shoved her stick back into her bag. "I have a feeling that curfew isn't going to matter pretty soon..."

At that, Cassidy hummed in soft agreement and pushed her things into the back seat of Douglass's car.

"Why do you have so much fabric?" She changed the subject lightly.

"Oh," Douglass scratched his head distractedly, tossing a bolt into the floorboards to make more room. "I was going to make a sort of..costume? For a convention coming up. Eyre-Con if you've ever heard of it."

Cassidy made a small 'oh' and nodded, then shook her head, prompting a shrug from the boy as he got into the driver's seat.

The drive there was simple enough, a few twists and turns but the backroads put them right at the edge of the park on the other side of the lake. Douglass kept quiet with his hands far too tight on the steering wheel and gear shift and Cassidy sat in the passenger seat, twiddling her thumbs while she struggled to come up with some kind of conversation to fill the silence between them.

"So, are we…just not going to talk about it?" Cassidy was the one to break it, pulling Douglass's attention away from the road and toward her.

"What do you mean?"

"About Oliver."

"Uh, yeah," he remarked, further tightening his grip as he shifted into fourth gear. "we're literally breaking him out of a fake mental hospital."

"I mean…" Cassidy failed to hide the frown that pulled at her lips, "I mean, with Theo."

Oh.

Douglass grumbled nothing words under his breath and shifted into fifth. "What's there to talk about?"

She eyed him, watching how he drew in a heavy breath and blew out through his nose. "I don't think I've ever seen you get that mad before."

"I'm not mad." He retorted gruffly. Though Cassidy was clearly hard pressed to believe it.

"You care a lot about him." She said, turning her gaze out the window at the passing trees. "Why?"

At that Douglass's nose scrunched. *What sort of question even is that?*

"Why wouldn't I?"

"Well..." Cassidy hesitated, "I just was thinking about how...you're going to all this trouble for him, but I've never seen him do anything of the sort for you."

"You weren't there when my sister died."

Cassidy drew in a soft breath at the statement, averting her eyes as Douglass allowed the thought to sink in. Though her discomfort at his exclusion of her made him sigh.

"He moved next door...right around my sister's last chemo sessions. They were in rooms next to each other at the hospital," he explained. "Jojo was...she wasn't gonna make it and it was tearing our— my mom and dad apart. She wanted me to make a friend. Before she...left."

Douglass shook his head, trying to hold down his anguish at the thought of it.

"And you picked Oliver?"

"Well...sort of?" He correctly gently. "He wasn't exactly enthused about being friends— threw a book at me the first time I ever talked to him."

"A book." Cassidy chuckled, bringing her gaze back to Douglass and the nostalgia in his eyes at the memory. "What made you keep trying?"

Douglass grew quiet for a moment and downshifted as they came to a stop sign by the cliff. "He's a really good listener."

The girl made a noise like that was something far too hard for her to believe. Likely because she had only ever seen Oliver doodling or sleeping in class and paying as little attention as possible.

"He is," Douglass affirmed, "when you don't ever talk, I figure you get really good at it. And well...he would just let me talk about anything and everything. Mostly my collection of manga or my books. But also about the divorce...and Jojo."

He laughed lightly. "There was this time, I was so upset because she'd moved back to the house for hospice and decided to throw away all her wigs, you know? And I wanted to practice this one braid— what was it? Something circa like, Regency Era? I don't know but back then, he had really long hair and he just...let me practice on him."

Douglass hummed softly at the memory, and the absolute disinterest on Oliver's face when he had shown him the little flower clips he'd intended to put in his hair. It made his stomach roll over with tender delight when he remembered just how promptly the kid had accepted them and pinned them into his hair himself. "He's not…anything like he is at school. And…how he is right now is…it's something else."

Cassidy gave a nod and Douglass noticed how she closed in on herself at his remark. "I..didn't know about your sister. I'm so sorry."

"Don't be," Douglass answered, forcing a smile. "If she hadn't had cancer…I'd have never met Oliver. And I'd probably be just as alone as I was in fourth grade."

They pulled to a stop in the Amelis parking lot, Douglass making a point to park far in the back of the complex.

Cassidy promptly reached into the back seat and pulled out the map she'd brought, unfolding it to plan their course of action.

"Alright." She pointed at the south wing on the map. "This building was constructed back in the seventies and it was originally some kind of retirement community. Because of that, there's a back entrance over here."

The girl glided her finger across the wing to another building a few hundred or so feet away. "The morgue. If I read the plans right, it has some kind of underground tunnel where they would move the deceased from their rooms. It's not in use anymore as a mental hospital, so it's our safest bet inside without drawing a whole lot of attention."

"Did you by any chance see what room number he was in?" Douglass questioned, digging in his bag for another anxiety snack.

"No, but the whole south wing was closed off, so he's probably in the east or west ones." Cassidy pointed out little red exes she'd drawn at the doors. "These are all our exits, but this one between the south dand east wing is a fire exit and it will set off an alarm so it's off limits…that leaves…"

She pressed her finger into three different doors. "Here, here, and here. There's no way we'd be able to get out the front door unless it's after hours, so I think we should just leave the same way we came in, through the morgue."

"Right." Douglass nodded, pulling his key from the ignition and readying himself for whatever might happen next.

***

Oliver stared out at the room before him. Unable to blink or move. It was orange and faded through the soft stinging juices of the plant he'd been trapped in for only a god knew how long. Or Poppy.

The ache of his skin and bones had dulled to a constant low throbbing, and he wasn't entirely sure how he was able to keep breathing.

He'd almost memorized the pattern of blinking lights on the machine that controlled the plant. It corresponded with colors that fit the hues Dindet turned when she ate his feelings. When it was blue, it washed him with uncontrollable sorrows. And bright yellow made him so unnaturally ecstatic that if he were free to move, he'd be jumping with joy.

Every now and then though, the lights turned black. And that feeling was much less of a feeling than it was a memory. It made him tremble with unconscious movements that alluded the Raflaesia's control and flooded his mind with the same breath stealing terror that Matthew did when he entered the room. The strangest of all of it though, was how quickly it faded.

"And you're certain this method will work?" An unfamiliar voice rose from the dark, beyond the blinking lights. It was followed shortly by Poppy's answer.

"It may take a few more weeks, but yes."

Into view came the mime and a person. They were tall and lithe, with silver hair that had been gelled back into gentle curls. They wore a neatly pressed suit and their smile never once faltered as they came close enough for Oliver to see the sharp canines in their teeth.

"Hmm..." the person's lips closed as they inspected him and the monstrous flora that had engulfed him. "How long has it been in there?"

"Four days, seven hours and thirty-two minutes." Poppy answered, visibly pleased with herself. "She should be touching down soon, within the next week, if memory serves. He won't be in there long enough to cause any lasting damage, if you're worried about the testimony."

Testimony?

The silver haired person stood straight and placed their hands behind their back. "The Archivist has been recording every loop thus far, our contingency plan in the event of damaged evidence is sound…though I wonder..how lucrative, if at all, is your operation?"

"Oh, *very*." Poppy smiled, moving to the machine on the right of the plant. Some contraption that sucked the juice from it and filled canisters similar to the one's Oliver had seen in the orchid laboratory in the south wing. She twisted one of them loose with an audible hiss of air and presented it for the silver haired person to inspect. "I have been able to feed Clowns in the far reaches of sector 67802 of the Peace Zone with these. And the by-products simply get sold to my shipping affiliates once they've outrun their use."

By-products..the people?! She's selling people in other dimensions! The urge to jerk away as the mime approached was quashed much to Oliver's dismay. Instead, he could only stare at her and her hideous grin.

"With more of these, we won't have to infiltrate the Dead Zones and assimilate en masse. It would protect us from other situations like…" Poppy gestured vaguely at the air. "This."

"And what of the Aurii?" The guest asked, turning their gaze directly at Oliver and staring him dead in the eye. "Their Embassador has formed an outreach program in Dead Zone sector 4283. Humans there are nearing probable safe travel…if they enter the Confederation, what sort of example would we be setting? Enslaving their kind and selling them for a fresh meal?"

"That will never happen!" Poppy retorted, casting an ugly glare back at the boy. "They are too selfish and reckless, you know that first hand— your…honor."

The mime bowed her head just slightly, taking a small step back when her guest's smile wavered. "It's…not my place to say but, I think it's too early to try to introduce Humans into the Confederation. I've seen the things they are capable of."

"And I have not?"

"That's— that's not what I meant, I mean…" Poppy's eyes raised, flickering from Oliver back toward the dark before she stood straight and gestured at him. "This one is a good example. The only reason it's here is because of the Scattering in the Cornucopia and the amalgamate's loop. It was *meant* to die. This entire dimension is *meant* to die. Because of their stupid and reckless endeavor to find us— find you. They practically eat their own young! How can they possibly be of any benefit to the Confederation? The only advocates they have are the Aurii and those tailed organics are only interested from an anthropological standpoint. We could make a million Human Artifs and they'd be content to study those instead."

The silver haired person stood quietly for a moment, the look of contemplation on their face unnaturally still as they continued to stare at Oliver in his cage.

"It is conscious?"

"I—" Poppy cut herself short, averting her gaze. "Yes. My prediction of the divergence was correct."

"I see." The person nodded, finally looking away from Oliver and back toward the mime. "How many constants have we reached now?"

"Two hundred and forty-seven."

"How many left?"

Poppy raised her head. "By my count..six thousand three hundred and seven. But..I don't know any of them past her return."

Breaking and Entering

Douglass and Cassidy trailed around the back parking lot, keeping themselves far from any windows as they rounded the morgue looking for a discrete way inside.

"It's bolted shut." He said, picking up the heavy padlock and chain wrapped around the main door. Cassidy moved behind him toward the chain link fence that segregated the property from the much larger medical center in the lot next door.

"Over here," she called, prompting Douglass to follow. She pointed up at a glass window roughly eight feet up and only about three or four feet wide. "I can break it with my nightstick, and we can climb the fence, you think?"

"You sure we can fit?" Douglass eyed the girls much wider hips. If she were Oliver's size, probably. But Cassidy had a good thirty pounds over him.

Her nose scrunched up at the comment and she promptly punched him lightly in the gut. *Yes, I can fit.*

The girl tore off her jacket, wrapped it around her waist and clambered up the fence, situating herself just so that she held her precarious balance with an outstretched foot against the brick building while she waved for Douglass to grab her weapon from her bag.

With one quick smack, the glass shattered in fat chunks and

Cassidy punched out the rest of the shards with the end of her stick before she hoisted herself up and through the window.

"There's some boxes and tables in here," she said, followed by the squealing of something metal directly before the rest of her slipped through the window with a loud clang and her own groan of pain.

"You alright?" Douglass asked, grabbing the fence and doing his best to mimic the way she'd managed to get up. Cassidy made it look a lot easier than it really was, that was for sure. "What's in there? Are you hurt?"

"I'm fine, I landed on a gurney and it slipped is all!" She answered back after a bit. "I hold it steady for you. Try to come in feet first!"

Feet first?! Are you insane?

Douglass let out an uneasy noise and slowly, very slowly, moved his foot up the wall, keeping a death grip on the fence so he wouldn't fall backward and accidentally skewer himself on the old rebar poking up out of the ground.

He managed to get the ball of his foot into the window sill and just as he did Cassidy's hand shot out and grabbed him to keep him steady.

"I got you! Just push it in a little further so you can get your knees in." She directed calmly.

"You sound like you've done this before." Douglass managed between his grunting effort to get his other leg into the opening. He felt Cassidy's arms wrap tight around his ankles, holding him in place so he could finally loosen his grip on the fence and hang out the window like a very confused bat.

"Back in my home country I used to play in this abandoned factory with my friend, Zuri. The only way we could get in was through the basement windows, so this is pretty much the same— if not a little taller than I'm used to." Cassidy grunted, tugging Douglass's legs until he sat in the window and gradually touched down on the gurney she'd placed below him.

The boy's legs kicked around for a bit before he slid in and down the wall, nearly causing the gurney to topple over with his weight.

"Okay," he panted, "I think we lost our primary exit strategy. Unless you saw a key anywhere?"

Cassidy shook her head, turning her attention toward a ramp that became a pitch black tunnel under the parking lot.

"I don't suppose you brought a flashlight?" She questioned, pulling out her phone to use as one. Douglass shook his head and followed suit.

"Sort of cliché, but it's kind of like a horror movie," he whispered, shining a light on the dusty and old boxes and lockers that at one point probably held dead bodies. "Oliver would probably get a kick out of that…"

"Yeah?" Cassidy stepped into the tunnel, shining her light around to check for obstructions. "He likes scary movies?"

"Only bad ones." He corrected, following closely behind. "We have this game where we try to work each other up for the jumpscares…what is that?"

Douglass stepped in front of Cassidy, shining his light at a massive water trough at the right side of the wall. It was filled with some dark and thick orange liquid that glimmered when the light hit it.

Cassidy drew close to inspect it, trailing her finger along a small plastic board. "It's labeled..but I've never seen any language like this. Look."

The girl gestured further down, rolling her light over the right wall at the row of other troughs filled with the same liquid.

"We should keep moving." Douglass urged, much more quietly. He took the lead, his pace quickening as the two of them drove forward in the shadows and an eerie silence fell around them. Dotted only by the occasional stumble of their footsteps.

The tunnel widened, fanning out until they reached another ramp. This one led to another room, pitch black through the grated windows.

Douglass pushed the door open and almost immediately doubled back at the horrendous stench that erupted from inside.

"Holy— it smells like dead animal!" He wretched, covering his nose and glancing back at Cassidy as she did the same.

She pressed forward though, shining her light into the room to see what could possibly cause such an awful odor.

"Douglass…" Cassidy breathed, casting light over a hideous and enormous plant. "I think I found Oliver."

The boy ceased his hacking and immediately looked up and toward where Cassidy shined her light.

A massive and almost pulsing fibrous bulb in the center of the plant, the membrane was thin enough that the light from her phone silhouetted a monstrous tentacle inside it. And hands. And legs.

Oliver?!

Douglass bolted around the other side of the plant, caught off guard by the noise of machinery and blinking lights illuminating the far end of the room. He swiveled around and clear as day, Oliver sat, or rather floated, entangled by the tendrils of the behemoth plant.

Cassidy followed shortly behind him, bending down to touch the massive fleshy petals of the Ralflaesia.

"A giant…carnivorous plant?" She glanced back at Douglass. "You said you had a pocket knife, right?"

Douglass promptly shoved his hand into his bag, sifting through it with increasing frantic until he grabbed something by the handle and ripped it out. "Just this."

He held up the screwdriver for her to see before already clambering up the slick petals to get to Oliver.

"Wait—" Cassidy was cut short the moment Douglass plunged the sharp end of the tool into the plant, tearing it down the side as a gush of steaming and stinging juice spurted and poured out of it.

Please be okay. Please be alive. Please…

He wrapped his arms up under Oliver's, pulling with every strength of his being in effort to loosen him from the plant's grip. Instead, all it served was to cause another gush of hot liquid to pour over him in his efforts while Cassidy stood dumbfounded.

"Help me!" He ordered, prompting the girl to scramble up to his side and start widening the hole he'd made.

She plunged her hands into the gore of the flora, wrapping them around it's captive's shoulder before she jerked back, eyes widened with horror.

"Stop, stop! You're gonna hurt him!"

"Wh-what?" Douglass let go of Oliver, watching Cassidy as she sliced up the side of the plant and forced the bulb fully open. She crouched down, wiping gunk and slime from Oliver's arms to show Douglass what she meant.

Massive and thick bruises that spidered down them like veins, swelling and pulsing under the boy's skin. Like something had crawled under it and latched onto him from the inside.

Douglass traced them delicately, up his shoulder where the massive tendril had fanned over and around Oliver's neck. It took him far too long to realize it. But his eyes were wide and open, staring at him.

Oh…my god…

Douglass grabbed his face, half pulling back as he felt the pulsing of veins under Oliver's skin. "He's not breathing!"

Immediately he began tearing at the large tendril, peeling it back and slicking the red and blotchy skin where it had latched onto. Cassidy followed suit, ripping off the pieces around his waist and legs until the only thing tethering their friend to this monstrosity was a three inch thick tube. A fleshy white proboscis of a sort that had dug itself into him.

"We have to cut it—"

"No," Cassidy interjected before Douglass could act on the thought. "We don't know what it does, we have to make *it* let go of him."

She scanned the room, searching for something, anything that she could figure was used to control whatever this thing was.

"There!" She pointed at a large computer, following the trail of chords and wires that stopped with barbed prongs that stuck into the base of the plant and slid down the petals to rip them out. As soon as she did, the beast of a plant rumbled and bulged, shaking vigorously until it deflated with a nasty high pitched squeal followed by a burst of the most noxious odor one could ever imagine.

Douglass felt the tendrils under Oliver's skin move, writhing before they receded so quickly and so violently that the poor boy was thrust into Douglass's arms.

He held him up and close, stammering and shuddering over his attempt at consoling him.

"You're okay, I got you. Please…be okay Oliver, I swear, I swear I'll keep you safe. I'll believe you and— and I'll even get you that really nice carving kit you wanted, and a new sketchpad. I'll make you your favorite curry if you promise me…promise me…" Douglass choked on his pleading. "You can't go..you can't—"

He was stopped by a cough. A very nasty, ugly sounding noise that made Oliver jerk in his arms before the boy very weakly lifted his hands and gripped the back of Douglass's shirt. His head raised slightly and just as quickly butted into Douglass's forehead.

"...Douglass..."

"Y-yeah?" He barely even breathed the word, lost in rapturous relief that Oliver had responded at all. He held him tight in his arms, he couldn't hold him close enough.

"I'm…naked."

What.

WHAT?!

Just as quickly as the concept crossed his mind, Douglass immediately shoved Oliver off of him, sending him tipping backward into the gore of the plant.

"Ow."

"Oh god, oh jeez, S— sorry!" Douglass cringed, raising and lowering his hands in frantic attempt to figure out what to do next. Thankfully Cassidy came crawling up the plant to save the day. She untied her jacked from her waist and dropped it over Oliver before plopping down next to Douglass.

"Are you okay?" She asked, though not expecting much of a reply.

"I'm alive. Dumb plant melted my clothes." Oliver grimaced, zipping up her jacket in effort to cover most of himself. He shook terribly. And both of them could see how much of a struggle it was for him to move at all.

"We should go. Before they find us." Douglass urged gently, he pressed his hand into his friend's shoulder but quickly pulled back at the wince Oliver gave in response to the touch. "Are you able to walk?"

Oliver gave him a look before his eyes trailed down to his legs and the thick and stringy bruises the plant had made on him. "...mostly? How— how did you know where to find me?"

For a moment the boy seemed to freeze, a look of absolute horror flickering across his face before his eyes flitted back to Douglass. He gripped the gore of the plant, attempting to pull himself away from the two of them.

"This is a trick."

What??

"I— no." Douglass leaned in, garnering a nasty glare in response.

"I'm not an idiot...*Poppy*." Oliver hissed, keeping his distance. "I'm not going to fall for it again."

"Oliver...it's not a trick," Cassidy corrected gently. She reached behind her, ignoring his anxious twitch at her movement. She pulled out one of the jelly buzzers she'd brought and held it out for him to see. "We're really here. To break you out."

Oliver's gaze flickered down and back up and a frown pulled at his lips, prompting the girl to shock herself to prove she was no alien imposter.

"Douglass," she directed, handing him the buzzer to do the same.

"Ouch— agh, you didn't tell me it would hurt that bad, Cas." He flapped his hand before returning his attention back to Oliver.

He stared at the two of them, and Douglass could almost see the cogs in Oliver's brain whirring as he processed what was happening. It shifted his look of disdain into shock, then relief. But it settled on horror.

"Kaylee...the other patients."

A Bit More Than You Bargained

"Who?" Cassidy shared a look with Douglass that Oliver flagrantly ignored as he started crawling, then tumbling head first down the slick petals of the plant. "My nurse, she was— aghck!" He winced, and the moment he even tried to stand his legs wobbled and fell out from under him, prompting Douglass to slide down to the rescue.

"Careful," he jeered, albeit compassionately. Douglass ducked under the boy's arm and hoisted him back up on his feet with little acknowledgement to Oliver's disgruntled huff. "You can barely move, we really should get you out of—"

"No." Oliver cut in, deliberately planting his feet on the ground to force Douglass to struggle against what strength he had.

"Douglass is right, though." Cassidy added, sliding down the petals and catching herself before she could trip on solid ground. "We don't know when Poppy will be back and the longer we stay, the more likely we'll get caught."

She came up and attempted to take Oliver's other arm before he jerked back, stumbling a bit before he caught himself and stood straight. Or, mostly straight. It hurt to move, far more than it had when he'd woken up long after Poppy had drugged him. A searing and burning sensation that struck every time his feet touched the ground or his muscles tensed at all. *All of them…she's doing this to all of us.*

"I said no." Oliver repeated with absolute conviction in the statement.

Douglass raised his hand to his head in clear frustration at his insane and easy dismissal. "Why not?"

At that, Oliver dropped his gaze, moving it from the machines to the plant before his eyes slowly trailed back to the two kids. "I just…we *can't* leave them here."

"Who??"

"Everyone. The patients. Nurses," he answered softly. "We— *I* can't just leave..knowing what she's doing."

Cassidy took a small step forward, her voice riddled with soft concern. "What is she doing?"

He answered with some small, barely audible word, prompting the girl to move closer. She cast a look back at Douglass who wore his impatience and fear plainly on his face. "Oliver…*what* is she doing to the people here?"

He swayed uncomfortably for a moment, gripping the hem of his borrowed jacket as he grappled with the concept, as horrific as it was. "She's..selling…them."

At his words, Douglass's look of frustration twisted into shock that mirrored Cassidy's wide eyes.

"This whole place," Oliver continued, gesturing feebly at the room. "It's some kind of— of farm. She drugs us— them. And feeds them to that *thing.*"

His eyes flickered back at the massive plant behind him. A shudder rippled through him that he could barely conceal. "She collects whatever comes out of it…and when she's done…"

Oliver raised his gaze, planting it somewhere between the two of them so he didn't have to see the horror on their faces. "I can't let anyone else get hurt."

Like Kaylee..or Cody. Or those people on the list. How many people has she taken already?

"Alright." Douglass wiped his face, keeping his gaze off of Oliver as he spoke. "We'll help you get them out…"

He said it as though he were upset. Though Oliver couldn't place just why.

"Okay, but how do we do that?" Cassidy asked, following Oliver as he made his way toward the doors that lead into the south wing.

He paused, briefly checking the window to ensure the hall was dark and empty.

"I don't know?" He answered. Honestly, he didn't think he would even have the opportunity to survive, let alone save the fifty odd patients trapped along with him. "What day is it?"

"Uhm.." Cassidy checked her phone. "Friday, why?"

"Good," Oliver pushed the door open with a wince, allowing Douglass to take the weight of it from him when he came to help. "She's at the school on Fridays, so she's probably pretending to be a person…" *which means she's not watching anyone, right?*

"Classes ended a couple hours ago," Douglass countered. "She could be here."

"I don't think so," Oliver retorted, making a beeline for the laundry room and hopefully more clothing than a jacket. "She— while I was in there— she came with some person and was talking to them about…stuff. Something about a court case? And she left with them. So I'm pretty sure they're preparing for something big." *Like Dindet coming back.*

"I don't think she's been here as often as before. She probably thinks I'm still.." Oliver hesitated, skirting around the topic and continued leading the other two toward the laundry room. "I'm gonna put some clothes on."

He nodded toward the lit door and dipped inside, grabbing the first pair of scrubs he could find and pulling them on before returning and pointing at the fire doors that connected the south wing to the rest of the hospital. "The front entrance is usually locked at night, but she uses the fire exits for her uhm..deliveries. I figure if we pull the alarm, the nurses will start pushing people out into the courtyard or something and we can sneak away in the crowd."

Cassidy drew closer, hushing her voice as the three of them crept toward the better lit main building. "You're certain that...*that* is what she's doing?"

Oliver gave a subtle dip of his head, staggering slightly before he caught himself by the wall. He directed his attention toward the other lit room of the south wing, prompting her to follow his gaze.

"That's where she keeps her stores and...information," he said. "I snuck in before. But Mat— I got caught."

At his stutter, Douglass spoke, his tone almost harsh. "He's here, isn't he? Matthew?"

Oliver nodded meekly, hoping to avoid the topic as best he could.

"How did you guys get in?" He changed the subject quietly, searching the darkness for a fire alarm. He found one on the wall, near the entrance to the south wing.

The lights were on in the foyer, and he could see people passing by, casting shadows into the hall that faded into the darkness.

"There's a tunnel behind that big flower, and we got in through a window in the morgue," Douglass answered, noticing Oliver stop at the fire alarm. He gestured at the foyer ahead of them. "No one will probably come this way when evacuating. We can just sneak back the way we came without anyone noticing."

Cassidy nodded in agreement and Oliver raised his hand, slight hesitation gripping him before he blew out a soft breath.

"Okay..on three, then we run?" He wasn't sure if he could manage that, considering he could barely manage walking at the moment. But going back through the tunnels was infinitely safer than trying to break out into the foyer, especially if Poppy and Matthew were anywhere in the main building.

Cassidy braced herself, and Douglass took a firm step forward, ready to catch Oliver if he stumbled.

"One..two..*THREE!*"

Oliver jerked down the alarm, setting off the high pitched ringing before a loud and nasty sounding beeping went off, followed by water jetting down from the ceiling. But they were already sprinting hard down the hall, Douglass had his hand wrapped tight on Oliver's wrist, dragging him far faster than his legs could move.

It hurt. Every step shot lightning from his toes to his knees and hips and they threatened to buckle under his weight as they raced down the hall. Cassidy slammed the doors wide open and beckoned them into the farming room.

Douglass moved so much faster than Oliver had anticipated, jerking him around the enormous plant and skidding in its gel that slathered on the floor. He didn't even take time to catch himself, instead his hand hooked under Oliver's armpit and he shoved him forward for Cassidy to catch before she backed through the tunnel doors, bathing the two of them in complete darkness. Aside from the blinking light of the fire alarm ahead.

"Are you alright?" Cassidy breathed in between her panting. Oliver merely nodded, trying to hide the wince on his face from how hard Douglass's fingers had dug into him.

The tunnel doors opened once more and Douglass ducked inside, quickly slicking off the slime from his shirt with a barely hidden 'blegh'. "We *should* be good now. There was no one in the tunnel when we came in."

Cassidy pulled out her phone, turning on the flashlight to provide light between the intermittent red flashes over the narrow hall. "Just straight ahead now.."

They walked now, as quietly as physically possible, down the tunnel. Cassidy took the lead and Oliver hobbled behind Douglass, trying not to gasp at how his bones wanted so badly to crack and shatter. His attention stayed on the two of them and their silhouettes, flickering in the strobing light.

"Ahh—" Oliver stumbled and drew in an ugly breath, prompting Douglass to whip around, prepared to dive under him to break a fall if need be.

"Cas…" he whispered, slowing his pace to that of Oliver's pained shuffling. "We should slow down—"

"No," he interjected softly. "It's fine, I'm fine."

Douglass shot him a look that in the flash of red light, Oliver quickly gathered was anger. He strayed away from him, resting up against the large trough at the side of the wall.

"No, you're not, you're—" whatever Douglass was going to say was cut short by something hard and heavy and fast. A shadow that bolted almost from nowhere and hands, large and strained that flew past the boy's face and straight for Oliver.

All he could see was the shock in Douglass's eyes before he was grabbed and thrust back, flailing in silent and frantic effort to get Matthew's hands away from around his neck and his head up from being plunged into thick and noxious liquid.

He clawed at his face and arms, struggling to hold his breath under the water before his head throbbed with lack of oxygen and Oliver impulsively dropped his jaw, dragging in a lung full of burning and horrifying familiar flavors. A mouthful of cinnamon.

Above the churning, he could see Douglass, standing in a stupor of shock before he grabbed Matthew by his shirt and yanked him away, tackling him and loosing his grip from Oliver's reeling head.

The boy hoisted himself up, struggling to maintain the desperate strength needed to pull himself to his feet. It was loud, yelling, and words. Poppy spoke and layers of her solidified in the flashing and dizzying lights where Cassidy stood.

No.

Oliver tilted his head, seeing the way Douglass ripped and cried out, some ugly and stifled noise when Matthew punched him hard in the stomach. Something clacked against the cement in front of him and he stared at it.

A…taser?

It sat right there. Right in front of him. Free for the taking while the walls grew arms and claws. They writhed and reached, pulling at Douglass and Cassidy. Oliver leaned forward, throwing a hand out and stealing the precious weapon away.

She's right…she's right there. I just have to…have to..

Oliver crawled, forcing himself to stand again, the walls and floor tilted underneath him and she was *right there.*

Deftly, he reached out pressing the prongs of the taser just under the surface of Poppy's matter.

And he pressed the button.

Electricity crackled, bright and loud, skittering amongst the screaming and the alarm. It spread up and through the alien's matter and in a brief second, far shorter than Oliver was prepared for, the creature erupted with an agonized shriek. He felt it, rattling his head and she spiked and jutted but he held the button down, praying that if he did so long enough, she would dissipate. The fighting would stop.

But instead, that awful and metallic shrieking persisted, and his brain caved in at it, this horrific burning feeling that shot down his spine and made him tremble until his mouth dropped open and he was enveloped by that same agony. Oliver shook and the jolt of electricity he sent coursing through Poppy reflected itself in him, followed shortly by Matthew, who reared up and arched his back over Douglass, crying out with the same visceral pain.

Keep going. Keep going until she— Oliver's thought dissipated, blinded by the expulsion of matter that splattered on the floor, landing in perfect little cubes that clacked and clattered around him.

Cassidy stood in front of him, her horrified face gasping with relief and fear so twisted up and contorted he couldn't quite tell if he had actually managed it. Managed to take her down.

A smile pulled at his lips at the thought.

"I...did it..."

Beast in the Hospital

Cassidy watched Oliver wobble, taser in hand with a dazed and soft expression of content on his face before his eyes rolled straight to the back of his head and he lurched forward, forcing her to bolt from her spot to catch him.

"RUN!!" She screeched, doing her best to pick the boy up as she sprinted toward Douglass and yanked him by the collar from the floor. He scrambled to his feet next to her and lifted Oliver out of her grasp and over his shoulder so she could increase her stride.

For a moment only did he look back, the flashes of red illuminating the tunnel where Matthew lay unconscious surrounded by cubes.

One flash passed. And the matter the mime was comprised of was already melted.

Then another. And it was congealing. Forming claws and smoke, billowing.

The third.

Disgusting gelatinous and narrow limbs formed, writhing and scrambling up from the floor.

Cassidy crashed through the doors to the farming room, barely stopping to breathe as she held it only long enough for Douglass to pull Oliver through and they ran, paces quickening with the burning of their lungs, skidding on the water that had pooled from the fire alarm as they forced their way into the foyer where so many bodies stood.

For a second, the girl stopped, forced by the distorted look of the patients. They bobbed and weaved, stilted and broken, like their arms and legs had been yanked and twisted, pulled from their sockets. There were streaking trails of black blood seeping from their mouths and eyes. No nightmare could be worse.

Until something slick and viscous burst forth from the door behind them and she stiffly swiveled around.

Poppy, with her monstrous nature revealed, squirmed, shrieking through the door as stick like arms shot forward, scrambling viciously to catch them.

"GET THEM" she ordered, the words so lost in her millions of voices that Cassidy only understood it when the nurses and patients moved. Disjointed and incongruous.

In an instant, she grabbed Oliver's other arm and jerked Douglass's breathless self forward, her attention solely on the glass doors at the front entrance of the building.

The bodies piled, rolling and clawing over one another as Poppy exploded from the south wing and the alien abomination clambered over them like a cricket over the piles of their dead brethren. Cassidy glanced back at Douglass, whose face had reddened with his sheer exhaustion, his focus only on following her and evading the horde of puppets under the alien's will.

Cassidy reached into her bag, whipping out the nightstick she'd had such precious forethought to bring and crashed it through the glass, sending shards scattering on the pavement as she twisted around and without a single utterance, pointed toward the large culvert pipe under the bridge.

Douglass nodded, though it was little more than a dip of his head before he shifted Oliver's unconscious body and the three of them broke from the parking lot to the road, to the bridge, hearing the nightmarish creature screeching after them until it stopped. Suddenly and abruptly.

The bodies that had piled up at the entrance of the hospital and the ones still chasing them ceased. But the kids kept running, sliding down in the mud and grass until Cassidy and Douglass both tumbled, Oliver in tow, and landed in the icy cold water still running from the pipe.

"In here!" Cassidy jumped up and quickly dipped into the pipe, grabbing Oliver's arm to drag him inside so Douglass had room to enter as well.

It was a brief and desperately deserved moment of respite. She heaved, trying to keep her breath quiet so she could listen for footsteps overhead.

Douglass tucked himself in next to her, breathing just as hard in the frigid night air. "I think…we lost—"

"Shhh!" Cassidy held her finger to her lips, drawing Douglass's attention and forcing his mouth shut when she raised her finger to point above them.

***

Poppy halted, her screaming mass folding and flickering as it condensed at the edge of the courtyard and her army of entrapped humans trampled ahead of her. Until she held out a hand and clenched her fist tight, forcing every last individual's muscles to contract and send them stumbling into the dirt or stopping altogether.

"There's no point," she said, the words stifled under her boiling rage. Her chin lifted slightly. "Everyone go back to your rooms. I don't need to catch them…I just need to wait for him to wake up."

***

It was dark now, and the only sound around was the crickets and cicadas that had just woken up from hibernation. Douglass and Cassidy trekked through the woods relatively aimlessly, at a pace one would probably go if they were to carry a whole unconscious person.

"I don't know how long he'll be out." Douglass attempted to catch his breath, but Oliver's dead weight was pulling him down further every step of the way.

"Doesn't— doesn't matter, we need to find a place to hide!" Cassidy panted, slowing to help him carry his friend. She ducked down and grabbed Oliver's other arm, shouldering a decent enough portion of his weight so that they could keep going.

Douglass gradually slowed, until his feet dragged and he lost his grip on Oliver, accidentally dropping him on the ground.

"You can't just drop him!" Cassidy crouched down, falling back on her butt and pulling the kid's hair aside to make sure he wasn't hurt too badly. Douglass sat down as well, heaving his breaths in effort to get back some kind of energy.

"You try carrying him then," he retorted through his panting. He smacked his palm on his leg, and began to get up before Cassidy pulled him back down to the ground.

"Are you okay?" She asked, resting her still shaking hands on his shoulders.

"No," he replied, "I just broke into a *human farm* fronting as a mental hospital to save my best friend, got the shit beat out of me by his dad and now he's unconscious and we just ran an alien blob monster that has an army of people puppets after us! I think 'being okay' is the least succinct way to describe what's going on. Dammit, *and* I left my sister's car!"

"I mean, are you hurt at all?" Cassidy rephrased, "that thing was trying to kill us."

"It's probably *still* trying to kill us, Cas," Douglass removed her hands from his shoulders and grabbed Oliver, hoisting his limp self over his back so he could carry him piggyback. "Come on, I know a place we can stay tonight."

Douglass led her through the woods, keeping close to the steep cliff side that inevitably led directly to his house. *Hopefully Poppy isn't aware of that.*

They came to a stop at a clearing, just past the suburbs and he veered off toward the left, until they walked right onto the dirt road that led to his house.

"Is this where you live?" Cassidy glanced around the dark road, then her eye caught the slight shift in color as the sun began to peek over the shadowed horizon. "We've been walking for hours! You couldn't—"

"Hush!" He snapped, crossing the road and quickly hiding behind the garage.

"What about your dad? He's gonna know if you just leave Oliver in your room," Cassidy remarked, more quietly this time. Douglass readjusted his friend and made his way around the back of the house, toward a small shed.

"He's not gonna be in the house," he answered, nodding for her to open the door for him.

The shed was dark, and littered with medical equipment, a small kitchen area, a miniature fridge, a broken television, and a bed that you usually see in a hospital in the back left corner. One that Douglass promptly tossed Oliver into.

He drew in a breath, holding it for a couple of seconds in effort to idle all the adrenaline in his veins before attempting to answer.

"We got this right around when my sister was in hospice, cause the house was getting too crowded," he explained, reaching up to pull on the light string.

Cassidy glanced around and immediately dropped her bag on the floor, heading straight for the old recliners across the television.

Douglass followed her, and plopped down on the increasingly more soft and comfortable chair. "My dad won't come in here anymore, and the only window is in the loft, so no one will know he's here except us."

"Plus," he let out a soft sigh of relief, "we can sleep now."

Douglass opened an eye, to see if Cassidy was listening, but she was already completely sacked out, curled up into a little ball on her side.

He closed his eyes again, ready to fall into probably the absolute best and most deserving slumber he would ever have.

Except his thoughts instead turned to Oliver and he winced, sitting up to swivel his head around and check on him.

He was out cold, in the same crumpled up position he had been dropped in before. Douglass glanced back at Cassidy for a moment, then got up, quietly moving to his friend to *really* make sure everything was okay. *Or as okay as it can be.*

He was bruised, pretty badly, and had little cuts and scrapes on his shoulders and face, probably from being dropped more than once. Douglass leaned in, hesitant to touch him, but all he could think about at the moment was the ear piercing scream he made when he electrocuted the alien. *God Oliver, what did you get into...*

Nervously, he glanced one more time back at Cassidy before tenderly pushing up Oliver's shirt to check for any particularly bad damage. He had a lot more scars than he anticipated, only one of which Douglass was certain came from Matthew's prior violence. The whole area was bruised though, not nearly as bad as he expected, but bad enough that it made him just a little sick to look at. They were wavy and faded near the edges, but built in darker and disgusting yellowed hues toward his back, where the plant had taken hold of him.

Douglass took a small step to the side, and quietly grabbed a spare blanket and pillow from on top of the mini fridge, throwing it over the kid and gingerly lifting his head up so he could shove the pillow under it.

"You'll be okay," he whispered, crouching down in order to see his face a little better. "You...you have to be okay.."

He stared at him, lingering just a moment longer before he stood up and headed back over to the recliner, dropping down and sinking into it for his desperately needed rest.

***

Douglass and Cassidy were both startled awake by an inordinately loud crash. The two kids jerked their heads up in search of the source.

Oliver wobbled next to the fridge, staring down at a bunch of glass that seemingly appeared out of nowhere in front of him.

"Warb! Warb warb warb warb warb!" Warblass warbed warb warb and warbed warbing warb Warbidy warb warba warb.

Douglass grabbed Oliver by the shoulders and sat him back down on the bed, "are you okay? Are you hurt?"

".....warb." Oliver lolled his head, clearly struggling to keep his focus on Douglass, as the boy bent forward and clasped his hands around his face.

"Oh my god your pupils are *huge*." Douglass glanced back at Cassidy, who was already throwing the broken glass into the trash. "What's wrong with him?"

Cassidy looked over, prompting him to twist Oliver's head to also look at her. He hummed some little murmur of laughter, before he dipped down into Douglass's chest.

"He mentioned she was drugging people, so that's probably what those big tanks were…at least he isn't dead," she remarked with a shrug. She tossed the last of the glass into the trash and came to sit nearby on the couch, "It'll probably wear off in a couple hours."

Oliver reared his head back, making some ungodly gurgling noise, before an uncomfortable amount of drool sputtered out of his mouth.

"DON'T STOP BELIE- ohhh wait, I think thas copyrighted…." He was exuberantly intoxicated.

He butted his head into Douglass's chest a few more times, at least until Douglass filed his hands between himself and Oliver's face in order to gently push him away. "You sure? We don't know how strong it is...or how much of it he—"

He stopped himself, the ugly flash of his memory forcing itself up. The way Matthew lunged forward. *He was going to kill him. He..wanted to kill him…* "we don't know how much he..swallowed."

Douglass glanced back at Oliver, who still dumbly pressed his slobbery face into his hand. "You think it might be permanent?"

Cassidy began grabbing her things, "you should read up more on drugs, if it was a sedative— which it probably is, considering she was hooking people up to that plant thing. Then it won't last more than a few days. He *should* be back to normal by like, Tuesday. "

"H-how do you know that?"

Cassidy narrowed her eyes at his stupid remark, "Jen is a surgeon. And Maman shows up to addict calls all the time for her social work, you just gotta keep an eye on him for a while and make sure he doesn't run off or something."

She backed up toward the door, slinging her back pack over her shoulder. Douglass reached out though, in a feeble attempt to stop her.

"Wait, you're just gonna leave?!" Oliver dropped face first into his lap, causing him to squeal a bit at the sudden extra weight.

"Uhmm…" Cassidy's eyes flickered from Douglass to Oliver and back. "Yes."

And with that, she left him.

Douglass heaved a beleaguered sigh and dropped back on the bed, lamenting the fact that Oliver was still totally out of it, and the only person capable of helping him just bounced. An alien clown was most definitely hunting them. And school started in a couple days.

Part of him dearly hoped that she wouldn't share any of this online. *What am I kidding? She probably has tons of fellow conspiracy theorist friends who would gobble up the news of alien influences the moment it hit the scene. She probably only helped for that reason alone.*

"Don't stop……belieeevin'."

Sweet god almighty.

"How you doing, Oliver?" Douglass asked, reluctant to lift his head or even open his eyes. He felt the boy sit up and slap his hand down on his thigh.

"I am…very *very* very very VeRy VERY *very*……..*very* good." He answered, plopping back down next to him.

It's gonna be a…day.

weekend with Oliver

"Stay right there, no— in here, right— ugh," Douglass grabbed the teetering boy and led him back to the recliner, forcefully sitting him down in it before even attempting to leave. He let go of his hands, and Oliver promptly tried to stand back up, only for him to lose balance and fall back into the chair with a delirious little giggle.

"Wh...her, where ya goin?" he asked, attempting to poke Douglass in the forehead, before he caught Oliver's hand and placed it back on the arm rest.

"I'm going to talk to my dad, I will be *right* back. Don't move, okay?" Douglass took a step back, awkwardly keeping his hands on Oliver's to make sure he stayed put before finally letting go.

"Can I get a treat?"

He let out a soft sigh and nodded, "what do you want?"

"Ruh..ruegihl—"

"Rugelach?" Douglass guessed, watching him nodd a little too enthusiastically. "Hanukkah is over, I don't have any left over from break, I'm sorry."

"Aww..thas okahy." Oliver leaned back into the chair and dropped his head, looking way more upset and pouty than he reasonably should. *Oh geez. That's adorable.*

Douglass averted his eyes, trying very very hard not to turn as red as he imagined he was and briskly nodded, "I'll get you something better, okay?"

"Mmhhmmmmokay."

Douglass backed his way out the door, slowly creeping it closed until he was absolutely certain Oliver wasn't going to get out and run off somewhere without his constant supervision.

Then, he dashed into his house.

"Dad?" Douglass called through the back screen door, leaning back to catch a view of the driveway and the distinct lack of his father's pick up truck. *He must…still be at work.*

The thought unnerved him, how close they were to danger.

But Douglass pressed on and made his way into his home, down the small hall that led from the back of the house toward the kitchen and began on a meal he was absolutely certain would ingratiate a very intoxicated Oliver into a hopefully more…subdued state.

Douglass dug into the pantry and began pulling out the biggest pot he could find before he was forced to stop by the inevitable lack of knowledge he had when it came to cooking anything that wasn't fall-apart latkes and pre-made oven lasagna. Oliver was a markedly better cook than him, and he wasn't entirely sure he could even come close to expectations mimicking Jon's feel good curry.

So, Douglass decidedly grabbed his phone to look up the closest thing he could find.

"Oh jeez," he groaned lightly at the list of ingredients he knew for a fact didn't exist in his own cabinets.

Douglass cocked his head. *I can probably find it in the cabin.*

With quick haste and a tad bit of hesitation, Douglass trotted over to the cabin to steal any and all spices and ingredients that he figured he would need.

He came back carting them precariously in his hands and trying to pull the door open with his feet before he turned heel and was met with a dopey and startlingly close Oliver.

"O— Oliver?! What—" Douglass juggled his armful of spices. "I told you to stay in the shed!"

Oliver merely blinked, one eye at a time while a wobbly smile spread across his lips.

"Whudyo doing?" He asked, shuffling to follow Douglass into the kitchen.

"I'm making you— us food, can you—" he paused to set his spices down on the nearest countertop and stop Oliver from putting his hand directly down the garbage disposal. "Can you *please* go back to the shed?"

Douglass tugged the boy away from the kitchen and toward the hallway, hoping to get him back into their hiding spot before he were caught outside for too long.

Oliver was seemingly under an entirely different impression though and instead of doing what Douglass wanted, he simply leaned into him, pressing the back of his hand to his forehead in the most dramatic way possible.

"They stood foh some time withouht speaking a wohd; and she began to imagine that their silence was to last through the two dahhnces, and at first was resssssolved not to break it." Oliver spouted off in a ludicrously posh british accent and Douglass felt the boy force all his weight on him.

"Are you—" Douglass cut himself off with a gracious eye roll and twisted around to catch Oliver before he fell straight back into the floor. "Are you quoting P and P?"

"Till sudd…dendly fancying that it would be the greater punish— punishment to her pahtner to oblaiiige him to talk, she made some slight observation on the dance." Oliver continued, throwing his head back with the most adorable giggle Douglass had ever heard in his life. He nodded lackadaisically and continued. "He replied, and was again silent. After a pause of *some* minutes, she addressed him a second time with—"

Oliver cut himself off, leveling his head, or at least trying to. "You say it."

"What?" Douglass blinked, shifting under Oliver's weight.

"It's your turn now," he replied with a level of seriousness one would assume belonged to a sober person.

Douglass nodded slowly, reaching back through the catalog of his memory in effort to figure out which part of Pride and Prejudice Oliver was reciting off.

Dance..dance….sounds like, uhm, volume one? God there are so many dances..

"It is…your?" Douglass watched the way Oliver's whole face lit up with pure glee at his quote guessing. "Your turn to say something Mr. Darcy?"

Oliver nodded vigorously and stood straight, albeit with a slight stumble, and pulled Douglass along with him to start into the most poorly coordinated dance one could ever dance.

"I talked about the dance, and you ought to make some kind of remark on the size of the room, or the number of couples." Douglass continued, opting to indulge a mock accent to match Oliver's slurred speech.

"Very well. That reply will do for the present. Perhaps by and by I may observe that private…haha…*balls* are much pleasantah than public ones. But now we may be silent." Oliver giggled and stumbled around Douglass as the two of them haphazardly waltzed away from the kitchen.

Though, a vast majority of their maneuvers were really just Douglass trying his absolute damndest to dance Oliver back to the shed. Despite the fact that his heart fluttered every time Oliver swung close enough that he could feel his breath on his chest.

"Do you talk by rule then, while you are dancing?" Douglass quoted softly, failing to hide the smile in his voice. He spun his friend out and gently directed the two of them into the garage.

Oliver's childish and dizzy squeals cut out for a moment as he twirled back into his arms and bonked his head on Douglass's chin. It did nothing to deter his enthused scene-play.

"Sahhmetimes. One must speak…uh little, y'know. It would look odd to be entahrely silent for half an hour together, and yet for the advantage of *some*, conversation ought to be so arranged as that they may have the trouboh of saying as littoh as as possible." Oliver replied giddily.

Douglass casually circled the two of them onto the back patio, until he had managed to dance Oliver all the way back into the shed.

He put his hands on Oliver's shoulders to press him back down into the recliner and watched the boy's face scrunch in slight frustration.

"I forgot what comes after." Oliver pouted.

"It's alright," Douglass consoled him and moved back toward the door. Oliver caught him with those big, tired eyes though, and held him standing half out the door.

"Remind me?"

"It's 'Are you consulting your own feelings in the present case, or do you imagine that you are gratifying mine?'" He answered sweetly, and the way Oliver's whole face seemed to beam with that bright and dopey grin made Douglass's insides rot like he'd eaten six pounds of candy.

"Ah....I love you."

"Hhh..."Douglass's breath hitched before he managed to finish his shaky inhale at how intoxicatingly sweet those words rolled off Oliver's tongue.

He stared at him for a moment. Lost on how to respond, whether he should at all...with what he wanted to.

"I...I love you too, Ols."

***

After grappling with...*that,* Douglass finished making his curry and swiftly headed back to the shed, pulling the door open with his elbow so he could get all the way in without having to make two trips.

"Oh my GOD, *OLIVER*⁉!" Thank goodness he chose lidded containers, because the second he opened the door he was greeted by a very confused, startled, and shirtless Oliver.

Douglass immediately covered his eyes, grabbing the nearest semi-long fabric and throwing it over him before he slid around the wall toward a small shelf full of old clothes.

"I need to rip my skin off," the boy complained through the blanket, blindly reaching out for something to grab and help balance himself.

"No! You don't!" Douglass replied, keeping his eyes firmly planted on the ground as he watched the sheet he dropped on top of him fall down, "you *need* to put clothes on!"

He felt a hand drop down on top of his head and quickly clenched his eyes shut, pulling an old T-shirt down over his friend's head before even attempting to open them again. When he looked up again, Oliver's huge eyes stared at him, dilating back and forth in futile effort to focus on something.

"You are *so* nice!" He grinned, coming a little too close for comfort. Douglass dipped down and around him, scrambling to grab the meals he brought and quickly shoved it into his hands.

"So nice...so...*soup*." Oliver plopped down on the recliner and set the container in his lap, apparently unable to comprehend opening it. Douglass heaved a sigh and took it from him, opening up the clasps and handing it back with a spoon.

"*Please*...keep your clothes on?" He begged quietly, moving to set up the dvd player so it could hopefully keep Oliver from undressing again. He didn't reply.

"Oliver?" Douglass turned around, and immediately saw the couple of seconds before the boy's whole face twisted up and turned red and blotchy with unfettered tears.

"Hey," he said, dropping the task at hand to try and comfort the sudden switch in the boy's mood. "Hey, I'm sorry, I'm not mad at you, I swear—"

"It's not fair!" Oliver cut in, struggling to hold his soup and also cry at the same time. Douglass gently took the container from him and set it on the end table.

"It's okay, I just wasn't—"

"Why are you so good?! You areh..arsuchagoodperson! You got me so-soup!? I love soup! Hhh-howd you know??"

Wait. What??

Douglass blinked, trying to figure out why he was crying over soup. He knelt down, and glanced at the bowl on the table.

"Uh..you said it was your favorite?"

"Exactly!! I like soup *sooo* much and you just knew it, and you made me some. That is just..so! Niiiiccce!"

"It's just soup?" Douglass shrugged, trying to come to terms with the current, very unusual friend of his. Oliver's hands grabbed his face, stealing his attention away from his thoughts and pulled him close.

"I want your skin." *That's...not creepy at all.* Douglass squirmed, prompting Oliver to wriggle off the recliner until he slid down to the floor, still staring into his eyes, completely unflinching.

The poor kid turned flush under his intoxicated gaze, and quickly dropped his eyes down to the ground.

That is, until Oliver pulled him even closer and stuck his tongue out, licking nearly half of Douglass's face before he even realized it.

He pulled away and shoved his hand over Oliver's head, to which the kid promptly licked that too, causing Douglass to yank it back and wipe the slobber on his pants.

"What is wrong with you?!" He snapped, staring back at him, utterly flabbergasted and completely flustered.

"I'm so jealous off yuu," Oliver replied, attempting to reach a hand up, which Douglass just as quickly pulled back down into his lap. "Yooouu..yor so so good, and kind and nice. And I'm so bad and mean, and I think yuer soho nic— righ, y know?"

His head lolled a bit, and he blinked a few times as if he were trying to stay awake. "Also you're reheal..like *really* real, a real one, and I'm... wanna be you so bad."

"...Oliver," Douglass softened his grip, finally understanding on some level what he was talking about, despite the horrendous slurring of his speech.

"Thas why— thas why I need tuh say sorry. But yooouuu can't say anything cause shell bee sososoSOo mad if you do, promis?" The delirious kid cupped his hand around his mouth and came close, fanning out his other hand as he pressed into Douglass's chest.

"For— for what?" Douglass felt his heart pace up lightly and he shuffled away from Oliver, who only leaned more into him.

"I'll do it," Oliver whispered through his hand, putting even more of his weight on the boy's torso.

"We can do sorry kisses—"

What?

Douglass pushed Oliver back on his knees, cutting him off with the abrupt change in position.

Oliver blinked, wriggling his hands in his friend's grasp, then he just stared at him. Like he was waiting.

Except he shook, ever so slightly, and Douglass wouldn't have even noticed if he weren't holding the kid's arms away so he'd stop trying to touch him.

"But," Oliver said, "it doesn't mean anything if I don't show you."

What are you trying to say?

Douglass watched the cogs slowly turn over in his friend's head, some visceral realization flickering over Oliver's face before he became very still and very quiet.

"I wish she stopped him."

They were small words, and there was so much sadness in his voice that Douglass felt compelled to give the kid a tight hug. He really deserved one.

"..Oliver, I—"

"I know, right? Ss's crazy!" Oliver cut him off with a heartbreakingly inappropriate giggle. He leaned back, holding himself up with his hands as he stared down at the ground. "Now I'm not evinah...person. issucks. BuddI'mgonna die soonly..."

Oliver's face twisted up with concern and he flashed a look of distress at Douglass before he leaned forward, clambering over him in an attempt to get to the door.

"I need to check on my babies!"

"Wh-what? What babies?" Douglass sucked in a gasp as Oliver's weight crashed down on him and he swiftly grabbed his shirt, then his hand, in case he tried to worm his way out of the shirt.

"Bacon, Pancake, Egg and Sausage they're muh chullren!" he replied, trying to wrench himself free from Douglass's grasp.

"Your *cats*?!"

"Mah bahbs!" Oliver cried, sitting back on his knees, "I missem sohhhuh muhuhuch!"

He began to sob again, plastering his palms against his face in a terribly bad effort to wipe away his tears. Douglass sat up and crawled around him.

"You can't, it's not safe."

"Don TELL me wut toh do!" He retorted, pulling him aside as he crawled toward the door and pushed it open. Oliver tumbled out into the grass and got up, staggering and stumbling haphazardly toward his house. "I am a *GOOD* dad!"

Imposter Syndrome

Oliver meandered in some erratic serpentine fashion toward his house until he stumbled onto the porch, and made a little mewling noise to call his cats. One by one, each and every one of them crawled out from under the porch and swarmed him, probably expecting a meal. Oliver had decided to make himself comfortable though, and laid down on the porch to stare up at the stars.

"You shouldn't be here," Douglass urged quietly. He glanced around, dreading that Poppy was anywhere nearby. "Come on, let's go ba—"

"Look, it's Dibdet," Oliver interrupted him with a content little hum. He flung his arm up and pointed at the night sky. "She's made of stars."

"That's cool, now—"

"Shhhuuuhhhshhh...she's *sleeping*." Oliver pulled his arm back and patted Douglass's face until he gave up on trying to convince him to come back. By now, all four of his cats had made themselves comfortable on top of him. And in his current state, Douglass doubted Oliver could muster the conviction to disturb a single one.

So, he laid back next to him and stared up at the sparkling sky as well.

"Why did she come here?" He asked, not really expecting an

answer. Nonetheless, Oliver turned his head to face him with a dopey, tired smile.

"Dunno, sheesaid I asked 'ertoo," he replied. He then looked back up at the sky and gestured exasperatedly toward it, "why *did* you come here?"

The sky didn't reply.

"Firgurs," Oliver huffed softly, resting his hand down on the fluffy Pancake to pet, and his currently very short attention span turned to the cat. "Pancake yuuh got fat."

Oliver rolled back in his back and picked up the cat so she stood like a little person on his chest. "Can oo be…preganté?"

"You think—"

"I was that…once."

…what?

Douglass turned his head to look at the boy, but his focus was solely in the cat as he fiddled with her paws quietly.

"Matthew made me, but issall gonnow cuz I went to the hospisle." Oliver continued softly, almost as though he was somewhat sober, and a silence drifted over the two of them.

Douglass sat up, that ugly realization dawning on him and making his whole chest ache. *That's what—*

His head burned at the thought, and it made his face fold and wince at the *lie* Oliver had told him. He sucked down a nasty little breath to hide his sob.

"Awweee," Oliver's voice drifted over the night and he pulled himself to his knees, crawling over to Douglass to press a compassionate hand to his back. "Don cry, why're you sad?"

Douglass's head dipped slightly, his aching heart turning over into soft rage at Oliver's delirium. *How could he? Why— why didn't he…*

"Issokay—"

"No!" Douglass shot, twisting out of the boy's intoxicated effort to console him. He stood up. "No, okay? No, it's not and you have to go back inside, Oliver. No more playing with your cats or— or talking to the *stupid* stars. I'm done. I want to go home."

Oliver blinked up at him like a toddler that had only just realized they were in trouble.

"..okay.."

***

"Cheri, Qu'est-ce qui ne va pas?" Naya stood in Cassidy's doorway as the girl furiously typed on her laptop. "You got home so early yesterday, did you and Lilly have a fight?"

"No," Cassidy replied, not even looking up from her computer, "everything is fine, I'm just doing some research, is all."

It was half a lie, she was definitely doing research, and things definitely were *not* fine. However, she was certain she hid the adrenaline induced shaking under her blanket.

"Don't lie to me, Cas." *Crap.*

Her mother shook her head, not believing it for a moment and stepped into the room, "you're shaking, did something scare you? Did someone try to hurt you?"

"Maman," Cassidy shot a subtle glare at her and pulled her legs into a criss-cross as her mother sat down on her bed. "I swear, I'm okay, personne n'a essayé de me blesser."

"D'accord, d'accord," Naya rubbed her leg gently, "I just want to make sure everything's alright with you, and if it's not I'd like for you to tell me, cheri."

Cassidy lolled her head and let out a soft sigh, "My friend got hurt recently and he's really sick right now, but Douglass is taking care of him."

It was a small admittance, but nothing that would tip her off to the real situation— *and even then, she probably wouldn't believe it.*

"Oh, is he gonna be okay?"

"I think so, Douglass was texting me earlier about him, and said he thinks he'll be okay tomorrow? But they're staying home from school anyways." Cassidy closed the forum page she was on and opened up another one to hide what she was looking at. "I'm just worried about him."

"I understand," Naya nodded and paused for a moment,

offering a reassuring smile, "I'm sure everything is gonna be okay, and maybe after school you can go visit him?"

"Maybe.."

Definitely not.

If she went to visit Oliver, either Naya or Jen would want to accompany her and their cover would most certainly be blown. For now, Cassidy prefered to relegate herself to simple reconnaissance. To make sure no one got close to them. *Especially since Poppy is still out there.*

***

The next morning, Cassidy made her way to school, gliding past the entrance and kicking up her board to shove in her bag before heading in. Every so often she checked her phone, hoping for a message from Douglass saying he was either coming or not, but from the looks of it, he was probably still asleep, and as far as she was aware, their bus was usually the last to arrive.

She hung outside by the flagpole for a while, glancing around to see if either of them were among the other students that filed one by one off the bus.

"Cas! Did you do the English homework? I completely forgot!" Her friend Lilly grabbed her shoulder, causing Cassidy to instinctively jump and throw her hand away.

"Oh my god, did you like, fight someone?" She remarked, pulling her hand back to her side at the girl's obvious startle. "Who was it? I bet it was Theo, right? Omygodsheissuchabitch!"

"No! I didn't fight anyone, and don't say that! You don't know her." Cassidy shot back, following her as she made her way into the building. "I just had a really wild weekend."

"Don't tell me, you and that weeb kid— Douglass right? You hooked up! I saw you go home with him, did he ask you out or something? Oh! Did you guys *kiss*?" Lilly prodded her, "isn't he neighbors with Olivia— I mean Oliver? Did you go to his house? Is it really a murder road?"

"I didn't, and it's not a murder road, he just asked me for some help with a school project." She lied, rolling her eyes at the girl's assumptions. "And he doesn't like me like that, and I don't like him like that either."

Cassidy narrowed her eyes with a sly little smile, "but if you're jealous...I *can* put in a good word for you?"

Lilly snorted loudly and shook her head, "No way. There's no way I would go for him cause like, me and Jonathan have it really good!"

"Right, *Jonathan*," Cassidy remarked sarcastically, "your very real boyfriend from Michiglenn."

"He is totally real! I showed you pictures and everything!"

"You do know photo editors are a thi—" Cassidy came to a halt, catching sight of Oliver just as he strolled into class.

"What?" Lilly circled around her, trying to follow her gaze to the kid that most certainly wasn't supposed to be here.

"Nothing." She lied, immediately pulling her phone out to shoot a text to Douglass.

Cassidy slowed her pace, cautiously making her way into the classroom while her eyes stayed trained on Oliver, who looked more or less the same as usual, if not slightly more grumpy.

Class went on as it almost always did, and no one seemed to bat an eye, and she hadn't gotten a reply yet from Douglass. *Where is he? What's going on??*

There's no way he'd just stay home unless something happened last night, right? Did Poppy get to them?

"Have fun at the crazy house?" Theo twisted around in her chair and flicked Oliver's nose, briefly pulling Cassidy's attention away from the message she was typing. Oliver glared at her but didn't answer.

"I saw the school therapist and you leave a few weeks ago, probably because *someone* had to do something." She readjusted herself so she could face him better, and donned an ugly mean smile. "I mean, obviously *something* is wrong with you."

At this point, Cassidy would be one to interrupt, but instead she stayed quiet, watching Theo reach forward to flick the boy again before his hand caught hers and thrust it down on the desk.

Oliver stood up and leaned forward, tightening his grip on her wrist.

"You're only rude to me because my existence confuses and frustrates you," He said, far too calmly, "you've been raised your whole life by your father to think that everyone has to fit into a specific little box, and anyone who falls outside of it doesn't deserve to live, *including* you."

"Hh-wh—" Theo's eyes flickered back toward the door and Cassidy sat up in her chair, turning her full attention to the two of them.

"And the fact that I exist so close to you reminds you of how terrified you are to fall outside that same little box, so you lash out at me to keep yourself in check. But no matter what you say or do, there is always that underlying fear. And your unjustified rage has led to some twisted kind of attraction, because deep down, you *know* you fall out of that box." Oliver leaned forward, and dropped his voice slightly.

"Here's a tip," he breathed, still keeping his grip on her arm as the girl anxiously leaned away from him. "Find a different person to like."

Oliver's eyes flitted back toward Cassidy and he dropped Theo's hand, promptly standing up to leave before the bell rang, signaling the return of a teacher.

Cassidy glanced down at her phone, praying that Douglass had replied within the few moments that whatever *that* was happened, but he hadn't, and she had a terrible hunch that this 'Oliver' was an imposter.

She waited until he left, and quietly crept out of her desk, ignoring the faces that turned to stare at her as she followed him out of the room. The class's hushed whispers grew as she closed the door, turning their attention away from the two of them and onto the recipient of the imposter's quiet wrath.

Cassidy sped up her pace, keeping sure to remain as far out of sight as she could while she tailed the kid. She even made sure to duck back behind the corners of the hall, just to be certain he didn't see her.

Oliver was mean, yeah, but never so scathing— especially toward Theo, who Cassidy was certain he didn't even bother to give the time of day. For as long as she knew him, or tried to at least, he wasn't one to confront her— or anyone for that matter, about their unpleasant views of him.

She was pretty sure he would rather just ignore it.

The other Oliver rounded a corner toward the bathroom, prompting Cassidy to follow. But the moment she made the turn, a blue ball came hurtling toward her, forcing her to dodge and stumble backward directly into him, where he definitely wasn't before.

The fake caught the ball and shoved her back against the tile wall, pressing his arm up to her neck with a terribly inhuman strength.

"You stole my bait," he hissed through gritted teeth, loosening his hold just enough for her to answer. "*Where* are you hiding it?"

"Like I'd tell you!" Cassidy spat, pushing back as hard as she possibly could, to no avail.

Poppy blinked, and cocked her head, "I don't need you to."

The alien pressed its fingers onto Cassidy's forehead, sifting through her thoughts rather effortlessly in order to find out where they had taken its leverage. Then, it let go completely, taking a step back before it vanished from in front of her.

Cassidy drew in a quick gasp, struggling to still her trembling as she fished for her phone. Immediately, she dialed Douglass.

"Come on, come on, come on! Pick up!" She breathed, trying to grab hold of her scattered thoughts. The ringing stopped.

"Hello!"

"Douglass! Poppy found me, she's pretending to be Oliver, don't go outside, don't go anywhere, and don't—"

"Sorry I missed your call, but it was probably important..uh, I don't know how to work the voice-mail so don't bother leaving a message, I guess. Bye!"

"Bon dieu!" *it went to voice-mail!?* Cassidy hung up and quickly made her way toward the fire alarm and pulled the lever, setting off a god awful ringing out and throughout the entire school.

The halls filled with confused students and teachers, who were scrambling to keep track of their classes as all of them headed toward the various doors, allowing Cassidy to slip in among them and easily leave the school entirely.

It would be at least forty-five minutes before they caught on that she was gone, and they'd probably call her moms, thinking she went home, but she was already tearing down the pavement straight toward Douglass's house.

Letting Go of Things

Oliver groaned, peeling his eyes open to stare at a vaguely familiar ceiling.

"Oh my god, I want to die," he muttered softly, trying to recollect what had happened between his rescue and subsequent escape.

Douglass sat on the recliner in the makeshift guest house. It was late, or at least he assumed, because the skylight was dark.

Douglass's head swiveled around to stare at him. "Hey, you're back."

"This is Jojo's old room," Oliver mumbled, glancing around the small shed, "we're at your house?"

"Yeah..." Douglass rubbed his neck, trying to hide the fact that he'd been sitting there for hours, thinking only about what happened while Oliver was at the hospital with Poppy...and Matthew. "I couldn't just take you home, and my dad never comes in here anymore, so..."

"Is..Poppy still out there?"

"...yeah," he admitted softly, "she hasn't come anywhere near here, so I think we're safe if we stay put."

Oliver hunched forward, and quickly sucked in a gasp at the wretched pang in his chest. He attempted to twist around, but buckled and winced with the effort, prompting Douglass to hurry to the cabinet for some high strength pain medication.

"You— you electrocuted her and passed out." Douglass offered him the pills, and headed over toward the microwave to heat up some leftover curry noodles. "When you woke up again you weren't really complaining about pain— I mean, you *did* say you wanted to rip your skin off, but I figured that was...for a different reason."

Oliver lifted up his shirt to inspect and drew in a small gasp at his mottled, bruised skin. He promptly dropped it back down once Douglass returned with the soup. "Are– are you okay?"

Douglass didn't answer, he simply gave a little lie of a smile and handed him a bowl of soup along with a spoon, then wandered back to the recliner to continue watching whatever movie he was watching.

Oliver stared at him for a moment. He could tell something was off, wrong. Douglass was abnormally quiet. It put an unease in him that made bringing it up hard to do.

So he focused on the meal he'd been brought. "This is coconut chicken curry."

"Yeah, you said you really liked it, so I made you some," Douglass mentioned, not looking up from the television.

"...Yeah, it's my favorite." He glanced up, turning his attention away from the meal and back toward Douglass, who was purposefully keeping his gaze on the TV. Oliver set his bowl down and slid out of the bed, only to close the bit of distance between them. "Why– why didn't you take me home?"

Douglass gulped, forcing down the soup so he wouldn't choke on his own reluctance to answer. "...They took Jon."

"Oh.." Oliver placed his bowl on the end table next to Douglass.

Douglass deliberately moved away from him, setting his spoon back into his bowl. "I haven't seen anyone at the cabin...for days."

Oliver hesitated, watching the boy quietly stir his food. He dropped down in the chair next to him and the two ate in incomparably awkward silence, at least until Douglass made a small noise and fished something out of his pocket.

"I almost forgot, since you're not all weird anymore," he opened his palm, showing off Dindet's little orange bean inside. "I figured you'd probably want it back."

Oliver stared at it, gently plucking the precious thing from his hand. "Thanks."

Another silence drifted over the two of them, and both Oliver and Douglass shifted uncomfortably in it, trying to find a topic of conversation that felt manageable. They couldn't. And Douglass couldn't leave his idle thoughts alone.

"You don't trust me," he finally said, glancing back at Oliver as he grew still with discomfort.

The boy stared at his curry quietly, stirring it every now and then as he worked to come up with a response.

"I don't...I don't understand?" Oliver asked, hesitant to take a sip from his spoon.

"You. Don't. Trust. Me." Douglass reiterated, his gaze never straying from Oliver's look of confusion.

"I—"

"No, *listen* Oliver," he cut in, setting his bowl down so he wouldn't risk spilling it. "You don't trust *anyone* and you lie, and pretend, and just act like— like everything is fine, when it's not. And I have been trying to figure out *why!* I can't tell if it's because you're afraid, or because you hate yourself *so much* that—"

"Douglass, I—"

"I'm not done, let me talk!" Douglass shot a small glare at him, forcing Oliver to close in on himself in preparation. "You *scared* me, you scared me so much when she took you. You pushed me away— like you always do. And I just— I want to help you, but you don't even want to help *yourself!* It's like as soon as something bad happens, instead of talking to anyone about it, you just wall yourself off and act like it doesn't affect you. And it just builds and builds until you blow up at the people who are actually *trying* to help! Why are you so— so *intent* on making sure no one wants to be around you? Why are you so mean to yourself? All it does is make you mean to everyone else. Do you like being this way?"

"I— no, Douglass, I'm sorry—"

"Are you?" Douglass cut in, his frustration growing as his

thoughts mounted up on each other. "Cause you say that, but I don't think it means what you think it means."

"I...what?" Oliver blinked, searching the boy's face for the meaning behind his words. Instead Douglass just wiped his mouth and looked away.

"Forget it."

"Douglass.." Oliver dropped his gaze, thumbing the small orange thing in his palm. "I— I don't..you shouldn't have to worry about me because—"

"No!" Douglass cut in, preventing Oliver from his attempt at any kind of misguided argument. "Why do you just– just make it okay?! How can you—"

"BECAUSE I HAVE TO!" Oliver shouted, forcing Douglass into silence as he ran his shaking hands through his hair. "I have to hurt because if I don't– if I don't, what else am I? How do I exist? How do I really know? What is left??"

He trembled and fidgeted, heaving short, painful breaths in effort to calm down as he tried to iterate why he needed so badly to be hurt. Why he deserved it. "I'm sorry...I'm *really* sorry."

"No, you aren't," Douglass huffed defiantly. "You apologize, over and over, but you don't actually change. All you do is justify the way you act, so how am I supposed to trust you, when you can't even be honest with *yourself*?"

"I can show you, I can prove it!" Oliver pleaded, "I can be sorry, I can do that! I can show you, okay? I'll be better I swear! I'll do anything!"

"Then *be* better, Oliver." Douglass shot a glare at him and closed in on himself, stealing away the boy's desire for comfort when he reached for him. "Show me you're actually sorry and— and *be* better."

Oliver sniffled and dropped his gaze to the floor.
Douglass was quiet for a moment, and when his eyes flickered up to see him, the boy was facing the television with a soft sorrow on his face.

"I...don't know how..." he admitted quietly.

Oliver slinked closer, drawing Douglass's attention when his fingers glided up against his arm and grabbed his shirt, as if to beg for his attention. "Please show me?"

Douglass stared back at him and his pathetic, tear stricken face. It was almost infuriating. He deliberately looked away from him and pulled Oliver's hand off of himself. "I can't."

"What?"

"I can't show you. I can't do it *for you,* and I don't want to, Oliver." Douglass drew in a breath and brushed his fingers through his curls. "I want...so badly for you to be happy. You have no idea how much I want that. And I am so scared, constantly, that I will never get to see that...because you won't ever let yourself *be* that. You are..so obsessed with this idea that some other person is going to come along and just fix you. Fix everything for you. If it's me, or Jon, or Dindet...or your mom."

Douglass paused, his gaze flickering back at his friend and his silent introspection. His anger had faded now, and he couldn't help but only feel pity for him. Oliver wasn't a bad person, but he wasn't a good one either.

"You're the only person who can fix you. But you have to want to."

Oliver stared at the floor, closed off and so incredibly quiet for so long.

"Douglass?"

"Yeah?" Douglass watched as the boy shifted slightly, the trembling of his arms that folded around his knees to pull them close. A few stray tears ran down his cheek, but he made no attempt to wipe them away.

"Can you...leave me alone for a while..please..." It wasn't a request, and Oliver didn't look at at him at all. So Douglass simply nodded and obliged, hoping that when he came back, the conversation could take a more positive turn.

After a while of looking for more bad romance movies to hopefully lighten the mood, Douglass pushed the shed door back open, and stopped in his tracks, searching the immediate area for the kid who was precisely nowhere to be found.

…no.

***

Oliver came to a stop at the edge of the same cliff he had gone up with Douglass before, except now it was dark out and the sky shone with a terrible brilliance that only reminded him of Dindet.

It was spring, but still cold enough that his bare feet had gone numb long before he reached this height. he could see the lights of the suburb a few miles away, and the cliff edge that continued along, snaking around the lake toward the other side of town.

He sat down on the cold ground, chucking little pebbles off the edge while he contemplated.

Douglass's words rocked around in his head. He was right, of course. Douglass was almost always right and it often hurt, but never so much as it did right now. It felt as though the hole Dindet spoke of had grown so large that he'd been long since swallowed up by it. And the prospect of even trying to combat that gentle sinking emptiness was terrifying.

Oliver rolled the little orange bean in his palm.

She's…better off without me.

He let out a discontent sigh, getting to his feet to stare over the cliff's edge. The ground was dark and inviting, and terrifying all at once. He was going to die anyway, but the idea that he had any choice in the matter was enticing. For a brief moment.

"Don't."

Douglass's voice stopped him, and he stumbled a bit from the shock of his voice in the night.

Oliver swiveled around to face the kid and he couldn't help but chuckle, in the way he did when it was the only option that wasn't crying. "I should probably be grateful."

"Were you going to kill yourself?" Douglass asked, this time softly, with no ounce of anger in his voice.

Oliver let out a soft sigh. He didn't want to answer him.

"I don't want to," he admitted, trying to smile through the statement so he didn't think on it too long. "Objectively."

"But I deserve it, right?" Oliver continued, "I break people... I broke Dindet...and Jon, and– and my mom...I'll probably break you too...if I haven't already...I wasn't supposed to last this long anyway."

Oliver folded in on himself, sucking in a quiet breath at how much it hurt to say. "So…being there...made it feel like I was getting what I deserved."

"Don't you think you've been punished enough?" Douglass questioned, pulling the boy's attention back to him with a small and empty gaze. "Sure, you do bad things sometimes, and push people away. You've hurt people. Everyone does at some point. So why should you have to die? It isn't fair."

"I'm going to regardless, Poppy said—"
"Poppy's full of shit," Douglass interrupted, causing Oliver to move his gaze over the edge of the cliff as his friend continued, "Poppy, or Matthew, they aren't the ones who should get to decide what you do, or how you live. That's a choice you make, right? So—"

"I'm *going* to die, Douglass." Oliver interrupted, briefly flickering his eyes back to the boy.

"I… I was *supposed* to die. That's why they came here, the Clowns. To stop her from starting it all over again." he continued.

The boy curled in on himself in the wind, digging his nails into his tender and bruised skin as the thought buried itself deep in his head.

"Our whole world, It's all a big loop. That's why… you can't worry anymore. You can't waste your time on me anymore.."

"Oliver," Douglass stopped him, closing the distance between them and filing his fingers between his. "You're the prettiest, and *dumbest* boy I've ever met."

Oliver blinked, completely unprepared for the remark, or the way Douglass wrapped his arms around him and pulled him close. It was gentle, and kind. And he was warm. Safe.

"You have *never* been a waste of my time." Douglass's voice was quiet, whispering in Oliver's ear as he stroked the knotted scar on his forehead. "Don't ever let yourself believe you are."

Oliver drew in a painful, staggered breath.

"Go home, Douglass…please."

"No." He answered flatly, causing the kid to take a step away. "I'm not gonna do that. Not without you."

"I–" Oliver's throat closed and a horrific, familiar sensation lit his veins on fire the moment all his muscles contracted and began to move without his permission. Tears pooled in his eyes.

Poppy.

His mouth clamped shut so tightly and abruptly that he could feel the grating of his teeth.

"Oliver?" Douglass blinked, caught off guard by the sudden look of terror that gripped his friend. "What's wrong?"

"S-stop.." Oliver attempted to glance back, feeling the traces of wet ice on his heels as he was forced to take a life threatening step backward. "Stop me!"

Douglass's eyes widened and he bolted forward in effort to close the small gap between them. His hands caught Oliver's shirt, just before he unwillingly tipped back, losing his footing.

The boy's fingers dug into Douglass's arm, and he struggled to balance himself and Oliver on the thin layer of ice over the edge of the cliff that seemed far more dangerous than a few very short seconds prior.

"Don't let me fall!" Oliver clawed desperately against the will forcibly imposed on him. "Douglass, please— don't let me fall."

"I won't!" Douglass heaved, gathering all his weight and strength into pulling the terrified kid back from the edge he half dangled over. He was heavy, and getting heavier by the second.

Every fiber of Douglass's body shrieked with the effort it took just to keep him there. Oliver's nails dug deep into his arms, stinging and burning them with the sheer pressure of gravity compounded by his weight.

Douglass's eyes flitted over the cliff side, how far it went down, hundreds and hundreds of feet, to a rocky death. Oliver followed his gaze, and grappled with the boy's shirt in a desperate attempt to keep his ever dwindling grip on him.

"Douglass." His voice was soft and quiet, and rattled with the unadulterated fear in it. It drew Douglass's attention back to Oliver and the two of them stared at each other.

"I'm scared."

"It's okay," he forced himself to smile, despite it feeling far more like a hideous wince, "I promise, I won't let—"

"I really have to do everything myself, don't I?" Poppy's voice cut in. The mime's black claws wrapped around Douglass's shoulder, effortlessly wrenching him away from Oliver's grasp as she tangled her fist into his shirt and jerked him close.

She narrowed her eyes at him as he clawed helplessly into her body in search of something solid that could possibly anchor him.

"*Please..*" Oliver breathed, "please don't—"

The alien thrust him back, and the ground under his feet disappeared.

Oliver scrambled to grab hold of something, anything.

And in the several terribly slow seconds it took for him to process that there was nothing there, that he was going to die, he heard a horrified shriek erupt from the cliff side just before all he saw were the stars.

Made of Stars

Time moves really, really slow when you're about to die.

He wasn't entirely sure how long he had been falling, or if he was just floating completely still in the air, at some point, he lost his grip on Dindet, and the two of them plummeted down toward the ground at a simultaneously achingly slow, and increasingly fast pace.

Oliver's focus though, stayed entirely on the night sky, if anything were the last thing he ever saw, at least it was pretty.

At some point, he heard Douglass scream, which meant he probably saw it happen, and that really sucked because Douglass was a good kid who didn't deserve to watch his friend die like this.

Oliver tilted his head, avoiding looking at the ground, and instead turned his attention up to the little orange bean that was about to die with him, and finally back up at the starscape above him, it looked like a galaxy, and it seemed to get closer and closer—which made it harder for him to tell whether or not he were flying or falling.

Then, it opened up, two giant white eyes in the dark peered down at him, as the night bled into the air and something like a fire, or maybe water, exploded out of it.

The little orange bean caught fire too, seamlessly blending into the sky as it burst, and twirled, and spun, and something familiar took form.

By then though, Oliver had closed his eyes and accepted the gruesome impact that had yet to come.

The fire and water and material of the atmosphere collided into itself and for a brief moment, Dindet hovered above him, trying to comprehend what was going on before she saw him. She dived forward, faster than the earth's terminal velocity, and reached out toward her friend.

"Oliver!" She cried, clasping her hands tight around his head as they plummeted ever closer to the ground.

In an instant, she spun, rolling in the friction of the air and tore out her arm, clawing into the fabric of time and space to gather even more of herself as some hopeful buffer for the inevitable impact.

The clown tumbled and grew, swirling up into an enormous black, sparkling mass that crashed into the forest floor and sent a gust of wind and dust flying out in the immediate radius.

Douglass ducked, bracing himself against a tree as at least fifty below were downed by the sheer mass of whatever fell from the sky. The moment the wind and dust settled he raced down the mountain side, catching himself on trees and tearing through the woods as his feet cut on the rocks and twigs he haplessly sprinted over to get to whatever had hit the ground below him.

"DOUGLASS!" Cassidy screamed, too slow to dodge out of the way when he ran straight into her. The two kids tangled up and tumbled a good thirty feet down the side of the mountain before she managed to catch herself on a trunk.

"Cassidy?! What are— you need to go!" Douglass stammered, scrambling to his feet to gain back the speed and precious time he'd lost. But her hand twined itself up in his shirt and yanked him back.

"What's going on?! I've been trying to call, Poppy is back—"

"I KNOW!" He cut in, jerking her grip away, "*Go*, Cas!"

Douglass pushed her hard, knocking her down on the ground and offering a short, regretful look. "She pushed him."

"*What?*"

Cassidy got to her feet, attempting to follow Douglass, who had already made a break for it and was sprinting down the mountain as fast as he possibly could go. She lost him.

***

The mass melted away, and Oliver was most certain he was dead, or if he wasn't, then he would be soon. Still though, he opened his eyes to see Dindet staring down at him, her face crumpled up with concern and fear, and every thought in her head screamed of worry.

"You...lost your hat," He mumbled, deftly reaching up to touch the soft and wild teal curls that poofed up around her head. Her face crinkled, and a tiny smile grew on her lips before it was interrupted with a broken little laugh.

"Yeah..."

"What a *touching* reunion."

All joy in the clown's face dissipated, quickly replaced by the tiniest flashes of fear before she turned a blackish crimson and twisted around to face the commenter.

"*You*," Dindet snarled, baring sharp teeth at Poppy, who stood at the edge of the crater she had made. "You *hurt* Oliver."

Poppy cocked her head, glancing at her newly formed claws.

"Well, you didn't exactly make it easy for me." She remarked, "if I had known better, I would have pushed him off a cliff sooner. I *am* working within a time constraint."

Dindet dug her claws into the dirt, struggling to not devour her rage at the wretched mime. "You hurt my FRIENDS!!"

The clown bubbled and smoked, boiling up and lashing pieces of herself out, slicing through the trees, and creating an even deeper crater in the earth as her weight consolidated around her.

"Oh, calm down," Poppy sighed, "if it makes you feel any better, I only did it to get to—"

Before she could finish, Dindet barreled into her with a horrendous metallic shriek, forcing the mime back as she clawed through the trees and sent them crashing down around her. Poppy dodged each blow, one after another until Dindet began to slow from some small amount of exhaustion.

"It's so hard, isn't it?" The mime halted, standing a few yards away from Dindet as she slowly returned to normal, already struggling to stay whole after all the effort it took just to get back. "Being so big, and only trying to use such a tiny amount. It must be *exhausting*. I was smart to make sure you'd waste all your energy just to get here."

"SHUT UP!!" Dindet slammed her fists into the dirt, forcing up the ground in a small seismic upheaval that buckled the forest floor and sent a crack up the cliff side behind her.

Poppy flitted from the edge of the upturned earth, directly beside her, forcing the clown to jump in between time and space to escape the swift swipe she had brought down.

"We don't have to fight, you know?" Poppy followed her, keeping pace with every jump Dindet made, until her claws dug into her matter and threw her down into the dirt. "We both know who will win."

"I DON'T CARE!!" She shrieked, tearing the mime's arm off and forcing her back with a hard kick. Dindet scrambled, making a break straight for the alien and forcing all her unquantifiable mass into the center of her as she ducked and rolled, catching fire with black, oozing matter that crashed hard into Poppy and forced her into the cliff.

The mime splattered against the rocks, losing whatever artificial appearance it had before Dindet trudged ever closer, deliberately slicing a tree in half to fell it between the fight and Oliver, who managed to plaster himself against the rocks in order to avoid being seen.

Poppy's grotesque ooze seeped down the side of the cliff, reforming into a slithering beast that roared in defiance, until it caught a glance at the position Dindet had set her in.

She was forcing her away from Oliver, trying to make sure the fight stayed far and away from him, in order to keep him safe.

In a split second, Poppy's glowing eyes flickered toward the child and Dindet immediately jumped through time and space, just as the entity flew toward the only thing she cared about.

"NO!" she barked, holding up her hands, the mass that

plummeted toward her broke, flying back and spattering on the grass and trees, and for a moment or two, it struggled to regain its consistency.

In those few precious seconds, Dindet wavered and stumbled, parts of her began to crumble and break, and she glanced back at her friend to make sure he was safe.

Oliver was crouched down, his head covered in brace for an impact that didn't come, and in the brief moment of pause, he glanced up just as the mime rematerialized behind Dindet and threw her back a good several hundred feet.

"Oh, *I see*," Poppy swiveled around, glancing back at Dindet a moment. "It's like your pet."

***

Cassidy balanced herself on a tree, ducking in brace against whatever wheighty atrocity that cratered the earth a few moments prior. Douglass had ran to wherever Oliver was— *if he's still alive..she pushed him. Off the cliff?!*

The girl made a quick break for it in between the rumbling of the ground, and sprinted down the last bit of mountain before she caught herself on a tree and veered left, straight for Jon's house.

Cassidy crashed her skateboard through the glass sliding door on the back of the cabin porch, but the entire home was empty and ransacked. She sprinted up the stairs, throwing open every single door in search of someone, anyone inside, but there was no one there.

She booked it out the front door, spinning around as her eyes flitted around the dark cul de sac, until they rested on the gleaming porch light of Douglass's house.

The girl ran across the road, not paying any attention to the bright lights that swerved and gleamed as she twisted around like a frozen deer. The car honked and slammed on its brakes beside her as a man in a lab coat jumped from the driver's seat.

"Are you insane?! I could have killed you!" Chris gestured wildly and filled with adrenaline at her soft stupor before he approached and grasped her shoulders. "Are you alright—"

"She tried to kill him!" Cassidy cut him off, twisting and wrenching out of his grasp, "Poppy pushed Oliver off the cliff!"

The scientist halted, his grip loosened around her shoulders and before she could comprehend, his face hardened with determination. "Get in the car."

Cassidy blinked.

"Now!" He commanded, prompting the girl to do exactly as he told and slide her way into the back seat of his truck.

"Wh— what are you going to—" She was cut short by Chris slamming the passenger door shut, already sprinting into the dark overgrowth toward the faint noise of screaming and crashing in the distance.

***

Poppy felled a tree, kicking it hard at the clown and forcing Dindet to shift consistency in effort to evade it. "You know, if I had known you'd be this bad at fighting, I'd have had you electrocuted eons ago."

In lieu of a response, Dindet growled, some guttural and horrendous noise that bubbled up from her as she solidified and launched herself forward, losing form in effort to shove the mime off balance and into the In-Between.

She swiped at her, quick and fast with long claws that grew even longer until Poppy twisted up and vanished from that liminal space, forcing Dindet to follow.

Oliver stood up, craning his neck in search of the clown when Poppy appeared behind him. She grabbed him tightly by the wrist and yanked him off balance as her other hand tangled itself in his hair and jerked him back.

"Let go!" He cried, blinking the quick tears from his eyes as he struggled to keep his feet on the ground. Oliver dug his fingers into her arm, attempting to hold himself up to keep the terrible sting of her unfiltered claws in his hair.

Dindet struggled to her feet, but the moment she caught sight of Poppy her exhaustion was eliminated, replaced by a disgustingly sweet wrath that boiled and bubbled inside her, and made her entirely content with murder.

The clown opened her palms, and brought back the terrible mass she had previously melted into some other place.

"Let. Him. Go." She said, almost too quietly to hear. The matter she gathered grew, melting away the trees and grass, and ground, and floating up in uncontrolled globs and bubbles in the air, only waiting for her to do something with it.

"Or what?" Poppy asked snidely, "you plan to crush this entire planet? Tear apart this whole dimension? That's what we want, idiot."

"LET HIM GO!!" Dindet repeated, clenching her fist as more and more matter pooled around her, bathing the entire area in a deadly, starry glow.

Poppy cocked her head and pulled the boy's hair taut, forcing him to let out a stifled cry while he struggled to keep his grip in her gelatinous body. "Come and take it, amalgamate."

Dindet barred nasty fangs and she flashed forward, some singular and empty thought, only the desire to destroy that which obstructed the thing she wanted. The thing she came here for.

She didn't see the vicious grin that ripped open the mime's face and how—

Dead Flower

lood splattered.

There was this soft, breathless noise. And Dindet stared, eyes wide with absolute horror.

She could feel it. Every ounce draining into her talons and how sweet it was. The rhythmic pulse of a heart lost among fractured and splintered bones.

Oliver met her gaze, his shock mirroring her own before her eyes flitted down, miniscule beats in each second, at where she had harmed him so.

Poppy rumbled with a hideous laugh, effortlessly removing the child from Dindet's blackened and bloodied claws.

She held him up, pressing her fingers into the hole in Oliver's chest and forcing his heart to continue beating.

"It's delicious, isn't it?" Poppy mused, only briefly drawing Dindet's attention away from the scattered remains of her thoughts. That unforgivable action.

You failed. Clear as the night sky. Marie's voice echoed, untouched by the distortion she had created in attempt to evade it.

You failed.

You failed.

You failed.

You failed.

You failed.

"It's almost…addictive…isn't it?"

Her mouth watered, disgusting hunger. Starvation. And it tasted so *good.* It was flesh. And blood. Human. That craving she had been longing for. The desire to consume all of him and leave nothing left. It screamed in Dindet's mind and made her crack and crumble with the concerted effort she made to control herself.

"You can barely even contain yourself." Poppy's head tilted and Oliver's grip loosed from her arm, swaying and drawing the clown's gaze. His colors flickered. Precious. And fleeting. They tasted like nothing compared to the blood coursing through Dindet's matter. Devoured and assimilated into the very fiber of her being in much the same way it had been countless times before.

"Go on…take a bite."

She tensed. Trying so very hard not to let that aching hunger consume her.

"HEY!"

Dindet's head jerked up and she drew in a gasp.

Poppy swiveled her head around, just as a small rock shot through her and hit the ground. Douglass glared at her, huffing and panting from the run down the mountain.

"LEAVE HIM ALONE!!" He scooped up another rock, chucking it straight at her and hitting the mime smack dab in the nose. She rippled, and for a moment, so did Oliver, and her attention turned fully toward the other reckless child.

Poppy dropped her leverage, tearing out her claws and barreling straight for Douglass. In the half second between the moment she reached him, Dindet crashed into her, sending the two of them flying back into the treeline as Douglass dove to catch Oliver.

"Oliver!" Douglass cried, wrapping his arms around the kid in order to break his fall. His hand reached up, cupping the back of his head as Douglass pressed into him. He held him as tight as possible and planted an overjoyed kiss on his forehead.

Oliver's eyes grew wide, and in a split second he was thrust back into the world. He stumbled back, gripping Douglass's shirt tight in effort not to lose his balance, and the taller boy dug his heels into the dirt to keep the both of them from hitting the ground.

"You're okay!" Douglass sobbed, sniffling through his relieved tears as he held him safe and secure in his arms. "You're okay!"

The kid pulled away, only briefly before he brushed the tangled mess of hair out of Oliver's eyes and held his red hot face. "I was so scared. I was so scared I lost you..."

Oliver could really only stare at him though, as he desperately clung to him in some wild effort to understand how he went from most certainly about to die, to being safe in Douglass's arms.

***

Dindet hurtled alongside Poppy, frantically fighting for the upper hand, only to be tossed and pinned down into the ground by her claws.

"You look tired," the mime remarked, digging her talons into the dirt around her and preventing any easy escape. "Haven't eaten in a while, have you?"

Poppy leaned a little closer, donning a terrible grin, "you seem *hungry*."

Dindet clawed at the dirt, kicking her feet up in effort to push her off, until her strength buckled and she struggled even harder to maintain control of herself. Flakes of her began dissolving in the air, prompting Poppy to let out a triumphant laugh.

"All I have to do is out-wait you! You'd be dead before the sun rose!" She cackled, pressing further into Dindet, until she was almost completely smothered.

The clown fell limp, allowing Poppy's weight to sink into her and begin to crumble the ground beneath them.

"This was too easy—"

Dindet's claws struck out from underneath her, startling the mime into silence. The clown's talons grew heavier and larger as they pierced the earth, creating deep, jagged crevices that snaked out as her matter bulged and grew.

It spilled over the edges like magma and the alien gurgled and grumbled, a terrible, guttural clicking noise erupting from underneath Poppy, forcing her to realize what was happening. She released her deathgrip, twisting around and scrambling to flee.

The mime clambered back, staring up at the monstrosity Dindet had turned into. A ravenous, drooling, hell beast that stared at her with empty, starved eyes.

"Do it then," Poppy breathed, narrowing her eyes as though she expected as much from the animal.

"DO IT!" She shrieked, louder this time, pulling the thing's wild eyes back down to her.

Dindet hesitated, wavering as though some last ounce of consciousness struggled against the insurmountable hunger and rage that blazed through her. And for a moment, that consciousness almost won.

"You're nothing but an animal," she chided, straightening herself in the face of what she understood was her end. "A dumb, starving animal. Smile is going to—"

The creature lurched forward, tearing its claws through Poppy's matter, consuming it in an instant, and cutting her size clean in half.

Poppy let out a hideous, metallic shriek.

The mime stumbled backward, opting to find an escape route. Her options grew increasingly limited as Dindet— or what was once her, tripled, then quadrupled in size.

Poppy turned, accepting her fate. The cruelty of it. And that it did not go wasted.

"Fine then," she said, lifting her chin with vindictive pride. The beast in front of her gurgled with its layered noises. "Do your worst. *I got what I wanted.*"

Dindet crashed her oscillating, razor sharp maw down on top of her, ripping and shredding apart each and every molecule.

The beast gurgled and bucked, shuddering as it consumed every atom that belonged to its sister species, until some vague scent wafted in the air, drawing the monstrosity's attention.

Talons dipped into the earth, four, then five, six, seven, eight limbs clawing up the dirt as the nightmarish and lovecraftian abomination tilted and churned, undulating and heaving, tasting the flesh and blood of creatures dwarfed by its mass.

As it moved, the ground shook, trees toppled over one another and the oozing slime of its stars floated so high that in the night sky it was a god of singular and all consuming death.

Dindet's blind and insatiable gaze rested on her prey. And she lumbered forward, drifting the mountains aside like sea foam as she waded. Unceasing. Starving.

***

Oliver's pulse beat in his head, throbbing and aching and slowing faster than he could comprehend. Douglass held him still, spewing apologetics and begging for him to be okay. To stay alive.

His focus drifted past the boy's red and sobbing face to the trees. They lurched and folded. He could hear them splintering and the splintering growing louder as what he knew with no shadow of doubt in his mind, was Dindet, drew near.

"Douglass," he croaked, the name barely audible on his tongue. Douglass rambled on, about what, it didn't really matter. Most of his words were garbled up with the thumping of Oliver's heart and he could feel how whatever Dindet had done, it had stopped Poppy's forceful push and pull on his arteries. It hurt. Incomprehensible pain. But it was also numbing.

The trees faltered and crashed down closer now.

"Douglass, you need to move…you need…to run." He couldn't. But Douglass could. And at the moment, that was the only thing that really mattered.

"Oliver, it's okay, you'll be okay, I can— well get you to the hospital, we'll fix you up and you'll be okay, it will be okay."

It didn't matter.

Bright and white eyes rose like the moon over the horizon, and one enormous clawed and starry foot catered in the earth ahead of them. *You have to move Douglass. She's going to kill you.*

"Douglass," Oliver repeated, even softer, raising his hands in effort to grab the boy's attention. There was little time. He needed to *make* him move.

A visceral, static and nightmarish howl burst from the beast. It could see them. It was going to eat him if Oliver didn't do something. Anything.

"Douglass, MOVE!" Oliver gripped Douglass's shirt tight, ripping him off of himself and using every last ounce of strength he possessed to jerk the boy from his stupor and shove him as far away as physically possible.

He moved too, or tried to. Tried to get out of the way.

In a split second, he watched Douglass's startled gaze flicker back before his face twisted with terror and he attempted to lunge forward, only caught by his father's strong hands, wrenching him away from that immediate and certain death.

"OLIVER!"

Dindet dove down, mouth agape and glowing, she scooped into the earth, displacing the ground and leaving a hole where her prey had stood. She would consume it wholly. Devour it and cherish the flavor of which only flesh could provide.

Oliver was far too slow and far too weak to stop it, to do much of anything but flail and reach out, grappling in the abyss of her in effort to find the one thing he could reach her with. Her heart beat fast and hard. Swirling around him and in his whipping galactic and cosmic monstrosity, he found it rolling in her matter and grabbed hard at it.

The creature erupted with a piercing shriek, one that engulfed his brain and nearly drowned his tired heart.

He couldn't breathe. And he couldn't speak. But he had her there, in his hands, safe and sound.

Dindet…it's okay.

The beast wailed and a wave of matter burned and melted around him, boiling up again as it moved further toward the rest of the town. Further toward food.

I'm so sorry I let you get hurt. I'm so sorry I let you go. And I didn't think about you or…or everything you've done for me.

You're lost…and angry, scared…right? Hungry…
But I'm right here. I'm right here. And I need you.
Please.. I…

"I need you to come back."

Silence fell, soft among the static and whirling rage and hunger. Oliver felt himself falling somewhere, before his feet touched the ground and he stood, hunched forward, pressing his dear friend's heart so close to his chest. She could feel his heartbeat. Taste his love and honesty.

Dindet stood in front of him. Some ten or twenty feet away, staring back at him, her face painted with dread and sorrow and unceasing adoration.

Oliver lifted his head just slightly, an exhausted smile on his face the moment he saw her return to that familiar form.

"…hey…"

It was such a soft and gentle greeting. He wondered how many times he'd said it before now. How many lifetimes had passed.

At it, Dindet's soft look of love broke with a shattered smile and she moved, slowly, at first. Hesitant as she always was to touch him. Then faster.

He wanted so badly to move too. To give her some sort of embrace that would show her how much he missed her and how much he *needed* her.

Instead, he stumbled, simply falling into her arms and letting himself sink into the comfort of her static.

She wasn't a monster. Or some evil and ungodly thing that only served to consume him. She was his friend.

Oliver's knees buckled, finally giving way and Dindet dropped down to soften the fall, gathering all of him up in her arms.

"Oliver," she said so softly. Her voice like honey with how sweet and riddled with sadness it was. "You're hurt…"

"It's okay," he replied. "I missed you…Dindet..I missed you so…."

***

Time moved innumerably slow.

Seconds ticked by, feeling far more like hours and Dindet couldn't focus on anything other than the sound of blood hitting the ground, until she caught movement in her line of sight.

All the soft and gentle glow of Oliver's pink dwindled away in front of her.

He swayed as his head dipped, and his arms, once wrapped around her shoulders, fell to his side.

It happened so slowly. And she couldn't figure out why she wasn't able to do anything.

Dindet stared ahead, holding him, her friend, as he rested his head so lightly on her shoulder.

No one moved. No one spoke. Or screamed, but she could taste the shock of them all around her. Or she could only taste her own.

All his colors. They were just there, she could taste them, see them, even the little black hole in the center of him. And now they just...weren't.

"Oliver?" Dindet brushed the hair from the boy's eyes and pulled in a jagged mock breath. They were open and he stared at nothing. He didn't blink, or move.

"Oliver wake up," she forced out a small laugh. *It wasn't real. This was just a trick, a false alarm. Like last time. They all were.*

"Please?"

She tried so hard. *Every single time.*

"Oliver, it's not funny."

She moved everything around. *Started over. Over and over again. Just to make sure.*

"Oliver!" Dindet moved him, staring into those hollow and empty eyes as she began to lose the hold she had on herself. *No one was doing anything. No one was trying to help. There weren't any screaming cars or rolling beds.*

"Wake up..please?" She shook him, pressing her thumb into his cheek in an effort to get some kind of reaction.

Only his mouth parted, and some terrible and agonizingly soft gurgle sounded from him as the last few ounces of blood in his throat rose with the awful exhale.

"I can— I can fix you," Dindet stammered, pressing her palms into the cavity of Oliver's chest. "I can help!"

The clown clenched her eyes shut, drawing every ounce of strength she had in effort to recall all the little details of him. She had done it so many times, brought him from place to place. Surely she could remake what stopped being there.

Her skin flaked and cracked, and her fingers crumbled with the increasing pressure she used to try and control herself. To manipulate all of him and bring him back.

"Please, I just need— I just need more time!" She begged his quiet body, "I promised, I promised I would come back— always...I promised to keep you safe, so you can't—"

Dindet fell silent, stopped by the Jester's gentle hand that rested on her head. Their gaze drifted from Oliver to her and it spoke quietly, kindly.

"You don't have the energy to do that."

Her eyes flickered up at Smile, but the enormous jester only stared at her, that grin unchanged.

Smile lifted their hand from her head and bent down in front of her. Beckoning her forward.

"No," Dindet argued weakly, "no, no, no, I— I have to. I have to try or— or I have to try again, and again, and *again!!* I have to make sure he's okay!"

"No," Smile corrected, "you don't. You are free now."

"NO!" Dindet barked, slamming her fists into the dirt and causing cracks to grow from the impact. "I'M GOING BACK!"

The earth around the clown swelled, bursting as it pressed and folded into her.

She grew, turning black and starry and the night sky poured down like fire and water, crashing into her and rejoining with its long abandoned host.

Tails and tentacles and talons formed from the mass, consuming

Oliver and the forest trees and grass in a heavy solid shadow that undulated and whipped in frenzied panic.

"I WILL START OVER!" The earth underneath the beast buckled, cratering with the weight of its matter and causing the crust of the planet to shift and sink as Dindet's true size built itself up in a horrific and condensed abomination.

"I can't let you do that." Smile reared back to avoid the shrieking atrocity Dindet had become in her unbridled grief.

The jester doubled around Dindet and slammed their fist into the ground, forcing up rocks and debris that sectioned off the town from the clown's rampage.

The creature's wild and pure white eyes opened up and she let out an awful noise, clawing against the mountains that crumbled under her weight in a frantic attempt to gather the rest of her and escape. Every tree and rock shattered under her steps. And Dindet grappled with her unruly body, desperate to form too many arms and legs to carry her and the thing so precious to her away.

The grieving alien leapt through time and space, crashing into dimension after dimension as it gathered its ungodly mass, leaving gaping holes in the fabric of the multiverse that had, at one point, been filled by her matter.

She would go back, she would start all of it over, just like she promised. And this time she wouldn't let him die. *It would be different.*

The raging beast let out a foul wail, crossing the wreckage of the Peace Zone into the In-between of this earth and the next.

She would destroy it all. *Every single time. Just to fix things.*

Some cosmic entity that bent and cracked the fractals of time, swirling it and all its glistening broken pieces into a mess around her. Dindet let out one last hideous shriek, a death rattle that reverberated amongst the stars as planets reversed their orbits.

Revolutions stopped and that deafening stillness fell around her.

I will start over. Over and over and over and over and over and over and over

~~*and over and over and over and over*~~

~~*and over and over and over and over*~~

The stars crushed, imploded and fractured, giant crystallized screeching

monstrosities ~~as~~ ~~the~~ ~~belt~~ ~~of~~ ~~existence~~ ~~folded~~ ~~back~~ ~~and~~ ~~that~~ ~~bright~~ ~~and~~ silent explosion

of ~~life began to draw inward on itself.~~

Dindet in her infinite and far too heavy brightness stayed near the center, grappling and stringing as her matter crumbled.

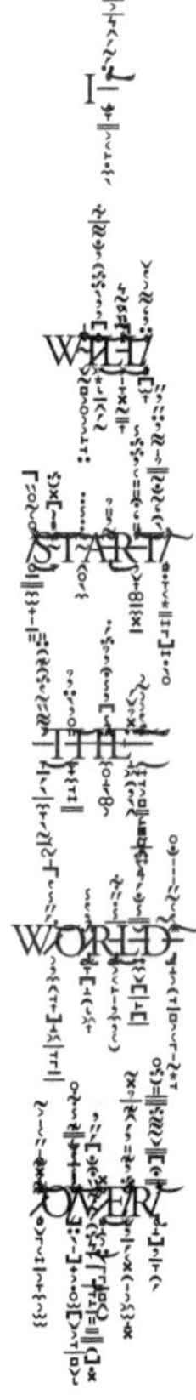

"No, you will not."

275

Epilog

Marie stood at the precipice of The Cornucopia, a ghostly, flickering body of light and color.

She faced The Abyss. A massive, undulating void of matter that bowed and bent when she turned her attention to it. As if it were conscious itself.

She wasn't supposed to be here.

The scattered woman pressed her palm to the surface of the darkness, puncturing that fragile surface tension and causing the reactive particles within it to light up in preparation for her intention. It could make anything, Smile had said. Anything she could ever want.

Or…almost.